ISBN 978-1-332-05167-0
PIBN 10276553

This book is a reproduction of an important historical work. Forgotten Books uses
state-of-the-art technology to digitally reconstruct the work, preserving the original format
whilst repairing imperfections present in the aged copy. In rare cases, an imperfection in
the original, such as a blemish or missing page, may be replicated in our edition. We do,
however, repair the vast majority of imperfections successfully; any imperfections that
remain are intentionally left to preserve the state of such historical works.

For support please visit www.forgottenbooks.com

English
Français
Deutsche
Italiano
Español
Português

www.forgottenbooks.com

Mythology Photography **Fiction**
Fishing Christianity **Art** Cooking
Essays Buddhism Freemasonry
Medicine **Biology** Music **Ancient**
Egypt Evolution Carpentry Physics
Dance Geology **Mathematics** Fitness
Shakespeare **Folklore** Yoga Marketing
Confidence Immortality Biographies
Poetry **Psychology** Witchcraft
Electronics Chemistry History **Law**
Accounting **Philosophy** Anthropology
Alchemy Drama Quantum Mechanics
Atheism Sexual Health **Ancient History**
Entrepreneurship Languages Sport
Paleontology Needlework Islam
Metaphysics Investment Archaeology
Parenting Statistics Criminology
Motivational

CASTA AȲ

ON THE

AUCKLAND ISLES:

A NARRATIVE OF THE WRECK OF THE 'GRAFTON' AND
OF THE ESCAPE OF THE CREW AFTER TWENTY
MONTHS' SUFFERING.

FROM THE PRIVATE JOURNALS OF

CAPTAIN THOMAS MUSGRAVE.

"AID UPON THE *SE...*

TOGETHER WITH SOME ACCOUNT OF THE AUCKLANDS.

EDITED BY

JOHN J. SHILLINGLAW, F.R.G.S.

AUTHOR OF 'ARCTIC DISCOVERY' ETC.

'How shall I admire your heroicke courage, ye marine worthies,
beyond all names of worthinesse!'   HAKLUYT.

LONDON:

LOCKWOOD AND CO., 7 STATIONERS'-HALL COURT,
1866.

THIS RECORD

OF A TIME OF GREAT TRIAL AND SUFFERING

Is Dedicated

TO

JOHN MACPHERSON, ESQ.,

MERCHANT, OF INVERCARGILL,

AND TO

THE HON. JAMES G. FRANCIS,

MINISTER OF TRADE, MELBOURNE,

AS

A TRIBUTE OF GRATITUDE.

a

From THE TIMES, *Dec.* 19, 1865.

" IN these smooth days of steam and rail to the uttermost corners of the earth, Robinson-Crusoe-like adventure does not seem to be very easy of attainment even to a man who may have a fancy for such experience. Nevertheless, some few desert islands still remain to us ; and the Auckland Islands, about 400 miles to the south of New Zealand, are among the number.   We had recently a visit from a mariner named Musgrave, whose diary of his nearly 20 months' stay on one of these islands is almost as interesting as Daniel Defoe, besides being, as the children say, ' all true.' "—*Times' Correspondent.*

INTRODUCTION.

FEW more interesting narratives of disasters at sea have ever been given to the world than the journals in which Captain MUSGRAVE records the wreck of the 'Graiton.' A great trial, bravely met, and gallantly surmounted, is therein told with a care and exactness which is at the same time singularly modest. Remembering the difficulties with which the devoted little party were surrounded, what reader can fail to exclaim, in the words which I have quoted on the title-page, '*How shall I admire your heroicke courage, ye Marine Worthies beyond all names of worthinesse!*' Indeed, the story of the wreck of the 'Grafton,' and of the sufferings of her crew, would have found a very appropriate resting place in the pages of that famous history of 'Voyages, Traffiques, and Discoueries,' side by side with many another pitiful tale of shipwreck, collected by the worthy 'RICHARD HAKLUYT, Preacher,' to be the delight in all ages of the school-boy as well as the scholar. The same feeling we experience in reading of poor WILLS, the hero of the expedition across Australia, 'waiting, like Mr. MICAWBER, for something to turn up,' animates us as we read how the Castaways on the Aucklands used to strain their eyes looking for that relief which never came. We hear the clink of RAYNAL's anvil far into the night whilst he is engaged forming out of old iron the bolts and nails necessary to repair the crazy 'dingy' for a perilous voyage of 240 miles across a stormy ocean.* Our admiration is compelled no less by the tinkering, tailoring, and cobbling ingenuity of the gallant French mate, than by the 'moral suasion' of the master, who employs himself in the evening in teaching his men how to read and write, and in compiling 'sailing directions' for a little-known part of the globe, to be 'sealed up in a bottle' for the benefit of future navigators of these seas. In his direst strait this modern 'Complete Seaman' finds comfort in some lines of THOMAS MOORE, and finally makes his last cast for 'Death or Freedom' with a truly Nelsonic touch.

Regarded as simply a marvellous tale of the sea—as a practical lesson of self-reliance—the story is sufficiently interesting; but it is no less an important contribution to Hydrographical Science. The limits of this small volume will not allow of the publication of a mass of barometrical and other observations collected by Captain MUSGRAVE. These will be forwarded to the proper quarter, and will doubtless receive the credit which they deserve.

It only remains to add a brief *résumé* of the steps which have been taken by the Government of Victoria, in conjunction with New South Wales and Queensland, to examine and set at rest the question whether there are at present any other unfortunates dragging out a miserable existence on the Auckland Islands. It will be seen from the journal of Captain MUSGRAVE that when he returned to the islands to rescue the two seamen he had left behind, he and others on board the 'Flying Scud,' on the 23rd

---

* The following extracts from *Lloyd's List*, which have come under the publishers' notice, will not perhaps be thought out of place here :—
"The 'Grafton,' Musgrave, sailed from Sydney for South Sea Islands Nov. 12, 1863."—*Lloyd's List, Jan. 9,* 1864.
"*Wellington, New Zealand, Aug.* 12, 1865.
"The 'Grafton,' Musgrave, from Sydney to the South Sea Islands, was wrecked Jan. 3, 1864, in one of the inlets of the Auckland Islands ; the master and two of the crew arrived at Port Adventure last month in a small boat of their own building."—*Lloyd's List, Oct.* 17, 1865.

August, 1865, thought they saw smoke on the eastern coast at a point shown on the map, which, however, they were not able to explore.

Subsequently they found the body of a seaman at Port Ross, who had evidently died from starvation. A slate which was found near him, seemed to have been written on, but the utmost ingenuity had failed to decipher the characters with any accuracy. On arriving in Melbourne, Captain MUSGRAVE waited on the Hon. J. G. FRANCIS, Commissioner of Trade and Customs, and explained his reasons for thinking that there might be still other persons on the island. As several vessels which had sailed from Melbourne were known to be 'missing,' Mr. FRANCIS, with a promptitude which does him great honour, immediately called for tenders for a vessel to proceed to the Aucklands, and finding that delay might ensue in sending a sailing vessel, at once ordered the equipment of H.M.C.S.S. 'Victoria,' Captain NORMAN. The 'Victoria' sailed on the 4th October, having Captain MUSGRAVE on board as a passenger, who thus, for the second time, put aside all personal considerations to carry out what he deemed to be his duty,—a self-denial which, considering he has not seen his family since November, 1863, is worthy of our heartiest sympathy.

The English Mail arrived after the 'Victoria' had left for Melbourne, and by it we received the intelligence that the ship 'Invercauld' had been lost on the Aucklands, on the 10th May, 1864, and that three of the survivors had been taken off by a Peruvian vessel on the 22nd May, 1865. In the Appendix will be found all that has yet reached us of the particulars of the wreck of the 'Invercauld.'

J. J. S.

MELBOURNE, 25th October, 1865.

NOTE BY THE PUBLISHERS.

Some additional particulars respecting the despatch of the 'Victoria,' taken from the *Melbourne Argus*, will probably interest the reader :—

" The Victorian Government determined to despatch the colonial steamsloop 'Victoria' to the islands, to discover and rescue the survivors, if there be any. The Governments of New South Wales and Queensland have undertaken to defray a portion of the cost of the expedition. The 'Victoria,' under the command of Captain Norman, left Hobson's Bay on her mission of mercy on the 4th inst. The instructions of the Government to Captain Norman were to proceed with all possible despatch to the isles, and search for and relieve any person or persons who may be there in distress ; and, on the completion of his mission, to return direct to Melbourne, or, in the event of fuel running short, or the weather being adverse, to make for the most convenient port in New Zealand for a supply of coal, which, it is to be presumed, will be afforded free of charge. Captain Musgrave, of the 'Grafton,' whose local knowledge will be of great value, accompanied the expedition. Should circumstances allow, Captain Norman will call at Campbell's Island, and also at Bounty Island, which are situate—the one to the south and the other to the north-east of the Auckland group. The crew of the 'Victoria' numbers fifty, and the ship is provisioned for three months. She also carries a supply of stores, bedding, clothing, &c., for any unfortunates who may be picked up. In order that people who may be shipwrecked on the Auckland Isles in the future may have within reach a supply of animal food, a number of pigs, rabbits, and goats have been placed on board by the Acclimatisation Society, to be turned loose on the islands."

Additional Note.

The *Times'* New Zealand correspondent, in a letter dated Nov. 15, 1865, writes as follows :—

" The Victorian war steamer 'Victoria' put into Otago on the 8th inst. for coals and provisions, having been searching the Auckland Islands for shipwrecked mariners. . . . . The whole group has, however, been thoroughly searched without success, no trace of human beings, dead or alive, being found. Provisions have been left in various parts of the islands for the use of future castaways."—*Times, Jan.* 13, 1866.

CONTENTS.

BREAKERS

True

ENDERBY I?

Green I?
Rose I?

Bank

SKETCH MAP OF THE

AUCKLAND ISLES.

Soundings in fathoms.

H.W.f & c 12h. 45m. Rise VIII ft.

LAT. E. ENTRANCE 50°. 56'.

LONG. D° 166°. 20' F.

1865.

NARRATIVE OF THE WRECK

OF

THE SCHOONER 'GRAFTON.'

From the Private Journal of Capt. Thomas Musgrave.

CHAPTER I.

ARRIVAL AT AUCKLAND ISLAND.—THE SHIPWRECK.—RESOURCES
OF THE ISLAND.

Wednesday, December 30, 1863.—Commences with fresh
breeze and dark cloudy weather. At 6 P.M. made the
Auckland Group, bearing N.W. about 25 miles distant.
Midnight, same weather; all sails set; water smooth under
the lee of the island. Barom. 29·80, 2 A.M.: Tacked to
S.W. From this time till 6 A.M. weather moderately
clear, but wind very puffy and treacherous. Took in fore-
.top-gallant sail; all the latter part, breeze unsteady;
weather unsettled and threatening, and a very ugly sea
getting up. Noon: Barom. 29·55, falling rapidly. Every
appearance of N. gale and a very heavy confused sea
running. South Cape, Auckland Islands, bearing W.N.W.,
distant about 20 miles. Lat. by observation, 51° 17′ S.;
long. by bearing, 166° 35′ E., therm. 60°. I think that
Mr. Raynal* is a little better since we left Campbell's
Island. Winds: 2 P.M., W.S.W.; 4 P.M., W.; 8 P.M. W.
by N.; 10 P.M., N.W. by W.; 4 A.M., W.N.W.; 8 A.M., W.

---

* Mr. Raynal was mate of the 'Grafton,' and had been seriously ill
whilst the schooner lay at Campbell's Island.—ED.

B

Thursday, December 31, 1863.—Directly after the sun crossed the meridian it came on to blow a gale. Immediately reduced sail to close-reefed topsail, foresail, and foretop mainstaysail. A dangerous, confused sea running, and breaking on board in all directions, and a thick fog set in, with drizzling rain, which continued up till 6 P.M., when the sea began to run more regular, but still much confused, causing the vessel to labour and strain heavily, and make a little water. From this time till midnight experienced a hard gale, high sea, heavy rain, and thick fog. At 2 A.M. bore to westward, and at 4 A.M. the gale moderated. Made sail accordingly. At 8 A.M. all sail set, and at 9 A.M. made Auckland Island again, South Cape bearing N.N.E., distant about 25 miles. As the wind will not permit me to weather the island, I have determined to go under its lee, and if possible cast anchor in ' Sarah's Bosom.' Mr. Raynal is much better to-day. Noon: Moderate breeze and cloudy. Took sights at 9 A.M., South Cape bearing N.N.E. by compass, variation 2 points E. Lat. 51° 8′ S. ; long. 166° 17′, and would put the South Cape in long. 166° 45′. This longitude does not exactly correspond with Bowditch, who gives two, which differ 20 miles, one being 166° 7′ and the other 166° 27′. Winds : 2 P.M., W.N.W. ; 10 P.M., W.S.W. ; 2 A.M., S.W. ; 8 A.M., W.

Friday (*New Year's Day*), 1864.—At noon one point of the island bore N. by W. ½ W., and South Cape bore N.E. by N., distant about 8 miles. As we approach the island I find that it bears precisely the same appearance as Campbell's Island, and the mountains are about the same height. At 3 P.M. entered a harbour which I suppose is ' Sarah's Bosom.' * First and middle parts of the 24 hours, moderate breeze and moderately clear weather. The entrance of the harbour runs east and west. We beat in, but found no bottom at 20 fathoms, even close in to the rocks ; kept under way all night.

---

* This is an error, it should be ' Carnley's Harbour.'—ED.

We saw great numbers of seals as we went up; at every tack we made they came off from the shore to look at us, and played round the ship like porpoises. 6 A.M.: Put the boat out, and sent her away to look for an anchorage, but found none. 8 A.M.: It came on to blow a strong breeze from N.W., which increased to a gale. Kept on heading up the harbour, to which we saw no end. At noon strong gale from N.W., with heavy rain; brought up on the N.E. side of the harbour, in 6 fathoms of water, close in shore, about 10 or 12 miles from the sea. We have had a very difficult job in heading up here, and are not yet in a good anchorage, but intend looking for one as soon as the weather moderates. We have got both anchors down, with 30 fathoms chain on each: this is all the good chain we have got. I consider her in a rather dangerous position, as there is hardly room for her to swing clear of the rocks should the wind come from the S.W. There is a swell on, and she strains very much at her anchors. The rain and gale continued till midnight, at which time this day ends, containing 36 hours. Wind, N.W. Barom., noon, 29·25; midnight, 29·3.

Saturday, January 2, 1864.—Very heavy gale throughout this day; first and middle parts almost constant rain, and during the latter heavy squalls. There is a considerable swell running, and the ship has been jerking and straining at her chains all day, and I expected them to part every moment. At 7 P.M., in a heavy squall, the starboard chain *did* part, about two fathoms outside the pipe, leaving about 38 fathoms on the anchor; and the other, or best bower, dragged a considerable distance, and then brought her up again, her stern in a quarter less two fathoms, about half a cable's length from the shore. She is lying almost parallel with the shore, and should the wind come from the S.W. she must most inevitably go into the rocks, and I have now made up my mind for the worst. I see no hope of her keeping clear. Barom., 28·90, and falling at 10 P.M. The wind is so that, should

I slip the cable with a spring, she would not clear the point, or I would slip and run out to sea. At every heave of the swell she is dragging the anchor home, and getting nearer the shore. From 10 P.M. till midnight the gale blew with the most terrific violence, and precisely at midnight the ship struck, but we hung on to the cable, in hopes that the wind would moderate as the tide rose, as it was then low water. Wind, from N.W. to W.N.W., and sometimes W.

Sunday, January 3, 1864.—After midnight the gale increased and blew with the most unimaginable violence, and we found that she was an unavoidable wreck; she lay broadside on to the beach, and the sea made a clean breach over her. At every surge we expected the masts to go over the side. We had veered out all the cable. We saw pieces of her keel coming up under her lee, and she made much water, but we kept at the pumps till we found she was filling fast, and the water was rushing into her like a boiling spring; this was at a quarter past 2 o'clock in the morning. We abandoned the pumps, and commenced getting the provisions on deck, which did not occupy much time, as our stock was very small. In a quarter of an hour she was full up to the top of the cabin table, and the sea was breaking heavily over her. The sea was so heavy on the beach that I considered it dangerous to attempt landing till daylight. We remained on deck, and at daylight commenced landing our provisions and clothes; we had much difficulty in landing; as it is a stone beach, the boat was in danger of breaking up. However, by 10 A.M. we had succeeded in landing the things most important without doing much damage to the boat. We brought the mainsail and gaff on shore and made a tent of it. We are obliged to lie on the ground, which is very wet. Raynal has walked about 100 yards to-day, from the beach to the tent. Wind, N.W. to W.N.W.

Sunday, January 10, 1864.—It is now a week since we landed here, and my time has been so much occupied in hard work as to leave me no time to make even daily notes; but Mr. Raynal, who is improving fast, keeps the diary. Indeed, he is so much better that he talks of going to work to-morrow. We have had a very stormy week; it has been blowing a perfect hurricane from N. to S. all the time, until yesterday, which was a mild, cloudy day, without rain (the first since we came here); the breeze light, from south.

To-day is also a very fine day, with a moderate N.W. breeze. Last Monday we went on board the wreck, and got all the boards we could muster to make a floor in the tent, as we had all got severe colds from lying on the wet ground. We also unbent the sails, and sent down all the yards and topmasts, and are using them for building a house, as in all probability we shall have to remain here all next winter; and if we want to preserve life, we must have shelter. We have all worked very hard, and although it has been so wet we have succeeded in getting up the frame of the house. There is plenty of timber where we are camped, and also a beautiful creek of clear water; but the timber is not long or big enough to make a proper log-house, so we shall put them (the pieces of timber) up and down. The seals are very numerous here; they go roaring about the woods like wild cattle. Indeed, we expect they will come and storm the tent some night. We live chiefly on seal meat, as we have to be very frugal with our own little stock; we kill them at the door of the tent as we require them. If we had been fortunate enough to have kept the vessel afloat, I have no doubt but in two months or less we should have loaded her. Mine appears a hard fate; after getting to where I might have made up for what has been lost, I lose the means of doing so. The vessel leaves her bones here, and God only knows whether we are all to leave our bones here also. And what is to become of my poor unprovided-for family? It drives me mad to think of it. I can write no more.

one hanging up, and it is no use for us to kill them for their skins, as whoever takes us away would not feel inclined to humbug with our seal skins unless we gave them to them, which, of course, they would deserve.

But we have other work on our hands at present. We must get a place to live in, for the tent we are now living in is a beastly place. I expect we shall all get our death of cold before we get out of it yet; and the blow-flies blow our blankets and clothes, and make everything in the most disgusting state imaginable. A kind of mosquito is very troublesome in the day-time also, but fortunately they do not bite at night.

We have several kinds of birds here also, two kinds of which are songsters, and send forth beautiful notes; and there is the green parrot and robin-redbreast. They are all very tame. We could put out our hands and take hold of them, but we do not disturb them. The robins are very familiar with us ; they come into the tent and chirp round us when we are at our meals, and are quite tame. While we were up the western arm of the harbour I shot a dozen of widgeon and young ducks ; and we picked up a piece of a studding-sail boom on the beach, which had evidently not been lying there very long. We also found a seal dead on the beach, which I shot about a week ago close to where we were camped. The ball entered just before the shoulder, but he was quite close to the water, and got in and away before I could get at him to kill him. Where we found him is about eight or nine miles from here. I have taken a sketch of the western arm. The water is very deep, with bold, rocky shores, 10 fathoms deep, 50 yards from the shore, and we nowhere found bottom with a 20-fathom line at a hundred yards from the shore.

Sunday, January 24, 1864.—The weather has been tolerably fine since I last wrote, although it has been blowing a westerly gale ever since, and on Friday it rained heavily all day, with thunder and lightning in the evening. We have all been busy about the house, and I think we shall be able to get into it towards the end of the incoming week. This morning I started to go on to the mountain which rises to the N.E. of us, to have a look round. I went alone, as my Norwegian friend, whom I had for a travelling companion on the other island, is sick; he was unable to work yesterday, and Mr. Raynal's legs are not strong enough for travelling yet. In going up I found seal tracks nearly to the top of the mountain, which I reckon is about four miles from the water; and about three miles up I saw a seal. I went about seven or eight miles and got a good view of the eastern part of the island, and I see that there is a sort of small harbour farther to the northward, but I don't suppose that there is any anchorage in it, as the mountains rise perpendicularly from it on both sides to the height of five hundred feet, and a considerable stream empties itself into it at the head; and it would not be fit for a vessel to go into if there was anchorage, as it is straight N.E. and S.W., and very much resembles the N.E. harbour at Campbell's Island, only that it is not so large. It is about three quarters of a mile long, and not more than a cable's length wide. All the mountains to the northward and eastward appear very precipitous, and there are only a few places where it would be possible to get either up or down them. They are covered with long, coarse grass, with here and there a patch of furze or stunted scrub, and there are numerous streams of water running out of them. In fact, the whole top of the mountain on which I stood was one mass of bog, and quite destitute of grass or herbage of any kind, but there is any quantity of granite rock. As I went up I found the travelling tolerably good, as I took the spur of the range, which is always the best; but, on coming back, I came down the face of the mountain, and encountered a number of swamps, through which I had considerable difficulty to get, until I arrived at the seal tracks, which do not go so far up here. They are not more than about a mile from the water, which is about the extent back of the

big bush. This 'big bush,' as we call it, is where the
largest timber grows; it extends about a mile from the
water all round the shores of this harbour, which, taking
all the bays, is not less than sixty or seventy miles. This
timber is all iron-bark and she-oak, but the bark of the
timber is not like that of the Australian. This is as thin
as brown paper, but the wood is precisely the same. It
does not grow straight; you can scarcely get a straight
piece out of it six feet long; it would make excellent
timber for the frame of a ship, and there are any quantity
of splendid knees. This is the iron-bark I am speaking of
now. The oak is not much good for anything but burning.

On Tuesday last I had a very narrow escape from being
shot. We were up the bush after a seal, which gave us a
very exciting chase. I suppose we followed him two miles.
They can run very fast in the bush. My gun had been
loaded for two days, and the powder had got damp. After
snapping three or four caps I got one barrel off, and the
ball went into his neck, and out again between his shoulders. However, as a proof of how hard they are to kill,
this did not stop him long enough for us to get up to him.
I did not stop to load again (and it is impossible to load
running in this bush), but pricked the powder up in the
other barrel, and tried it again. The cap snapped, but the
gun did not go off. I brought the barrel to my shoulder,
with the butt to the ground, in order to load the other
barrel again, when off she went, and the ball passed
through the rim of my hat. They killed the seal before I
got up to them again; but not, however, till he got on to
the beach. I thank God, who has protected me thus far,
although in His wisdom He has chastised me severely
lately, that He has again spared my life. The thermometer
is about 48° or 49° at midday now.

Sunday, February 7, 1864.—It is now a fortnight since
I last wrote, during which time we have had very bad
weather; there has not been one entire fine day, excepting
last Friday and to-day. To-day it is exceedingly fine; it

is blowing a light westerly breeze, with clear weather. Barometer at 29·30. On Monday last we had a most fearful S.S.W. gale. We had the boat afloat in the morning, and the gale came on so suddenly at noon that we could not attempt to haul her on to the beach, there was so much surf; so we left her moored to the wreck, but she got stove in there; for the sea struck her, and started all the ends of the planks on the port bow. We have not yet undertaken to repair her, as we have been too busy with the house. We kept at work at it, in spite of the bad weather, and we even worked at it on last Sunday. On Tuesday we came into it, and I am glad to say that we shall be much more comfortable. The house is 24 feet by 16 feet; the chimney is 8 feet by 5 feet, built of stone. We· shall be able to have a roaring fire in it in the winter, if we are so unfortunate as to have to remain here till that time; and God help those at home, whom it almost drives me mad to think of. We have, as yet, had plenty to eat, but whether they have or not, God only knows.

For the last three weeks we have killed a cow an a calf seal each week. We only eat the cow and calf tiger seals; the black seal is not good, and the bulls are all very rank. We killed a cow and her calf this morning; we got milk from the cow after she was killed, which is very rich and good, much better even than goat's milk. We have not had time to go fishing in the boat yet, but I have no doubt but there is plenty of fine fish in the harbour, for we have had several dishes of small cod, which we catch amongst the kelp at low water. We also get plenty of mussels at low water springs.

Up to the present time the men have worked well, and conducted themselves in a very obedient and respectful manner towards me; but I find there is somewhat of a spirit of obstinacy and independence creeping in amongst them. It is true I no longer hold any command over them, but I share everything that has been saved from the wreck in common with them, and I have worked as hard as any of them in trying to make them comfortable, and I think gratitude ought to prompt them to still continue willing and obedient. But you might as well look for the grace of God in a Highlandman's log-book as gratitude in a sailor; this is a well-known fact. They have not as yet objected to do anything that I have told them to do, but they did it in that manner which says plainly, Why don't you do it yourself? On Monday last the barometer was down to 28 inches, which is the lowest I have ever seen it. Thermometer stands at about 48° to 50°.

Sunday, February 14, 1864.—During the first part of the past week we had very heavy and almost constant rain; wind moderate, and generally from between W. and N.W. On Thursday morning we had a light air from the eastward, which is the first easterly wind we have had since we came here. Since Wednesday the weather has been very fine, with moderate westerly winds, but still not a day has passed without showers, more or less. This is a dreadful place for rain; but still we appear to have got to a place where it falls least. There is one place where it scarcely ever ceases raining; this is caused by the form of the land in that particular place (which we have named Rainy Corner), which is backed by a very high mountain, which bursts the low clouds as they pass over it. I have been working at the boat, and have got her in first-rate order—much better than when we got her. The men have been jobbing about the house, and cutting long grass to thatch the walls with outside.

Since we came into the house we have arranged that one man shall cook for a week, and that they will take it in turns; and as Mr. Raynal wished to take his turn with the rest, I did not object to his doing so. He was cook last week (they change on Saturday nights), and an excellent cook he is; he has set the others a good example for cleanliness and good cooking, and I hope they will follow it. He very frequently gave us four courses at a meal. (Anyone might wonder where we got anything to make four courses off, but we are like the shell-fish, we get the most at spring tides). One would be stewed or roasted seal, fried liver, fish and mussels. We got a young seal on Friday, but we have not had a large one since last Sunday, which we cut up and salted like bacon. It is now hanging up, and I think this will be the best way of keeping the meat. We have tried several ways to preserve the skins without salting, so as to make clothes of them, but we have not succeeded yet. We cannot get them dried without something on them, as the flies destroy them, and there is no bark that will tan. We have not had any seals about the tent or house since I shot the fellow in the stern. Since noon it has come on to blow stiff, with squalls from W.N.W. Barometer 29·30 ; thermometer ranging from 48° to 52°. Went out with the gun this morning, and got a few widgeons.

CHAPTER II.

REFLECTIONS SUGGESTED BY OUR SITUATION.—BREAKING UP OF THE WRECK.—A BATTLE WITH THE SEALS. — UNSUCCESSFUL FISHING.

Sunday, February 21, 1864.—I am in exceedingly low spirits to-day, and I know that one loved one in Sydney is so also ; for I have no doubt but by this time they have given me up for lost, and what is to become of my own dear wife and children ? May God, to whom only they can now look for comfort, watch over and protect them, is my constant and fervent prayer. I shall never forgive myself for coming on this enterprise, although strong inducements prompted me to the undertaking ; and although the chief object of my coming was a failure, the sealing would have done very well, and I should have made a good thing of it, had the old chains only held the ship to her anchors. I could have loaded her with skins in a month, and should have been in Sydney before this time. However, this was an accident over which I had no control, and God in His wisdom knows best why I am left here, and how long we may remain here ; but surely our friends will send some one to look after us by some means or other, for I told them before leaving, that if any accident did happen to the vessel, it was much more likely to happen in harbour than at sea ; so it is to be hoped they will exert themselves in finding some means of getting a vessel sent to look for us. But if they do send one, it is not likely to be before next October or November, as I suppose people would not come down into these stormy and unexplored regions in the winter, which is now approaching. And this is certainly a very stormy place, and the wind is almost constantly blowing out of the harbour, and blowing a gale; on an average there is not more than one day out of three that a vessel could beat up against it. During the last week we have had the finest weather that we have had since we came here. We have had no rain until yesterday, when it rained heavily from noon till 8 P.M. To-day it is blowing a heavy and very squally N.W. gale, with misty dark weather. Yesterday the wind was N.N.W. and a hot wind, such as is felt in New Zealand. We have had it before, but not so hot as yesterday. The thermometer was up to 60°, which is usually about 48°; barometer at 29·25.

On Wednesday we went across the bay in the boat, and in two hours and a half shot 150lbs. weight of widgeons and a one-year-old seal, part of which we had roasted for dinner to-day—it was delicious. It took three men a whole day to pluck the widgeons—I don't know how many there are of them. We have got them salted and hung up; they are in reserve for the winter, when we may not be able to go out to look for food. During the remainder of the time we have been occupied in laying ways for hauling up and launching the boat on, and making a jetty; cutting down and clearing the timber from about the house, and getting and tying in bundles of thatch for the sides of the house, &c. It will take an immense quantity of grass to thatch it round. I may here give a description of this castle of ours. It is 24 feet long by 16 wide. The walls are 7 feet high, roof 14 feet. The corner posts and centre posts, which are made of spars from the ship, as also the wall plates and ridge poles, are let three feet into the ground. The walls or sides and ends are made of timber out of the bush, placed upright, and let into the ground about a foot. They are far from being straight, consequently they are far from being close to-gether. This is why we are obliged to thatch them. They are now covered with old canvas outside, but it lets a great deal of wind through. The door is a very good one, made of inch boards. The floor is also boarded, and tolerably good. There are two small squares of glass, which were taken out of the cabin of the vessel. The rafters are sticks out of the bush, placed two feet apart. There is a double cover on the roof, with two sets of rafters and two ridge poles. The fireplace is built of stone, as high as the walls of the house; above, it is made of copper, tin, zinc, and boards towards the top, and is 15 feet high. The fireplace inside the walls is 6 feet, with four walls 1 foot thick. Furniture—stretchers to sleep on, six feet from floor; large dining table in centre, 7 feet by 3 feet, with benches on each side. I sit on a keg at the head. A table at one end, at which I am now writing, and where I keep my writing-desk, chronometer, barometer, books, &c. This, the north end of the house, is occupied by Mr. Raynal and myself; the men occupy the other end. A cook's dressing table stands behind the door which opens. towards the men's end. There are also two or three shelves round the place, which, with a pair of bellows and my looking-glass, complete the furniture. It is now just four o'clock in the afternoon (three in Sydney), and it has commenced to rain heavily, with every appearance of continuing for the night. We have trenches all round the house two feet deep, which keep the floor perfectly dry, and no water has yet come through the roof. The barometer is now at 29·15. Thermometer 48°, which is 16° above freezing and 6° below temperate.

Sunday, February 28, 1864.—Another dreary week has passed. We have had very bad weather. It has rained every day. We have not been able to do much at the thatching; but we made a commencement yesterday, and worked at it between the showers. Last night it blew a very heavy gale from S.S.W., with frequent heavy showers. On Wednesday Mr. Raynal went across the bay in the boat, and got a one-year-old seal and two dozen widgeons; these we find very good, salted and smoke-dried. He also tried fishing; but it came on to rain, and he was obliged to return without catching any. We have found a root, which is very abundant all over the island, and it is very good food; it makes a very good substitute for bread and potatoes. There is also a great deal of sugar in it. We intend to make sugar from it. We have also found a method of curing the seal skins without salt. This is by stretching them and fledging them clean, and rubbing them well with strong lye (made from ashes) two or three times a day, until they are perfectly dry; then scour them well with sandstone, take them down, roll them up tight, and beat them on something solid with a smooth piece of wood until they are quite soft. This does not injure the fur, and they remain quite soft. We shall be able to make either blankets or clothes of them. I sleep on one of them now, and it is very comfortable.

Amongst the birds with which the woods abound, there are three kinds of songsters. Some of them are so tame that they come and feed out of our hands, and come into the house and remain there for hours. They also fly to the house in flocks when the hawks are after them. We shoot all hawks that come near. We have killed five, and this encourages the small birds to come near. On Thursday it blew fresh from the eastward, with 24 hours' heavy rain. During the remainder of the week the wind has been westerly, until last night; and to-day S.S.W. Barometer 29·50; thermometer 40°.

Sunday, March 6, 1864.—The first part of the past week was very fine, and we got on tolerably well with the thatching, and got more grass; but since Wednesday we have had continual drizzling rain, with light westerly winds, until midnight last night, when it came on to blow a very heavy gale, and continued ever since, with frequent showers. On Thursday I went across to Figure-of-Eight Island (as I have named it from its shape), and I discovered a reef of rocks which are dry at low water. They bear about S.W. from the N.W. end of the island, and the centre of the reef, which is round and composed of sharp loose rocks; it is about a cable's length from the shore, and connected with it.   There is barely a passage for a boat, and very shallow water outside of the distance of a cable and a half, where the centre drops suddenly into eight fathoms, close to the edge, and deepens fast from that outwards. But I was not particular about sounding far from it, as it came on to rain, and we wanted seal, as our fresh provisions had been out for two or three days; so we landed on the island, and found three mobs of seals asleep. There were from 30 to 40 in each mob, and there were a great many very young calves amongst them.   These we wanted to get without killing the old ones.   I had only two men with me; so we took our clubs and each of us took a mob, and I suppose in ten seconds we had knocked down ten calves from two to three months old, and one two-year-old seal.   We had to go right in amongst them, and, although they woke up, we were so quick about the job that they stared at us in confusion for a moment, and then by a simultaneous movement rushed towards the water.   We could have got more, but one of the men was at this moment attacked by the only remaining one, which was a tremendous large bull—the largest tiger seal I have seen (they were all tigers), and he fought like a tiger. We immediately rushed to the rescue; the poor fellow was obliged to take to a tree till we came up, when all three set on to the seal, and he showed fight bravely.   It was as long as ten minutes before we proved ourselves conquerors: we should have been quite willing to get out of his way, but he would not give us a chance.   We were in a thick bush, so that he had a decided advantage.   However, we left him, as he was too big for us to attend to when we had so many little ones to look after.   This was the greatest piece of excitement I have had for a long time. We got our booty into the boat, which was quite a load for her, and returned to the camp.   We had also a lot of widgeons, which I had shot before landing.   I had left my gun in the boat, or else I should have shot the big seal. We salted all the meat excepting two seals, which we kept for present use; and this afternoon I found a young seal, not more than a month or six weeks old, sitting shivering at the end of the house. I took him in, and some of them wanted to keep him; but this of course we could not do, as he would eat nothing but fish, and not even that yet; so we killed him. I think he had lost his mother, for he was very low in flesh and had nothing at all in his inside. So this is more fresh meat. God is certainly good in sending us plenty to eat. I hope and pray that He will soon send some one in here that will take us away.

The ' Grafton ' is breaking up fast to-day. There is a heavy surf on with the gale. Her decks are coming up. The barometer has been very high throughout the week; it has not been below 29·50 until to-day, when it fell, from 10 o'clock last night till 9 o'clock this morning, from 29·58 to 28 at 9 A.M. The thermometer has been about 48°, till to-day it is 47°.

Sunday, March 13, 1864.—My heart beats fast to-night as I sit down to write, somewhat similar to what it might do if I was about writing a love letter. I know that many a bitter tear has been shed for me by this time, and most likely to-day, as this is the end of another dreary month since I left those I loved so much; and how many more must pass, or how they will pass them until we meet again, or whether we shall ever meet again on earth— Heaven only knows. These thoughts, and such as these, which now prey continually on my mind, are maddening. I feel as if I was gradually consumed by an inward fire. I strive, by occupying my hands as much as possible, to dispel these sad feelings; but it is utterly impossible. A melancholy is getting hold of me; I am getting as thin as a lantern, and some disordered fluttering and heavy beating of the heart, which causes a faintness, is troubling me. I have felt this before, but only on one particular occasion, and that is some time ago. Were it not for the hope that

I shall yet again be of service to my family, I think my spirit, if not my health, would break down; although under my present afflictions my continual prayer is that God may soon deliver me out of them. During the week the weather has been variable; wind generally from N.W.

On Wednesday we had a very heavy gale, similar to the one the 'Grafton' went on shore in; wind baffling between N.W. and S.W. On Friday Mr. Raynal and others went to Figure-of-Eight Island; they killed seven young seals. There were great numbers on the island. They might have killed any quantity, but we did not want them; we salt and dry what we cannot use fresh. Barometer 29·70; thermometer 48°.

Sunday, March 20, 1864.—During the last week we have had nothing but a succession of westerly gales, which only cease for a few hours and then blow again with great fury; and it has also rained almost constantly until yesterday at noon. Since then we have had very frequent falls of hail and snow: some of the mountains are now quite capped with snow. I fear we shall have a great deal of this sort of weather in the winter. However, we have got a good stock of meat hanging up in the house, and so long as we can get to the roots we shall not starve; but these roots will not keep long out of the ground. We are obliged to pull them as we want them. We had a few hours of moderate weather on Friday, and we went to Figure-of-Eight Island, and found the seals, both young and old, very numerous; but this time we had a regular pitched battle with some thirty or forty of them on the beach. We vanquished them, and got seven young calves. There were four of us; Mr. Raynal had the gun, but I did not want him to fire at them if we could avoid it, so he stood by as a reserve while we poured on to them with our clubs, and there was not a shot fired. We killed a number of old ones; but these we had to leave, as they would only have been an incumbrance to us, and the seals were running around in such numbers, and in such a threatening manner, that we hurried away as fast as possible. There was a great number of young ones left on the island, and there is no doubt but they would have landed with increased numbers, and attacked us again. The very young seals do not like to take the water, as they cannot swim very well. When they first go into the water the old cow carries them on her back, or rather carries it, for I have not seen any of them with more than one calf, and they have a great job to get them down to the water at first. I have known a cow to be three days in getting a calf half a mile to get it into the water. When you surprise the calves when they are staying at the edge of the water, they will always run on shore and make for the bush. The last time that Raynal went without me the seals were very savage. In the water they attacked the boat ; one left the marks of his teeth in an oar, and another one was going to jump into the boat, but Raynal shot him. When they are killed in the water they sink like a stone.

We have got a nest of young parrots. I think we have had them at the house a fortnight now. The steward attends to them ; they are getting on very well. I think it very strange to find parrots here at all, and it is more surprising that they should have young ones at this season of the year. The common field mouse is also here. I do not know whether they are very numerous all over the islands or not, but there are a good many about the house. We have not been able to do anything at the thatching this week. About one-third of the house is finished, and the grass is all bundled for the remainder. We are only waiting for weather to put it on ; but whether it will ever be favourable again or not I cannot say. In going to and from the island, on Friday last, I sounded all the way. I found a bank with eleven fathoms on it in the middle of the harbour, and well to windward of this is good anchorage ground. It will be, however, in the chart I have in course of construction ; and as I have not yet named all the points, it is useless to note down any bearings here. We cure all the skins; we shall soon have enough to make a suit of clothes each. This is seals' blood that I am writing with now, as our black ink is done. I think this will do very well. There is no getting it out of our clothes, although we use strong lye and soft soap, which we made ourselves. Monday is our washing day. We have strict regularity in all we do. Barometer 28·78; thermometer 36°.

Sunday, March 27, 1864.—During the first part of the last week the weather was very boisterous, and a good deal of hail and snow. The wind was generally from W.N.W., barometer sometimes as low as 28·62, and the thermometer was so low as 35°. Since Wednesday the weather has been tolerably fine, with fresh westerly winds and cloudy, though mild and pleasant weather. We have finished thatching the house, and find it very warm and comfortable. It has taken 5000 bundles of thatch, each bundle weighing a pound, so that the total weight of thatch on the sides and ends of the house is about two and a quarter tons. The roof remains covered with canvas. To-day I went in the boat up the harbour; I have not been there before. This harbour is rather narrow, but quite broad enough for any ship to work up. It is about half a mile wide in the narrowest place, which is about the entrance, and in some places it is about one and a half miles wide. I find that this is the proper place to anchor a vessel in; it is well sheltered from the prevailing winds, and there appears to be none of those sudden gusts of wind which are so frequent and dangerous in this part of the harbour. The depth of water in the middle harbour is from thirty fathoms at the entrance, gradually decreasing, and good anchorage will be found in from twelve down to four fathoms (stiff blue clay), about one mile and a half from the head of the harbour, and the water shallows so gradually for this mile and a half that a great deal of the head of the bay must be left dry at low water. It was half flood when I was up there.

There are several streams of beautiful water emptying

into the bay ; two of them are the largest I have yet found in any part of the islands. We tried fishing, but unsuccessfully. We killed one seal and a number of widgeons, and then returned home. We did not see any seals on shore, but we saw great numbers in the water. I suppose, as it was a fine day, they were all out fishing. There must be great numbers of fish in these harbours to supply so many seals, but we have not yet found out how to catch them. All the fish we have got as yet we have picked up amongst the seaweed and stones on the beach at low water. During the last day or two all the snow has disappeared from the mountains. I hope we shall have some fine weather yet before the winter sets in. The barometer is very high to-day, 30·20 ; and the thermometer 47° in the shade. I have found another small bottle of black ink, so I shall use it while it lasts; for I see that the seals' blood fades away very much.

CHAPTER III.

VISIT TO FIGURE-OF-EIGHT ISLAND.—DOGS DISCOVERED.—
ROYAL TOM. — BIBLE READINGS.

Sunday, April 3, 1864.—Since last Sunday we have had tolerably fine weather, although we have had two days of rainy, misty weather, but mild withal. The wind has generally been very light from the westward, but at midnight last night it shifted to S.W., and has blown a fresh breeze, with occasional showers of hail, throughout the day. The barometer has kept very high, and the thermometer has been about 50° until to-day, when it was 40°; at noon, barometer 29·92. On Monday last we went to Figure-of-Eight Island to get some young meat. We found the young seals as numerous as ever, if not more so ; and this time they would not take to water at all. We were obliged to go right in amongst them, and they showed fight bravely. However, we got three young ones without killing any old ones. This was as many as we wanted, as we do not intend salting any more down, as we generally get one fine day in the week, when we can go and get more ; and we can keep the meat a week very well now, for the flies are nearly all gone, and we keep it hanging at the top of a high tree, where they do not touch it.

While on the island we found a place where some party had camped at some time. There is no doubt but that they were killing seals, as we found a number of bricks, which no doubt had been used for their fry works. There had been two tents pitched, and, from the appearance of the ground where they had their fire, I should judge that they had remained about a week. The ground all over these islands, except on the mountains, is of a turfy nature, and burns away wherever a fire is made ; it is by this means that I judge from the place where the fire has been how long they have remained. How long it is since they were here I am unable to conjecture, but it is evident that ships visit this harbour sometimes; very probably it has been a whaler come in for wood or water, and finding the seals so numerous has taken a few. I am delighted to see even this sign of ships coming here : there is no doubt but we shall be released from our bondage some time—perhaps sooner than we expect. May it please God for it to be so! We sailed all round one of the heads of this harbour, taking soundings all the way, and I find anchorage in 10 and 11 fathoms ; but there is an excellent anchorage in 15 fathoms, between Figure-of-Eight Island and Round Point.

On Wednesday Mr. Raynal and I went to try fishing from the shore. We caught one very nice little cod, about three pounds weight, but the seals were round in swarms, which drove the fish away. We found a place about three miles from the house, where a fearful rush of water has come down from the mountains very recently, tearing away trees, earth, and rocks in its track to the harbour. We now found only a very small stream trickling down its bed, and if the terrific rush of water which has made this havoc has been caused by the thaw of the little snow which was on the hills a fortnight ago, I don't know what we may expect after the winter's snow. However, our house stands on pretty high ground ; I think it will be out of all danger.

Sunday, April 10, 1864.—Another month is now nearly gone since we commenced this unfortunate voyage. The days are getting short, and a long, stormy, dreary winter is before us, without the slightest prospect of getting away ; and how those dear ones whom I left manage to battle with the misery in which my ambition and folly has plunged them, I dare not think. Oh ! if they were only here with me, how happy would be my condition compared with what it is; for I am provided with a good shelter, and plenty to eat, and I should then think that they shared these blessings at least; but as it is, I know not to what extremities they may be reduced. My urgent prayer to Heaven is that I may be permitted to retain my health and reason through this fearful and distressing trial. During the past week we have had very little fine weather. Monday was the only fine day we have had; and on this day we went to Figure-of-Eight Island, and without much trouble got four young calves. The seals were as plentiful as ever on the island. We took two without getting amongst the old at all. The other two we were obliged to go in amongst a mob to get, but it was admirably done. We are getting quite expert at the business. Myself and one of the men ran in amongst them, and knocked down and dragged away the two young ones before the old ones had time to collect themselves sufficiently to offer any resistance.

On Tuesday morning it was quite calm. We went down to the harbour to look at the flag we put there some time ago. We found that the flag was entirely blown away; and the staff, which is a stout pole, and was well set into the ground, was nearly blown down; and the bottle, which was well tied to it, was also shaken down and lying on the ground. It requires something exceedingly well fastened in the ground to withstand the almost constant and terrific gales which blow here. I intend to put up a white board, in such a manner that it cannot blow down, on the first fine day. Before we arrived at Flagstaff Point it commenced to blow from the N.N.W. We had no time to lose, but returned as quickly as possible, and it was as much as we could do with three oars and me sculling to get across the bay, and under the lee of the weather shore; indeed several times, when we were losing ground, I thought we should have to run back and beach the boat somewhere. However, we managed to get across, pulled nearly to the head of the harbour, and, taking in ballast, sailed across to the house, where we arrived at 5 P.M.

drenched with rain and spray, and fainting with hunger; for we had had nothing to eat since breakfast.

Our first intention in going afloat was to try fishing; but being unsuccessful, and the morning so fine, I determined on going down to look at the flag. It is almost impossible to catch fish here with lines, as the seals are attracted by you, and come round in such numbers that they drive the fish away. In going down the harbour I took a number of soundings, and I have discovered another reef of rocks, which are dry at low water spring tides, and might prove very dangerous to anyone working up for the Middle Harbour, where the best anchorage is, as they lie about a cable's length from the southern point of its entrance; and a vessel would naturally bring that point, so as to weather in as far as possible on the first board. Their position is marked by kelp, which always should be avoided in this harbour. Barometer 29·50; thermometer, 47°.

Sunday, April 17, 1864.—The first and middle parts of the past week were very fine, with a high barometer. Wind generally from the west and W.N.W.; but yesterday and to-day it has been blowing a hard gale from the N.N.W.; and about four o'clock this evening it backed into north, and is now (8 P.M.) raining heavily, and blowing a hard gale. We have found another place where the seals assemble in great numbers; it is on this shore, about a mile and a half from the house. We do not intend to disturb them, unless on account of bad weather during the winter, when we cannot get to the island.

On Tuesday morning one of the men came running in, in a state of excitement, and told me that there were two dogs in the bush; he had left the other man in the bush to watch them till he came and told me. I immediately went to the place where the other man was left, but when I got there the dogs were gone. I saw their tracks, and was satisfied that they had seen dogs; and from the men's description of them I think they were sheep dogs. One day, about three weeks after the wreck, we heard what we all supposed to be a dog barking; but as we had not heard or seen anything of dogs, we had almost forgotten all about it. But it is now evident that there are dogs on the island. At a short distance from where they were seen we found a dead seal calf, which they had evidently killed; so it appears that they subsist partly on seals' meat. We find that there is another small four-footed animal an inhabitant of this island also; this animal burrows, and undoubtedly only comes out at night. We have set snares, but have failed to catch them: their footmarks are similar to those of a pig. We catch small fish in the creek, which are delicious eating; they resemble the trout, but are very small. It would take four of the largest we have yet caught to weigh a pound, but they are very numerous. Barometer 29·50; thermometer 50°.

Sunday, April 22, 1864.—During the past week the weather has been exceedingly fine and mild; we have had some misty and frosty weather, but no disagreeable weather to speak of. The wind has been generally from N.N.W. On Wednesday and Thursday the wind was light from the S.E., which is something very unusual. On these two days we went down to Flagstaff Point, and erected a board 4 feet long and 2 feet 6 inches wide, painted white, with a large letter ' N ' painted blue on it, to indicate that they must turn to north. I also secured a bottle to the board, to notify to anyone where we are, and giving them some instructions for working up the harbour. But should they not be able to send a boat on shore to get the bottle, the letter ' N ' will indicate which way they are to turn; and when they are round the point we shall see them, and I shall get on board as soon as possible. The board is elevated about sixty feet from the mean level of the sea, and will be visible at some distance outside the Heads. While we were down there we caught a few very nice cod-fish, and I took a number of bearings which I had not been able to get before. I also sounded in all directions; my line was only 35 fathoms long, and in many places I could not get bottom.

On Monday we went to Figure-of-Eight Island. We did not find the seals as numerous as previously; the day being very fine, and it being flood tide when we were there, no doubt they were fishing. We took a bull and cow seal, both yearlings, very large and fat. During the week the barometer has been very high; on Wednesday it was at 30·36, to-day it is 29·50; thermometer, 51°.

Sunday, May 1, 1864.—We now enter upon another month of imprisonment, which is commencing with bad weather. During the last three days it has been blowing a very heavy gale of wind, between S.W. and W.N.W. Sometimes there is a lull for about four hours, and then it comes on with great fury. The squalls are terrific, and accompanied with hail or rain. Sometimes the hills are quite white, but it soon disappears. The last month, on the whole, we had exceedingly fine weather—much finer than any we had at midsummer; but I suppose we may now expect winter to set in in earnest.

On Wednesday we went to the island for fresh meat. There was not a great number of seals on shore. It was flood tide, and I find that this is their fishing time. They are more numerous on shore during the ebb tide. They appear to assemble in greater numbers on the island than anywhere else, exactly at the head of the western arm, which is too far away for us to visit them there; but we also know many other places where they camp. Certain mobs collect and camp on their own particular ground, and also keep together in the water, but do not confine themselves to any particular part of the harbour. This I have ascertained from observations. There is one seal which we all know particularly well wherever we see him; he appears to be the king of the mob which belong to Figure-of-Eight Island. He is a very large dark coloured bull, of the tiger breed; we have named him Royal Tom. He is not at all afraid of us when we see him on shore; if the seals around him run away, 'Tom' will not move, and takes very little notice of us. One day some of the men tried to drive 'Tom' into the water, but he would not move for some time; but after some trouble I suppose they got him to start. He went leisurely down to the water, and there he remained scratching himself; 'Tom' had a dry coat, and did not fancy wetting it just then, and into the water he would not go. He is too big and old for use, therefore we did not wish to kill him; indeed I do not allow any seals to be disturbed at all excepting those we intend to kill; but as I was not there myself I suppose the boys wanted to have a little fun to themselves, which would have cost them a reprimand had I heard of it in a direct manner. But they kept this to themselves; I only heard of it in an indirect manner, and so I let it pass. I have adopted a measure for keeping them in order and subjection, which I find to work admirably, and it also acts beneficially on my own mind. This is, teaching school in the evenings, and reading prayers and reading and expounding the scriptures on Sunday to the best of my ability. We have done this for some time now, and I am happy to say with much greater success than I at first expected. They are all getting particularly fond of reading, and hearing the Bible read. Some of them cannot read yet, but they are learning very fast, and I have not heard a profane word spoken for a long time. So much for moral suasion. I trust that the result will be beneficial to all parties. The barometer has been about 29·60 to 29·90 through the week; to-day it is 29·30, and rising. I hope we shall have finer weather to-morrow. Thermometer 40°.

Tuesday, May 10, 1864.—For some few days back I have not been very well. To-day I have had a very severe headache, but as it has now left me, and as I did not write on Sunday as usual, I shall do a little of it this evening; and, moreover, as this is the anniversary (32nd) of my birth, I have made it a point for some years back to

pledge my mother on this day in a bottle of good old port
—but unfortunately it is out of my power to do so to-day;
but I have not omitted to pledge her for all that. I have
done so in a glass of beer of our own making, and what
we use as a substitute for tea. It is not very good, but
still it is preferable to cold water. It is made from the
root which now forms a very material part of our food, and,
as I have before stated, contains a considerable quantity
of sugar. To make the beer we grate the root on a large
grater (as we do for eating), boil it, let it ferment, and
then put it in a cask and draw off as we use it. In using
the root for food we fry it in oil (seal oil). It eats something like sawdust, but we are very thankful that we have
it, otherwise we should have to live entirely on seals' meat,
fowl, and fish, as our little stock of provisions which we
had when we were wrecked has long since been exhausted.
Nothing remains of it but a few crumbs of biscuit, which
are regularly placed on the table, but only to look at—or
' point at,' as Paddy would say—for no one touches it.

We find that we can catch fish in great abundance, but
we have only very recently found out the secret of catching them, which is done by fishing amongst the rocks with
a short line tied to the end of a stick. The best time for
catching them is the first quarter flood. One man can go
out, and in an hour will return with sufficient fish to last
us three days, and we eat them at every meal; and since
we find that we can get them so easily, we eat very little
seal meat; and the root, which we call sacchrie (from its
saccharine property), eats better with fish than anything
else.

Our parrots, which we have now had for some time, are
getting on very well, and are beginning to talk; but, unfortunately, yesterday they all got out of the cage, and we
have lost one of them—two remain.

Since I last wrote the weather has been very boisterous,
and a good deal of snow has fallen. Yesterday everything
was quite white, and it lay quite thick on the mountains;

but to-day the wind has been from the N.W., heavy gale
with rain, and has taken it all away. We have not yet
actually had frost, although the thermometer has been
down to 33°, which is only one degree from it. The flies
have not left us yet; the blow-flies are not so bad, but what
is most extraordinary is that the mosquitoes are almost
as troublesome as they were in the summer; they bite
like fury, with the thermometer at 35°. We have not seen
the dogs since I mentioned them before, but we frequently
fall in with their tracks; they do not come near the house.
On Saturday last the barometer was very low—28·46 ;
to-day it is 28·80 ; thermometer 44°. I felt inclined to
write some, but my scholars are troubling me, so I shall
quit.

CHAPTER IV.

WINTER IN AUCKLAND ISLAND.—THE MOUNTAINS.—AN
EQUINOCTIAL GALE.—A WEARY JOURNEY.

Sunday, May 15, 1864.—Six long and dreary months
have now passed since I left Sydney, and the idea of the
sad lot which may and must have fallen on those I love so
much, wrings my soul with agony, and a remorse which I
fear is crushing me fast to the earth. Oh, my God! how
long is this to last? Oh, release me from this bondage!
Night and morning, daily and in my dreams, I offer up my
prayers to Thee. Oh, hear me! and release.me that I may
flee to the succour of those dear innocent ones who are
now suffering for my folly. Give me but an opportunity
of making amends for this and many other thoughtless
acts—the hope of which only at present sustains me.
Were it not for this hope, I should pray for death, or
perhaps seek it by my own hand. What is life to me, but
for their sakes? A mere burden. I have already lived a
long and chequered life in a few short years; I should feel
satiated with it, but for their sakes may it please God to
spare me, at least as long as them. But set me at liberty
to provide for them, I will be content even with separation;
but let me not have doomed them to wretchedness and
misery. Hear my prayer, O Lord! and grant my release.

During the last three or four days we have had the most
varied and extraordinary weather that ever I remember
witnessing. There have not been two hours alike during
the whole time, except in the general calm or very light
airs, varying from all points of the compass; but chiefly
from S. and S.E. One hour the sky is clear, with bright
sunshine, and only a few bright fleecy clouds visible,

D

almost without motion. Then suddenly rises an imperious cloud, which immediately covers the whole sky, and down falls a pelting shower of rain, sleet, or hail, generally accompanied with a thick fog. Thus it continues night and day. The barometer has kept very low; yesterday it was down to 28·30, but it has been rising rapidly since, and is now (11 A.M.) at 29·18, which is the only apparent indication of a change. There is snow on the tops of the mountains. We have not yet had frost where we are, although yesterday at noon the thermometer was as low as 34°. This morning, about six o'clock, we felt the shock of an earthquake; it was not violent, but the tremor continued about a minute. Eight P.M.—The weather continues as before, only that the showers are now alternately sleet and snow. Barometer 29·45; thermometer 33°.

Sunday, May 22, 1864.—The weather continued as before described until yesterday morning, since which time it has been dull, cloudy, and foggy; but wild, with N.W. airs. On Friday morning the ground was all covered with snow; but now it has disappeared even from the tops of the mountains, and the birds are again singing blithely. The blow-flies are busy again, and I begin to think that the winter will not be severe enough to banish them entirely. The small flies, or what I have called mosquitoes, will evidently not leave, for on Friday, with the thermometer at freezing (32°), they were biting. We have seen one of the dogs again, and we have also seen one of those animals which I have before mentioned as burrowing in the earth. The one that we saw was up a tree, and the dog was barking at him; but on seeing us they both made off. The animal had short legs and short ears, a long tail, and grey-coloured fur like a cat, which he somewhat resembles, only that his body is long, and not so big round as that of a cat. This animal evidently lives upon birds and eggs, from the fact that we frequently find feathers and egg shells about their holes. Speaking of eggs, we have not as yet found any; but probably we arrived here too late in the season

The seals do not appear to come on shore in the day-time so much as they used to do. We very seldom see any on shore now, unless we wait for them coming up late in the evening, or go before daylight in the morning, and get them before they go into the water. To-day the barometer is 30·3, thermometer 46°.

Sunday, May 29, 1864. — It has been blowing a very heavy gale during all the past week, with continued hail, snow, and rain, and yesterday thunder and lightning : the wind was from between S.W. and N.W. It has been impossible to launch the boat, or even to go out of the house, and we have to live entirely on salt seal, roots, and cold water ; for we have been obliged to abandon the beer, which I have before mentioned, as it gave us all the bowel complaint. But yesterday I sauntered out with one of the men, and we managed to kill a seal ; but we had to carry it on our backs a distance of about two miles, which is no joke, over these rocky beaches, and through this thick bush. However, we were glad to have it for the carrying. Mr. Raynal is again laid up, with a sore finger, and one of the men is also laid up, with a sprained ankle. Since noon the weather has moderated : the glass is rising, and I think we shall be able to get out the boat to-morrow. The barometer was at the lowest on Friday, 28·60 ; to-day it is at 29·40 ; thermometer 34°.

Sunday, June 5, 1864.—Since last Sunday the wind has generally been very light, from between N.W. and W., with a great deal of fog and drizzling rain. The barometer has been as high as 30·30, and the thermometer about 40°. On Monday we went up to the harbour, and paid a visit to the island, to look for fresh meat ; but to our disappointment we found no seals there, and the island has evidently been deserted by them for some time. Neither do they appear to go on shore anywhere now so much as they did in summer ; but they appear more numerous in the water than I have ever seen them. We managed to get some mussels and two seals, but we had a long hunt for them. It was late at night when we returned to the camp. We have now got some good roads made about the house, which was very necessary, for the ground is so soft that after any part of it has been trodden a little it becomes mud, which in this damp weather never has a chance to get dry. We are also getting a considerable clearing round the place; for we burn a great deal of wood —not less than a large cart-load a day. Consequently it is getting cut down very fast. Light airs from N.W. and thick fog to-day. Barometer falling, 29·50; thermometer 40°.

Sunday, June 12, 1864. — During the past week the weather has been bad. We have had a good deal of S.W. and southerly gales, with snow; but this has all disappeared again. Yesterday we went out in the boat to look for something to eat; but unfortunately (and for the first time) we got nothing but half-a-dozen small fish. We were not able to get any mussels, as the tide was not low enough (it being now neaps), and we did not see a single seal on shore. They appear to keep in the water almost constantly. Now, as the water is warmer than the air, and they only come on shore in the night, after dark, to sleep, and go into the water before daylight, it would be madness for us to go through the bush to look for them in the dark. They are very numerous in the water, and if we actually get hard up for something to eat, I shall fasten to one with a harpoon. But our boat is only a dingy, and so frail that I am afraid she will not stand it, or else I would have tried it before this time; for 'tis now a fortnight since we got one, and for the last few days we have lived on pickling. We have to look pretty sharp after our bellies now, and I fear very much that we shall go hungry yet before the winter is out.

It is very fortunate that the weather is not severely cold, and I am somewhat surprised at it; for we have scarcely had frost as yet, and it is now mid-winter. On Friday morning we found ice in a tub, about as thick as a shilling, which is the first actual frost we have had. Our parrots are beginning to talk, but I think they are the ka-ka-po, a very rare bird, which is found in New Zealand and on some of the Philippine Islands, and eagerly sought after by naturalists. In the spring, if God spares me, I intend to get as many young ones as I can. Mr. Raynal has had a very bad finger. It was a fester, and I thought at one time he would lose it; but it is now out of danger. The man who sprained his ankle is also well again. It is now seven months since we left Sydney. I shall not attempt to give expression as to what I feel on this point; but I may say that I begin to look forward to the coming of summer, when surely we shall be relieved. The barometer has been low, 28·60, during the week, but it is now up again. Wind N.W., was S.E. outside; barometer 29; thermometer 30°.

Monday, June 20, 1864.—Since Thursday last we have had remarkably fine weather, with a slight frost, and very light easterly airs and calms. This is the first easterly wind we have had to continue more than six hours. On Tuesday and Wednesday the wind was S. and S.S.W., light, with dark gloomy weather, fog, and drizzling rain, which is something very extraordinary with southerly wind. On Monday morning two of the hands went before daylight to a place where we know a mob of seals frequent in the night. They found great numbers on shore, and just as the day began to break they began to go into the water. They killed two cows. It is evident that they only come up for a few hours in the night to sleep, and stop in the water all the day.

On Friday we went down to Flagstaff Point, and, finding our signal-board right, we caught fish and got mussels until dark, when we returned home with a load of mussels, but only a few fish. We can manage very well for provisions when the weather is fine, but still we have to look very sharp after it, for the days are very short (they are now at their shortest). We have only eight hours daylight, and we have taken nearly all the fish and mussels that were anywhere within two or three miles of the house ; and we cannot very well go any farther along the shores without the boat. Besides, the mussels are very scarce anywhere excepting at low water spring tides ; and at that time it is always dark now, as it is high water on full and change days about noon.

Yesterday we all (excepting the cook) went on to the mountains to the north, taking the same track up that I took on the 24th January. We travelled on until we reached the top of a mountain which is situated about the centre of the island, and is, I think, the highest part of the land. From here we had a full view of the whole group. The south island, as I noticed on 13th January, is scarcely disconnected, and one to the extreme north is at some distance from the mainland—perhaps six miles, and it may be about six miles in circumference. The whole extent of the group from north to south I judge to be 30 or 35 miles, and about fifteen miles east and west at the widest part. The western shore is high and bold, particularly the southern end, carrying almost a straight line N.N.E., and with one or two small islets (perhaps there are more ; I saw two) off the middle of the island, but close to it. To the eastward of the extreme northern part, there appears to be a number of dangerous sunken reefs, on which the water breaks heavily, although it was calm, and has been calm, or nearly so, for the last four days. Some of these reefs extend to a distance of not less than ten miles from the land.

On the eastern side of the island, from about the centre of the coast line, the land trends away in a N.W. direction to its northern extremity. This part of the land is much lower than the southern parts, and from the western coast slopes away in undulating ridges to the N.E. shore, which is cut up by indentions, small bays, and chasms. From the appearance of this part of the island, I have no doubt but it is swarming with seals. The shores are clad with scrub and stunted timber, similar to the shores of this bay. The view from the summit of the mountain on which we stood, at an elevation of about 800 or 1000 feet, is something grand and magnificent; a prospect so rude and craggy I have never met with. The summit of the mountains consists of nothing but rocks, that are totally barren and naked, and are thrown up in every possible variety of shape and ruggedness. There are chasms and perpendicular precipices, hundreds of feet deep, down which it is fearful to look ; and looking from these to the sea, which is visible all round, gives a beautiful relief to the eye. I have an outline sketch of the group. We were seven hours out. The travelling on the top of the mountains was very good, as all the springs and soft places were frozen over. In coming back I caught a bird something like a water-hen. Barometer, 30·20 ; thermometer, 32°.

Sunday, June 26, 1864.—I closed my note of last Monday without furnishing the details of Sunday's excursion. The mountain which we went on to we have, ever since we had the misfortune to come here, distinguished by the name of the Giant's Tomb. Its summit, when seen from the bay, bears a very striking resemblance to an immense coffin ; and since I have been to it, I find that it will bear the same appearance from the offing on the eastern and N.E. sides of the island. On arriving there, we found this apparent coffin to be a solid wall or ridge of rock, about 100 yards long and 20 feet thick, running in a N.W. and S.E. direction ; on the S.W. side about 20 feet high, and on the N.E. side not less than 45 feet high. In its S.E. end, which overlooks a valley, is a large cavern. This valley is about a mile long, and appears not to be more than 200 yards wide. It is bounded on both sides by precipitous rocks, rising to a height of from 600 to 800 feet. Its head is bounded by a semi-circle of the same precipitous nature, but rising to the height of about 1,000 feet; and at the summit is the before-mentioned cave, into which we managed to get, though not without exposing ourselves to the danger of falling from top to bottom. On our return we found a plant, which we have not seen anywhere else on this island; but there is plenty of it on Campbell's Island. We brought some of it down and cooked it, and found it very good to eat, and particularly good to put in the soup, which is very purging; and we find that this vegetable has a contrary effect. Everything here is evergreen, even the grass. Some of the trees have blossoms now, and there are small red berries which are at present ripe; they are very good, and the birds are very fond of them. I am reserving some of the seed; I have no doubt but with cultivation they may be made a very nice fruit.

On Thursday morning we went down the harbour in the boat, and at the break of day we landed and killed a seal, the only one we saw on shore, although there were plenty in the water. At low water we got a load of mussels, and then went to select a place for keeping a look-out for a vessel, when we begin to expect one. And now that the shortest days are past, I begin to look forward with hope towards the time when we may expect one. Last night we heard one of the dogs barking close to the house. During the whole of the week, and up to four o'clock this afternoon, the weather has been very mild—calm in the night time, and very light northerly N.W. airs in the day; but the weather generally dark, and gloomy, and foggy, with the barometer about 30·0, and thermometer 44° at noon. At 4 P.M. to-day a breeze sprang up from the westward, and is now blowing a strong breeze, and squally, with frequent showers. Barometer 29·20; thermometer, 30°.

Sunday, July 3, 1864.—Blowing a strong gale at W.N.W.; barometer steadily rising from 29·50, where it stood when the gale commenced; but before the gale commenced it had been down to 29·25. 8 P.M.: Barometer standing at 29·96; gale continuing to blow steadily. Midnight: Barometer perceptibly falling; weather showery and foggy. It has been stormy during the whole of the past week. On Tuesday and Wednesday a considerable quantity of snow fell—all the ground was covered; but since midnight of Wednesday we have had a heavy gale from the W.N.W., with much rain, which still continues; but the barometer has been rising to-day. Very likely the gale will take off at midnight. I find that in the locality of these islands, as also on the coast of New Zealand, the barometer is of very little service to a stranger, and would, to say the least, lead his judgment of the weather into error, by its strange irregularities. It frequently falls below 29 inches, with light southerly airs and fine weather, which continue so long as the barometer keeps down (sometimes 60 hours); but immediately after the barometer begins to rise, and gets above 29 inches, it is followed by a gale commencing at S.W., and blowing between S.W. and N.W. for generally three days, and dies away at north. The gales following this, with a very low barometer, are the heaviest, and generally accompanied by rain, and blow with great fury. When the barometer falls to 29·25 and again commences to rise, a strong gale may be expected from the west, where it continues sometimes seven days, and until the barometer has risen to 30 inches, when it may be expected to die away suddenly. Again, the barometer at 29·50 and lowering dark weather, a N.W. or northerly gale may be expected; and these gales are accompanied by much rain, and invariably haul to the southward, and die away with a rising barometer, and are of the shortest duration. But I should recommend the stranger navigating these parts to be ruled by his own judgment, independent of the barometer; but use great caution, as these gales come on very suddenly.

The only time that the barometer can be implicitly relied upon is when it is above 30 inches. Then the weather is fine, with light airs, generally southerly, but sometimes east and north-east, which does not continue more than two or three days. After this very fine weather, a gale seldom comes on suddenly. A south-east gale, or even fresh breeze, we have not yet had. As far as my experience goes, I find the summer gales heavier, of longer duration, and more frequent than those of the winter. In winter, or in this winter, we have had the most moderate weather ;. but fogs (which are frequent all the year round) are more prevalent, and excessively dense during the latter season, almost constantly enveloping entirely the land, and rendering its approach dangerous. On Thursday morning we got three seals, after going out every previous morning without success. We killed them about two miles from the house, butchered them, and hung them up, carrying as much as we could home with us. The weather has been so bad ever since that we have not been able to launch the boat to go for the remainder.

Monday, July 4, 1864.—Gale continued till 3 P.M., when it backed to N.W. by W. and increased to a whole gale, which has continued to blow from the same point with great violence throughout the day. Weather dark, foggy, and showery. Barometer: 9 A.M., 29·92; noon, 29·90; 4 P.M., 29·88; 8 P.M., 29·94; wind W.N.W., gale unabated; 10 P.M., 29·95; wind N.W., gale unabated.

Tuesday, July 5, 1864.—The gale continued until 3 A.M., and died away suddenly. Nine A.M.: Barometer 30·9, light northerly airs, and foggy dark weather, though very mild. Noon: Barometer, 30·11; thermometer, in open air, 47°. Thus, if the barometer gets above 30 inches, the gale is done, and a day or two of fine weather may be expected; but should it fall the slightest before it arrives at 30 inches, whilst the gale is blowing, the wind will haul again to the westward, and blow harder. But after blowing hard from the westward, when it backs, and gets to the northward of N.W., it invariably dies away, independent of the state of the barometer. To illustrate Sunday's note on the weather and barometer, I shall insert at full my observations since that time.*

---

* One of the equinoctial gales of September, 1864, commenced on the 6th, from the north-west, with the barometer at 29·75; but it immediately

Sunday, July 10, 1864.—Tuesday last was a fine, mild day, with light northerly airs. The barometer rose to

fell to 29·25, and again rose to 29·30, the gale gradually hauling to the southward ; and on the 8th was at south, and remained there 54 hours. On the 9th it again backed to the westward, barometer fluctuating between 29·75 and 29·40. On the 11th it was at north-west, where it stood 36 hours. During this part of the gale the weather throughout was dark and gloomy, and generally foggy, with almost constant alternate falls of hail, snow, and heavy rain. On the 12th the gale backed farther to the northward, and was accompanied by constant heavy rain, and black, impervious fog. At 9 P.M. on the 13th the barometer was down to 28·65, wind at N.N.W., gale moderating. From the 8th up to this time it blew with great fury, and without the slightest intermission ; great numbers of trees were torn up by the roots. 11 A.M.—Calm. Noon.—Breeze from the W.S.W., rain and fog continuing, barometer rising rapidly. 1 P.M.—Strong gale from S.W.; weather as before. 6 P.M.—Barometer 29·25; rain ceased, but fog continued. At 3 A.M. on the 14th the wind came from the S.E., and increased to a brisk gale, gradually working to the eastward ; cloudy, misty weather, with frequent showers ; barometer, 29·60. 15th.—Strong north-east gale and constant heavy rain ; barometer 29·24. 16th.—Wind moderate from the northward ; weather cloudy and misty until noon ; barometer falling rapidly. From noon until midnight, wind high from N.E., with constant heavy rain ; barometer 26 inches. 17th.—Calm and cloudy until noon, with the barometer at 28·82. From noon until 3 A.M. on the 18th, wind light and puffy, between W.N.W. and N.W., and steady rain ; barometer still slightly falling, 28·82. 18th.—From 2 till 9 A.M, wind light and fitful from W.S.W., and heavy rain. 9 A.M.—Wind S.W., and detached opening clouds ; rain ceased, but occasional showers fell throughout the day ; barometer 28·82. At 4 P.M. the glass commenced to rise ; strong breeze. 8 P.M.—Strong breeze and squally, with hail ; barometer 29·15. 19th.—Fresh breeze from S.W., light scattered clouds, and fine weather, with three showers of hail, until sunset, when the wind fell very light, and the sky became beautifully clear. At 8 P.M. it again increased from S.W., and blew a hard gale, with squalls and frequent showers of hail, until 3 A.M. on the 20th, when it again moderated to a fresh gale, and remaining at S.W. Hail-squalls continuing at 9 A.M.; barometer standing at 29·86. Noon.—Barometer at 29·70, weather dark and cloudy, gale inclined to increase. 8 P.M.—Strong and dark, misty, showery weather ; wind inclined to westward ; barometer 29·80. During the night it blew a very hard gale from W.S.W., with frequent heavy squalls and showers of rain. 21st.—At 9 A.M. barometer stationary at 29·80 ; weather as last described. Noon.—Wind

32·25 and fell again suddenly, and was followed by a strong north-east gale on Wednesday, which lasted 24 hours, with dark cloudy weather. On Thursday we had a hot wind from the N.N.W., and rain during the latter part. Thermometer at noon stood at 52°, barometer at 29·22. Since Thursday the wind has been north-west by north, fresh breeze, and almost constant rain; but the weather has kept very mild—in fact it is much more like summer than winter; and to-day, with its alternate sunshine and showers, has put me very much in mind of an April day at home, although the present month corresponds to January in the northern hemisphere. I had expected to find the winter very severe, but thus far I am agreeably mistaken. I hope I may be mistaken on the whole. The birds continue their merry song, and the blow-flies are quite troublesome again. The mosquitoes, or, more strictly speaking, sand-flies, have never ceased to be troublesome. To-day we heard the dogs barking, but they were at the other side of the bay. Barometer rising, 29; 8 A.M., thermometer 48°.

Sunday, July 17, 1864.—During the past week the weather has been very variable, but without any hard gales. About three weeks ago we commenced to look for

---

west, weather as before; barometer 29·82. 22nd.—Strong S.W. gale, with passing temporary showers. 9 A.M.—Barometer standing 29·82. Noon.—Wind N.W., fresh gale, and foggy, wet weather; barometer, commenced to fall. 8 P.M.—Barometer 26·60, fresh gale, and fine, clear weather. 23rd.—At 3 A.M. barometer 29·30; brisk gale from north-west; rain commenced to fall, and fell heavily, accompanied by thick fog. 9 A.M.—Barometer inclined to rise; wind a little to the northward of N.W. At 11 A.M. the gale died away suddenly at N.N.W.; calm till noon, when a light breeze came from the southward. Heavy rain, and fog still continuing. Barometer 29·40. This will sufficiently illustrate my remarks of July 3rd on the weather and barometer; and by carefully perusing these notes, it will be seen that that statement may, as a rule, be admitted, but that the workings of the weather and barometer are so eccentric that it is almost impossible to connect their inferences with any degree of certainty.

a place suitable for keeping a look-out, when we began to expect a vessel; and as we did not succeed on that occasion, we have occupied nearly all the past week in the same object. I think we have at last fixed on a place, although the place we have chosen is not a very good one for a look-out, as we shall not be able to see a ship until she is inside the heads; whereas I should have liked to have been in some place where we could have seen clear out to sea. But, under our present circumstances, I find that this would be impossible; for we can find no such place where those keeping the look-out would be able to provide themselves with food; for seals and roots are not to be found at all places in the harbour, and where they are to be found would be out of their reach.

Travelling along the shore is at the best tedious and difficult, and in many places impossible; so that they would have to depend entirely on the people at home for supplies; and as the weather is so bad and uncertain, should we go to what would really be a good place, those who were there might, perhaps, starve before supplies could be got to them. Besides, there is no safe place for keeping the boat should she be caught down there in a breeze, and unable to get back. As, for instance, on Thursday, Mr. Raynal and I went down by ourselves in the boat, and while down there it came on a strong breeze, and we could not pull the boat back again. We moored her in the safest place we could find, and, taking the sail on shore, made a sort of shelter, lit a fire, and sat by it all night. And a sorry shelter we had, for it came on to rain heavily. The sail is an old thing, full of holes, and we got quite wet. This, it may be easily understood, was not very comfortable in 51° south latitude, in the middle of winter. However, we were obliged to put up with it. We were on the east side of Flagstaff Point. We had brought a little cold seal and roots with us, which had all been eaten on that day. On Friday the breeze was stronger, and the rain continued to fall heavily all day. In the morning we shot two widgeons

—one we roasted, and the other we stewed by piecemeal in a quart pot, which is used as a bailer for the boat. We waited till about noon, expecting the breeze to take off; and as there was no prospect of it doing so, I was obliged to undertake the journey on foot to wind up the chronometer, which, if neglected, would run down on the following morning; and as, although the boat was in danger, one of us could do no good by remaining alone, we decided on both of us going. It is needless to detail our troubles in getting through the scrub and grass in a pelting rain. Suffice it to say that we were six hours in going the distance of five miles, and arrived home an hour after dark. We had not a dry thread on us, and were almost sinking with exhaustion from fatigue and hunger. The men had been very uneasy about us, for they were afraid we were blown out to sea. Fortunately they had killed a young seal of this year on that morning, which was quite a treat, for it is the first young seal we have got for a long time, and assuredly we did ample justice to it; immediately after which we went to bed, and required no rocking to put us to sleep.

We rose on Saturday morning, without feeling any further bad effects than a slight stiffness. After breakfast we started back again to look after the boat, about which I had felt very uneasy; for should we lose her we lose our means of getting a living. We took about a day's provision with us; we should have found it impossible to carry more. A strong breeze was blowing when we started, and the grass and scrub were dry, as there had been no rain since midnight; but before we had got half a mile from the house it commenced to rain, and continued until we arrived at the boat, which fortunately we found as we had left it, only that she was about half full of water. After bailing her out we made a fire, stripped off our clothes one piece after another, and managed to get them dry some way or other, and had something to eat in the meantime. As the night came on the breeze died away,.

and towards midnight we started off, and got the boat home safe and sound. But we must not hazard leaving the boat again: therefore I have decided on keeping the look-out on the hill about two miles from the house, where we can see a long way down the harbour, and we shall be able to make a signal from the house for them to bring the boat down should a vessel come in to look for us—and surely one will. On the first day of October I intend to go to keep the look-out myself. I shall remain there until we give up all hopes of any one coming. It would be a relief could I only feel sure that some one would come to look after us. To-day is a beautiful day, with a very light southerly air, and light scattered clouds, and the atmosphere is particularly clear; barometer, 30 inches; thermometer, 40° at noon. The barometer quite deceived me on Thursday morning. From the appearance of the weather I should have expected a fresh north-west breeze, which actually came; but the barometer was at 30·20, which indicates light southerly or easterly airs.

Sunday, July 24, 1864.—Throughout the past week the weather has been exceedingly fine; wind (when any) generally from the south, or eastward; very light airs, but frequently calm. On Thursday, and only for six hours, the wind was very light, from the N.W. The thermometer from last Sunday has been gradually, and almost imperceptibly, falling, and is now at 29·50. It will be seen that with the barometer between 29·50 and 30 inches, we have frequently had strong gales, so that this is another instance of its deceitfulness, and almost uselessness, in this locality; but at the present moment, from its state, and the appearance of the weather, which is dark, gloomy, and misty, I have every reason to expect an easterly or N.E. gale.

On Tuesday, Wednesday, and Thursday we had sharp frost. The thermometer was as low as 22°, and when it was at 29°, which is 3° below freezing, the flies were blowing, and the sand-flies were biting furiously. I give up all hopes of their ceasing hostilities during the winter, so it may be imagined what an annoyance they are in the summer, as all my descriptions would fail to convey an idea of its extent. It is almost impossible to do anything for them. Yesterday I was repairing the boat, and the sand-flies were so troublesome that I was compelled to take refuge in the house two or three times before I could complete my job. They are worse near the water.

On Monday morning we went up the bay in the boat to try and get a seal, as our fresh meat was just out. We arrived some time before daylight, near a place which we knew was frequented by a mob. We lay in wait until the day began to dawn, when they began to come down to the water, and we had the good fortune to kill four—three young ones, and one cow, which was in calf. We might have got one or two more, had we wanted them. But these were more than we could use whilst fresh. One of them we salted. Our greatest difficulty was to find out where the seals are, for every time we kill any they shift their camp, and I fear much that they will disappear altogether before we get away from this infernal place. We have heard the dogs barking several times during the last week, but we have not seen them. We frequently see their tracks in the woods, but not near the house. I think it very strange that they don't; for I feel convinced that these precise dogs have been left here by some one, for, had male and female been left, there would have been more now.

CHAPTER V.

THE AURORA AUSTRALIS.—OUR DAILY FARE.—HEAVY SNOW-
FALL.—FAILURE TO REPAIR THE SCHOONER.

Sunday, July 31, 1864.—It is seven months to-day since
I entered the harbour, and during the past week we have
had more easterly winds than during the whole of the
previous time. I shall note down my slate notes whilst
these easterly winds are blowing; as, given in full, they
will better serve the purpose of a reference. On Sunday
last, July 24, at 3 P.M., the breeze coming from north-east
increased to a strong gale, which continued 36 hours, with
drizzling rain and thick fog (black north-easter), barometer
steadily falling. Monday, 25th—8 P.M., 29·14. Tuesday,
26th—3 A.M., the north-east wind died away, calm until
noon, latter part light breeze from west north-west, drizzling
rain and thick fog; barometer, 8 A.M., 29, 8 P.M., 29·12.
Midnight, calm. Wednesday, 27th—Until 3 P.M., fresh
south-east breeze and fog; at that time the wind became
fitful and gusty, hauled to the eastward and to the north-
east, steadily increasing to a brisk gale, with drizzling
rain and thick fog; barometer rising rapidly after 3 P.M. ;
8 A.M. 29·12, 3 P.M. 29·15, 9 P.M. 29·28. Thermometer in
open air at noon, 46°. Thursday, 28th—The north-east
breeze continued until 3 A.M., fog and drizzling rain, and
then became puffy, and hauled to S.S.E., blowing a strong
breeze until 3 P.M. Latter part, moderate breeze from
the same point. Detached opening clouds, and occasional slight falls of snow, with a clear atmosphere, and
rapid rising barometer through the day; 8 A.M., barometer
28·28, 8 P.M. 29·76; thermometer at noon 35°. Friday,

E

29th—Light airs from the S.S.W., and fine clear weather throughout these twenty hours. Frost in the evening.

This evening we saw the most vivid and beautifully brilliant Aurora Australis that I have ever witnessed; indeed it was as bright as ever I remember seeing the Aurora Borealis. We frequently see these southern lights, but only showing a pale light; whereas on this occasion they shot up from the horizon to the zenith in streamers of magnificently varied shades of light. Barometer standing at 30·50; thermometer, 30°. Saturday and to-day light westerly airs and foggy weather; barometer, 30·10; thermometer, 38°. On Friday I went up to the Giant's Tomb. I was alone, and started early in the morning, and did not get home until dark. I came back by the head of the bay, which made it a long and difficult journey. I took nothing to eat with me, as I had no intention of being away so long; but I kept myself from feeling hungry by eating a quantity of roots and drinking water, which, thank God, is very plentiful, and acceptable in the absence of anything better. The ground was frozen, and the travelling up and on the top was very good; there was snow on the top, but in returning I had a most horrible road. The weather was particularly clear.

8 P.M.—About four o'clock I had to drop my pen in a hurry, and go in the boat to get a seal that one of the men had killed about three miles from the house. We have just finished supper, so I shall pick up the thread of my yarn. I had a much clearer and better view than I had obtained on my last visit, as on that occasion, although the weather was very fine, there was a slight deceptive haze in the atmosphere, which I found deceived me a little: for I find that there are several small islands at the north end of the group. They are small and low, and to attempt a passage through them with anything but a boat would be attended with great risk, as the channels appear to be full of rocks, and the islands surrounded by sunken reefs and banks, some of which are dry at high water, and on

which the sea breaks heavily. These dangers are visible
only from where I stood, amongst the islands, and on the
east side of them, and are not so far from the land as I
have before described them. Still, the north end of the
group should be approached with great caution. I am
now of opinion that there is a bay, or perhaps a harbour,
on the west coast, opposite the small islets which I mentioned in my note of 20th June. I intend to go farther
the first time the weather permits, and determine this
matter, unless we should be so fortunate as to be picked
up before such opportunity presents itself.

I think I have never described our precise mode of
dragging out this miserable existence, for I cannot call it
living. Breakfast—Seal stewed down to soup, fried roots,
boiled seal, or roast do., with water. Dinner—Ditto ditto.
Supper—Ditto ditto. This repeated 21 times per week.
Mussels or fish are now quite a rarity; we have not been
able to get either for some time. The man who killed the
seal to-day had been fishing nearly all day, and had caught
one small fish. The men have stood it bravely thus far,
but it grieves me unspeakably to hear them wishing for
things which they cannot get. I heard one just now wishing he had but a bucket of potato-peelings!

Sunday, August 7, 1864.—During the whole of last
week the weather has been very bad: it has been blowing
a very heavy gale from between west and north-west, with
either hail, rain, or snow continually falling. From noon
yesterday till three o'clock this morning the gale was at
its height; it blew a hurricane, and was the heaviest I have
ever seen while on shore. Our house is elevated about
30 feet above the mean tide level, and is about 50 yards
from the water; and during the height of the hurricane the
spray was frequently dashed against it in heavy showers.
Had it not been well built and secured it would inevitably
have been blown down, and we should have been house-
wrecked as well as shipwrecked. It is exposed to the full
fury of westerly gales, although it is well sheltered from

every other quarter ; but after standing this severe gale it will stand anything. I have determined on trying to get the schooner higher on the beach, so as to look at her bottom. It may be that it is not impossible to make something of her yet : she is evidently very strongly built, for she still holds together in spite of all the gales which have blown since she was stranded, with the exception of a portion of the decks, which came up some time ago. Had we any tools I should have made an attempt to do something with her as soon as we had got ourselves sheltered for the winter, and found it not so severe as I had anticipated.

As the spring is setting in, and Mr. Raynal thinks he can make tools, I have determined to take her up, if possible, and see what can be done. At the commencement of the past week we had spring tides, which is the only time we can do anything. On Monday and Tuesday we employed ourselves at tide-time in clearing away the rocks and boulders off the beach up above where she now lies, and where she must come up, if she comes up at all, which I consider as very doubtful ; but rather than remain here another winter, I think I shall be tempted to risk my life in the boat. We shall not be able to do anything more until spring tides again. The barometer has been very low all the week—lowest on Friday, 28·65 : during the hurricane it rose or fell as the wind lulled or increased in violence, and is now 29·40 ; steadily rising. Thermometer 38°.

Sunday, August 14, 1864.—Since last Sunday we have had what we call very fine weather—that is to say, we have had no gales ; but otherwise the weather has been very variable, with frequent showers of rain and snow. Atmosphere alternately hazy, foggy, or clear, aud the sun peeping through the clouds once or twice a day, or, perhaps, not more than half-a-dozen times during the whole week ; with light airs, generally from the westward, but more frequently calm. This is what we are obliged to call fine weather in this part of the world. It will be a glorious change if ever we get back to the land where the sun shines every day; and it is to be hoped we shall, and that before very long now. I don't know how it is, but for the last few days I have felt unaccountably fidgety and uneasy, as if I were every moment expecting some extraordinary occurrence.

Yesterday I got to where I could see well down the harbour, and sat on a rock all day, expecting to see a vessel coming in. This morning I walked all about the beach, expecting the same thing; still I have no right to expect such an event for at least two months to come. We have not been able, on account of the neap tides, to do anything at the 'Grafton' last week; but in the middle of the incoming week we shall have the full moon springs, when I hope we shall be able to get her a little higher on the beach.

On Tuesday morning we went in the boat, about four o'clock, to go seal hunting. We were unsuccessful at the first place where we had expected to find them, and took a turn farther up the bay to try and get some mussels or widgeons; and luckily, about eleven o'clock, we found three seals on shore, and killed them. Two were cows in calf, the other this year's calf. These are the only seals we have seen on shore in the daytime for a very long while, but as the weather gets milder no doubt they will come up to sun themselves. On this day there were also great numbers in the water, and we saw our old friend, 'Royal Tom,' whom we have not seen for a long time. It is to be hoped they will return here again towards calving-time. First part of the week the barometer was high, 30·30. Since Wednesday it has been down to 29·40, and is now rising, 29·65; thermometer about 40° at noon.

Sunday, August 21, 1864.—During the greater part of the past week the weather has been very fine. On Monday the wind was light from south-west, with light scattered clouds and clear atmosphere. This was a truly fine day. On Tuesday the barometer fell to 28·65, although the wind was at south, and very light. On Wednesday, at 9 A.M., the wind shifted suddenly to south-east, and increased to a hard gale (the only south-east gale we have had since we came here), with sleet and much snow, and lasted 18 hours. The snow lies yet thick on the ground. This was the heaviest snow-fall we have had during the winter. When the gale was at its height the barometer began to rise rapidly, and when it died away the wind hauled to north-east. Barometer 30·2, where it has remained up to the present time, with fine and generally clear weather, and frost during the night. Whenever we had frost it has been with light north-east winds, and this (or any easterly winds) never occurs excepting at or about the full of the moon.

All the week we have been working tide-time, night and day, at the wreck, and a precious miserable job we have had ; for we were obliged to be up to our middle in water all the time nearly, with the thermometer from 2° to 5° below freezing, which was anything but comfortable. But I was determined to try what could be done towards getting her a little higher up on the beach. The men worked with great spirit and energy, fully expecting that we would be able to get her up and repair her, so that, in case no aid comes for us, we could make her carry us to New Zealand. However, the result has proved contrary to their expectations, though precisely in accordance with my own. I had given them too much encouragement to hope, which was perhaps wrong ; for they have been very much disappointed since yesterday, when we had fairly proved that it was out of our power to do anything with her, except it be to break her up, and, as a last resource, try and make something out of her remains that will take us away from here, if it only be to drown at sea. After getting all the ballast out of her, we tried by pumping and baling to keep the water down, but found it impossible. We then, with considerable difficulty, got her thrown over on the other bilge, and found a number of holes in her, some of her timbers broken, and the main wheel gone from the stern to about the main rigging. This was done when we first struck. The holes have no doubt been chafed through since. We threw her back on her sore side again. Nothing more can be done. Barometer falling, 29·90. Thermometer, noon, 36°; midnight, 24°.

Sunday, August 28, 1864.—All last week the weather has been very fine, with easterly or southerly winds. On Friday it blew a strong gale from the south, which lasted 24 hours, but the weather was dry and fine, although cloudy. On the whole the weather has been much better during the winter than it was during the latter part of last summer. Indeed, from the 1st of April to the present time, we have only had one very severe gale, which was on the 6th and 7th of this month; whereas, from the 1st of January till the 1st of April, on an average, we had one fine day out of seven. So that it may be concluded that the weather during the winter months is more moderate, with more easterly winds, but unfortunately more frequent and denser fogs than during the summer months—at least the latter part of the summer, which is as far as my experience and observation go. I hope and trust it will not be extended throughout the whole year. I do not expect a vessel here until the middle of October, and I don't think that my anxiety after that time can surpass what it is at present for that time to arrive. I have commenced clearing away a place where I intend to keep the look-out, and Mr. Raynal and I purpose going and taking up our quarters there on the first day of October.

I am glad to find that the seals are becoming as numerous as ever, if not more so. On Wednesday morning we went out early, with the boat, to look for some fresh meat, and at the peep of day we got four young ones, and we saw upwards of 50 within a distance of half a mile. The shores appeared to be literally crowded with them. Had we wanted to kill seals, I have no doubt but we might have killed a hundred in this short distance, and more elsewhere had we wanted them. And now, as my book is full, I shall continue my journal page 138 in another book. The barometer has been about 29·50 all the week, and is now rising, 29·80. Thermometer at noon 40°.

CHAPTER VI.

SCARCITY OF FOOD.—TENACITY OF LIFE IN SEALS.—FURTHER
EXPLORATIONS IN THE ISLAND.—RESOLVE TO BUILD A VESSEL.

" *Sarah's Bosom.*" *   *Sunday, September* 4, 1864.—It is
now eight months since I had the misfortune to be cast
away on this miserable island. And how tardily they have
passed, and what anguish of mind I have suffered, would
be impossible for me to describe, or any one else to
imagine, unless they have been similarly situated ; and how
much longer it will last God only knows. Surely some
friends (if we have any) in Sydney will bestir themselves,
and have us looked after by some means or other; and if
they exert themselves a little, and go about it properly, I
have no doubt but that the Government will take the
matter in hand. But as the time approaches nearer when
I may reasonably expect a vessel, I am getting daily
more uneasy and dubious about it. I take so many
conflicting views of the matter, that sometimes my mind
is almost (and I am not sure if not quite) wrought up to a
state of frenzy.

I have employed myself all the week in working at our
new place, and I am going to much more trouble than is
absolutely necessary, so as to divert my mind as much as
possible from melancholy thoughts and forebodings. To
judge by the pains I am taking with it, any one would
suppose that we intended to pass the remainder of our
days here, which may be the case ; but if life and health
are spared me, I shall not remain here another twelve

* As already pointed out, this is an error. It should be ' Carnley's
Harbour.'—ED.

months, if I go to sea in a boat and drown like a rat—
which would be the most probable result—which mode of
getting out of this world could not be termed suicide ;
although by those who are aware of the risk in so doing it
might be considered systematic self-destruction, which I
hope I shall not have occasion to adopt. If we had any
carpenters' tools we would soon knock up something that
would carry us to New Zealand, out of the wreck of the
' Grafton,' if it was only a scow. Mr. Raynal has been shoe-
making for the last fortnight ; he has made a pair for himself and a pair for me, and, considering the material he had
to work with (seal-skin uppers, and old boots picked to
pieces for soles), and having had no previous experience,
he has made a surprisingly good job of them. The seal-
skin is too thin for mocassins : we wore out a pair in five
days or a week. The men make wooden clogs, but they
are very dangerous amongst the stones on the beach. The
weather continues fine ; we have had the wind high, and
moderate, from the south, or the eastward, throughout the
week ; atmosphere moderately clear. Barometer has been
down to 29·50, but is now rising, 29·90 ; thermometer from
40° to 50° at noon each day.

Sunday, September 11, 1864.—We have had quite a
change in the weather since last Sunday. On Monday a
gale came on from the north-west, and it has continued to
blow very hard ever since, with heavy squalls and showers,
sometimes hail and snow. On Thursday morning the
ground was covered with snow, but it did not lie very
long, for there has been a great deal of rain falling also.
The wind hauled to the south, and veered again to the
north-west, from which quarter it is now blowing a very
heavy gale, with constant heavy rain, and very dark,
gloomy weather. It has been a very miserable week, and
there is no prospect of any change for the better. I have
no doubt but we shall get bad weather in earnest this
month with the equinox. When the gale commenced the
barometer was at 28·75. It has since been at 29·25, and

as high as 29·80, constantly rising and falling, and is now at 29·50; thermometer 44°. I have done nothing at the new place this week; the weather has been so bad that it was not fit to go outside the door if it could be avoided: but we were obliged to go out on Monday and yesterday to look for meat, and, as we could not launch the boat, we had to carry it a distance of about three and a half miles. We killed a cow seal each day; they were both in calf.

Sunday, September 18, 1864.—The weather has been very stormy, with almost constant hail, snow, or rain throughout the past week, and we are again hard up for something to eat. We have been obliged to turn out in the midst of the bad weather to look for grub, and if turning out was all it would not be worth mentioning; but I am sorry to say that it is not to be had so easily as it used to be. We were out in the boat three times in succession —Thursday, Friday, and Saturday, from four o'clock in the morning to six in the evening; and, by dint of great industry and perseverance, we managed to get as much widgeon, fish, and mussels as kept us going, and a small surplus, which will barely last us to-day. To-morrow we must boat it again, whatever the weather may be; and it is not at present very promising. The barometer is very low, with every appearance of a heavy S.W. gale.

About three weeks ago I had every reason to hope, from the great number of seals that were in the harbour just then, that we were going to have abundance of seal meat, which is our principal food; but I find myself sadly disappointed, and I fear very much that they were only mustering at that time for a final leave-taking, for at the present time there is not a seal in this part of the harbour, and whether they have left the harbour entirely or not I cannot say; but as soon as the weather subsides a little we intend to go up the northern arm and see if we can get any there. They were numerous up there on the occasion of our visiting that part of the harbour. It is twelve miles from here; therefore it is quite an undertaking for us to go there.

The present state of the weather has prevented us doing anything at the new place. If provisions were so plentiful as not to occupy all our time in looking after them, we might be able to do something towards it. Certainly we have dried meat and widgeon, but it is almost impossible to eat it. If we are compelled to have resource to it, and I find I can subsist upon roots, I shall certainly do so in preference to eating it. I must do the men justice in this, that, with all our hard fare, which is no doubt much harder than anyone that reads this journal might be inclined to imagine, they have not as yet made any open complaints. But since we have been so very much pinched, they have had to be pulling about in the boat, in the storm and wet, from morning till night, and then scarcely getting enough to subsist upon.

Wednesday, September 21, 1864.—On Monday morning the weather appeared promising, although the glass was very low, giving indications to the contrary ; but, as forage is getting so scarce, I thought we would venture to start for the western arm. We had the wind from the S.W., which was ahead in going, and detained us so much that by nightfall we had only got a short distance into it—about eight miles from the house. Here we spied a seal on shore, and as yet we had only seen one in the water, and it was an old black bull. We landed and killed the one on shore ; we also found another, which led us a chase until dark, and we were near losing her. They were both old ones. We now made up our minds to camp here for the night, and in the morning go farther up, and see if we could find any more ; but it came on to blow, with hail and rain, and the night was bitter cold, so about midnight we made up our minds to return home. Although it was blowing a hard gale, it was favourable, so we started, and arrived at home about two o'clock on Tuesday morning, wet through, and almost famished with cold. Seeing the black seal gives me hope that the others have not left the harbour altogether, but are at the head of the western arm; for we supposed that the black ones had left entirely, as we have not seen any for a very long time. Tenth anniversary of my marriage.

Sunday, September 25, 1864.—From the commencement of the gale mentioned on Wednesday, until Friday evening, it continued to blow very hard from between S.W. and N.W., accompanied by hail, rain, and snow. There has been more snow on the ground this week than at any time during the winter, and it lies thick on the mountains yet; but it will not lie very long, I suppose, for the sun begins to feel very warm again. Yesterday and to-day have been two very fine days, with a light breeze from the southward. It would have been an excellent opportunity for a vessel coming here to have made the land and got in, for the atmosphere has been particularly clear. The island might have been seen at a great distance. However, I don't expect anybody here until after the 15th of next month; then I shall look for some one coming every day, if we are not starved to death before that time.

It is evident that the seals have left this part of the island entirely. We were out in the boat yesterday, but did not see one. I have often thought I could get across to the western shore of the island by a valley at the head of the bay, where I imagine it is not more than three miles across. We started in the boat the first thing after our breakfast, and landed at the place where I intended to cross. We left the boat, and the three men who were in her started to go with me; but the travelling was so horribly bad that when we had got half a mile two of them turned back, leaving the other man and myself to pursue our way without them, which we did for about a mile farther; and I may say we had accomplished this distance by creeping on our bellies, very seldom getting as high as our hands and knees. I have described some bad roads before. This beats description, and it also beats me; and this is the first time I have been beaten in getting through the infernal scrub and swamp. The time which we occupied in going and returning this mile and a half may give some idea of what sort of travelling it was : we were about seven hours in doing it! I got a severe cold over it, which was the only reward of my trouble (fatigue and scratched face and hands excepted). On our return, I shot three widgeons and two young ducks. There are ducks here, as I think I have before remarked ; but they are very few, and they are so shy that we cannot get within gunshot of them. What we have got have been young ones, before they could fly. The widgeons, or what we call widgeons, are getting scarce also. We must go up the western arm again to-morrow, weather permitting. Barometer, 29·85 ; thermometer, 38°.

Sunday, October 2, 1864.—The long looked for month has arrived at last (God send relief before it passes). It is nine months to-day since the wreck. I shall make no comments how they have passed, as they could only have a tendency to rekindle the internal fire which has almost consumed me, and which fresh hopes have in some measure quenched ; still, the dying embers require but a slight blast to make the flame burst forth afresh.

On Monday morning last the weather appeared promising, although the barometer was at a doubtful altitude. We started at an early hour for the western arm, to look for fresh meat, and fortunately for us we had to go no farther than its entrance. On the small island there we found and killed four seals, and amongst them was our old acquaintance, 'Royal Tom.' Had meat not been so scarce we would not have killed him. Another was a great calf about four months old. We killed a cow in milk the Monday previous, which, without a doubt, was its mother. This is the only instance that we yet found of them having calves later than January. December, I should say, is the month in which they generally calve. I am inclined to think that these seals, with the two we killed the week before, have composed a family, which, perhaps on account of the young calf, have not taken their departure with the rest, for

I fear much that they have all gone; for we have not seen a sign of any others. However, it is to be hoped that these will last till we are taken away, which event I fully expect between the 15th and 20th of the present month; for if anybody has exerted themselves at all on our behalf, I have no doubt that the Government would despatch a vessel to look for us not later than the 1st of this month, after the equinoctial gales have subsided. Had we not been so fortunate on Monday, in falling in with seals so soon as we did, it would have been impossible for us to return yet, for it has blown a gale of wind ever since, which would have prevented our doing so.

At 9 A.M. on Monday a breeze came from the N.E., which soon increased to a gale. This is only the second N.E. wind we have had at any other time but the full of the moon, and both those have happened at about the last quarter, but did not stand long before it hauled, by north to the westward, and has continued to blow a very heavy gale from between S.W. and W.N.W., and is now at N.W., with the barometer 30·20. We have had another instance of a low barometer preceding a S.W. gale, but this is the first time I have known it to be above 30 inches with a N.W. wind. A great deal of rain has fallen throughout this week also: on one occasion it rained harder for about two hours than ever I remember seeing it do anywhere, except it may have been one of those heavy showers we get on the equator sometimes. The thermometer has been low, 36° to 40°.

Sunday, October 9, 1864.—The past week, up till Friday, was very fine. Light north-west wind, and, although the sky is generally clouded, the atmosphere was particularly clear. This would have afforded an excellent opportunity for a ship to have made the island and got in here. It is to be hoped that we shall have moderate weather for a time now, for goodness knows it was bad enough last month to suffice for some time; but I suppose we must take it as it comes, without grumbling. However, the barometer is now

up to 30·20 ; we shall have good weather for a few days, no
doubt.   In that time there is no telling what may trans-
pire ; perhaps we may get away before any more bad
weather comes.   At midnight on Thursday it commenced
to rain, and continued without ceasing until midnight on
Friday.   At 4 P.M. on Friday the wind shifted instantaneously from N.W. to S.E., and has remained at S.E.
and S.S.E. ever since ; moderate breeze and passing
clouds, with frequent showers of snow.   The tips of the
hills are once more white, and it is very cold: the thermometer is down to 38°.   We planted some pumpkin
seed at the beginning of the week, but I am afraid it will
stand a poor chance.   We tried some last summer ; it did
come up, and that was all.   Corn would do very well here,
I have no doubt—also potatoes : we have got two or three
which we intend to try.

Sunday, October 16, 1864.—Another week of fine weather
has passed, and here we remain yet.   Surely not more than
another week at the outside will pass before something
arrives to take us away ; that is, if anyone has thought
anything about us, or done anything towards having us
looked after.   But I am afraid that those who should have
felt interested in our fate are either dead or sleeping, or
else something would have been despatched to look for us
at the latest on the first of the present month, in which
case, had they come here direct, as I instructed Mr. ——
they should do if anything happened that we did not
return in reasonable time, they should have been here
before now : and I think I made him understand clearly
that an accident was much more likely to happen in harbour than at sea ; so thus their consciences will scarcely
allow time to let the matter rest without discovering by
some means what has become of us.   Besides, they don't
know but their own personal interest is at stake, which
in itself would stir them to action ; still I do not for a
moment doubt they will be doing something towards
finding us.   I think I may question their energy, for had

they applied to Government as soon as they gave us up—which they must have done, at the outside, five months after we sailed—I feel convinced that we should have had relief before this time; for the New South Wales Government is not slow to move in such matters. In this humane age, the probability of saving the lives of five men becomes a matter of immediate and energetic public interest and action; therefore I am inclined to think that our friends, who should at least have given us an opportunity of condescending to receive succour from public benevolence (we are not too high-minded now to accept of assistance from any quarter, neither would any-one else be so if they had lived as we have done for nine or ten months), have been, to say the least, wanting in energy; but, for fear of doing them an injustice, I will say no more on the subject at present.

As I have already remarked, the weather during the past week has been fine. On Monday morning the snow lay thick on the ground, but was soon dispersed by the sun. In the afternoon of that day we had a strong breeze from the westward, which lasted till midnight. Since that time the wind has been light from the southward and south-east, with scattered clouds, but mist almost con-stantly enveloping the high parts of the land. To-day the wind is moderate from N.N.E., with passing clouds and clear atmosphere. The barometer has been steadily rising all the week, from 29·50 on Monday to 29·90 to-day; thermometer at 53°, which is below temperate; but we feel it very warm. The weather has been so fine, and I am so sick of remaining here, that Raynal and I proposed taking the boat to try to reach New Zealand in her; but the men at once opposed this project, as they did not wish to be left alone here; and as I do not wish to risk unne-cessarily anyone's life but my own, and perhaps relief may not after all be so far off, I have for the present abandoned the idea. Perhaps I am unreasonably uneasy, but it is impossible for me to be otherwise.

F

On Monday morning last we started at daybreak for the western arm, to look for seal. On Masked Island we saw one tiger seal, but we could not get him; and he was the only one we could see until we arrived at the head of the arm. About noon we landed, made a fire, and got something to eat, and then proceeded on our way; but immediately after noon we got a strong breeze from the westward, which was dead a-head. We are very unfortunate, for every time we go out in the boat a gale of wind comes on before we get back. However, by about 4 o'clock in the afternoon we had managed to get nearly to the head of the arm, and we saw a large black seal lying amongst the rocks close to the water—so close that it would have been impossible for us to have got him if we had landed to attack him : and the meat is getting so scarce we were glad of only half an opportunity of getting him, and only afraid that he would escape and we should not be able to get another one. He was not asleep, but sat up and looked at us; and we lay on our oars and looked at him, not daring to move for fear he would take the water—and a musket ball seldom has any effect on them when they are so near the water, further than it may confuse them, when you must be ready to attack them at once with clubs; and we were as yet too far from him to shoot. We made a few bold strokes towards him; he did not move until the boat was near touching the beach ; then he started : but Mr. Raynal let drive at him with the gun and staggered him, knocking out three of his canine teeth, the ball going up into his head: but this did not kill him. In an instant we were on him with our clubs, which had the effect of quieting him for a short time; but, strange to say, the very time occupied in pounding him to make sure of killing him gave him time to revive again, and he nearly escaped into the water before we got his throat cut. He was a very large seal, one of his teeth measuring $3\frac{3}{8}$ inches long, $1\frac{1}{2}$ inches in circumference at the gum, and 5¾ inches at the base.   Mr. Raynal has some larger than this.

It is a surprising fact that the nearer to the water a seal is killed, the more tenacious it is of life.   I have actually seen one of these black bull seals, with two bullets in him, his head split open with an axe, and his brains hanging out, dragging the men along the beach, who were trying to keep him out of the water by hanging on to his hind flappers ; and he would have got away had not another man at that moment come to their assistance, and chopped off his head entirely with the axe.   But when they are at any great distance from the water a slight tap on the nose will stun them, and if struck immediately they will probably die without the slightest muscular motion.   But in striking these fellows it is necessary to make sure of your blow, for if you miss they will have hold of you, and they would undoubtedly break the limb they got hold of.   None of us as yet have got bit, thank God ; but they have on one or two occasions taken the club out of some of our hands. After getting our seal into the boat, we went as far as the western head or entrance, where we got another black seal, and saw there three others, which we could have killed, but the two we had already got were a load for the boat.   We also saw about half-a-dozen in the water, all black seals.   Not very long ago we thought it would be impossible to eat this kind of seal ; and indeed they are not by any means fit for food, for the strong smell of the meat is enough not only to disgust but to stifle a person. But what are starving men to do ? and we may consider ourselves such.   Hunger is certainly a good sauce.   We were all in a state of excitement over the seal that was shot, for fear we should lose him and not· be able to get any more.

After taking a good view of the entrance, we returned to the boat and set sail homeward (as I must call my prison-house), with a strong fair wind, as much as we could carry the whole sail to, and were not more than two hours and a half in running back, and arrived about an hour after dark. The distance is fourteen or fifteen miles. I may here give a description of the western arm of this extensive harbour, as I think I have not as yet done so. About seven miles from the eastern entrance heads is Musgrave's Peninsula, which lies nearly at right angles with the entrance and Flagstaff Point. Its S.E. entrance bears from between the heads W.-half-S. (Here our signal board is erected). The elbow, which turns off from the direct line to the heads, and into the western arm, is called Point No. 1, and bears from Flagstaff Point S.E. by E.-half-E. From Point No. 1 the arm runs, in a S.W. by W. direction, a distance of about five miles, to Point No. 2, where it turns its direction to W.N.W., about two miles to Point No. 3, and follows nearly the same bearing from this point to a point along the northern shore to its head, a distance of about three and a quarter miles farther. From Point No. 3 to Break Sea Point (which is on the east side of the passage out), W.-half-N., about one and three quarter miles.

On the eastern side of the passage (from the sea) are standing two isolated rocks, not less than 200 feet high, which from seaward would appear to be one, and which I am of opinion are synonymous with the rock placed on the general chart immediately off the South Cape, and named Adam's Rock. This entrance, I am fully persuaded, is precisely on the South Cape, although I am not at present able to assert such as a positive fact. The passage runs N.N.E. and S.S.W., about one and three quarter miles in length, and one mile wide at its entrance, narrowing very regularly and gradually towards its head, where its width is not more than half a mile, which space is almost entirely occupied by an island, which is situated almost exactly in the centre, leaving on each side a very narrow but deep channel. The one on the east side appears to be the best; it is about 100 feet wide and 300 feet long.   .

On the inside, immediately off Break Sea Point, stands a rock which only shows at low water, unless occasionally when the sea breaks on it. A considerable portion of the point is covered at high water also. The island, which from its singular appearance I have named 'Monumental Island,' is a peculiar feature of, and would be an unmistakeable finger-post to, this entrance. The eastern head, for a distance of nearly two miles, is a perpendicular wall, averaging not less than 120 feet high. The western head rises to a height of not less than 400 feet, and is not quite so perpendicular as the eastern one, but shows an unbroken face. This passage, if properly examined, might possibly be available to a vessel entering or leaving this harbour; but, in my opinion, it would be in no wise recommendable.

Masked Island bears from Flagstaff Point S.W. by S., and could not, by a vessel bigger than a long boat beating or sailing in, be discovered; indeed, I passed it once in a boat without discovering the fact. There is a snug nook on its south side, where a vessel might very easily be secured, and would be well sheltered from both wind and sea. I would recommend laying down two anchors ahead, in about 12 fathoms (not less), and hauling her stern as far in to the N.W. as the depth of water will allow (there is eight feet rise and fall; high water on full and change days at 12 hours), then moor with four good hawsers to the trees, or the rocks if preferable. I would prefer this place to any other in the harbour. There is a drift to the S.E. of about one mile and a half, but the wind from that quarter is not felt; the very high land off the south island entirely breaks it off, and when it is blowing a heavy gale from any other quarter there is scarcely a breath of wind in this quarter. From this island the western arm has on its north side six bays, from half a mile to a mile deep, and at the head of each is a small stream of water. The shores are generally rocky, and clad with stunted crooked timber, similar to the shores of the north arm where we live, running to some distance up the mountains, which rise abruptly from the water to the height of

1,000 to 1,500 feet. The south island attains in one place a height of not less than 2,000 feet. I have not visited the south side of this arm, excepting at its head. It carries an average width of about one and a half miles. The south side has a number of small bays, but nothing near so deep as those on the north side. I have sounded along the north side, but nowhere did I get bottom with a 20 feet line at 90 yards from the shore.

On Thursday we were out in the boat all day. We went down to Flagstaff Point and re-painted our signal board, and spent the remainder of the day in fishing, and getting mussels and widgeons. We got three small fish, a basket of mussels, and a dozen widgeons. We saw two small seals in the water. It is evident they have left the harbour altogether. God only knows what is to become of us ; we shall starve outright if we remain here much longer. I expect the few black seals that remain will be off now also.

Sunday, October 23, 1864.—Week passes on after week. Another one has passed like its predecessors, and thus I suppose it will continue till time shall be no more. Each day passes, and we know not what the next may bring forth, or whether we shall see it or not ; and probably one of the best gifts of Providence is the veil that conceals futurity. My eyes are positively weak and bloodshot with anxious looking. Since last Sunday I have scarcely slept, for night and day I have been constantly on the worry, expecting that a vessel would come in. The weather was moderate during the first and middle of the week, but since noon of Friday it has been blowing a hard gale from S.W. and W.N.W., with much rain and dirty thick weather, and at the present time has not the slightest appearance of subsiding ; so that if a vessel was now in the vicinity of the island it would be impossible for her to get in. It would be impossible for me to convey to any one an idea of my present state of mind. I am anything but mad ; if that would come it would very likely afford relief in forgetfulness. I was mad once, though, and no doubt people are made accountable for their actions in that sort of mad-ness ; and perhaps I am suffering the just punishment of my folly.

     *   *   *   *   *   *

I have still one consolation remaining, in those beautiful words of Thomas Moore :—

> Let fate do her worst, there are relics of joy,
> Bright gems of the past which she cannot destroy ;
> That come in the night-time of sorrow and care,
> And bring back the features that joy used to wear.
> Long, long may my heart with such mem'ries be filled,
> Like a vase in which roses have once been distilled.
> You may break, you may ruin the vase as you will,
> But the scent of the roses will hang round it still.

On Tuesday morning, Raynal and I set off at five o'clock in the morning to go on to the mountains to the northward and have a look round. The night had been beautifully fine and clear, and when we started there was not a cloud in the sky, and scarcely a breath of wind. A finer morning could not have been, but before we arrived at the top clouds rose from the westward and passed rapidly over, till the whole sky was covered, and a mist began to settle on the land, which soon became a dense fog, with heavy rain. It continued for several hours, and we were very glad that we had not got to the top, and made our way back again as quickly as possible. It would be exceedingly dangerous to be caught on the top of these mountains in one of those thick fogs ; for sometimes you cannot see two yards before you, so that you would be obliged to stop until it cleared away, and in so doing you might perish with cold and wet. The alternative would be almost a certainty of falling headlong down one of these immense precipices, which I have mentioned before, 1,200 to 1,500 feet deep.

On Wednesday morning, about the same time, we made another attempt, and succeeded. The day was dry and clear, but there was a haze about the horizon which prevented us from seeing so far as we otherwise could have done. However, I suppose we had a clear view all round of not less than fifty miles; but no sail blessed our longing eyes. We went much farther to the northward than we have been before, and nearly over to the western shore, and saw several detached conical shaped rocks, and small islands scattered about close to the shores, which are high and rugged, with here and there small indentations or bights. But I find that this western coast line does not run, as I have previously noted, N.N.E. and S.S.W., but nearly north and south. It has, however, an elbow about its centre, which lies somewhat to the westward of its north and south extremities; and I am now inclined to think that the passage out from the western arm is a little to the northward of the South Cape. In other respects the description I have given before is correct, only that the mountains are higher than I at the time supposed them to be. I have since measured some of them, which enables me to judge more correctly the height of the others.

The Giant's Tomb is about 1,800 feet high, and the highest part of the land is on the south island, and is about 2,000 feet high. I also find that some of the chasms in the north-east angle of the land penetrate nearly (perhaps some of them go entirely) through the island, and are very narrow, with the mountains rising perpendicularly from the water to the height of 1,200 feet. Indeed some of them are so narrow that it appears as if a person could jump across at the top. The great height and extraordinary steepness makes the distance appear much less than it actually is. It would be difficult for me to judge how high they are; however, they vary very much in every feature. I hope no vessel will go humbugging about these places looking for us. The reefs before mentioned, lying to the eastward of the north end of the group, I may here mention again, for they are undoubtedly exceedingly dangerous, and should be carefully avoided. On this occasion there was a long line of breakers (with several dry places) running in an easterly direction, and extending (as I first stated) not less than ten miles from the land. I have now seen them from several different bearings, and I conclude that their distance from the land is not less than ten miles. I should also have stated that there are a number of sunken rocks, which do not always show, lying about and across the mouths of the bights and chasms on the north-east angles. All this part should be very carefully approached. As we returned we set fire to the grass on the homeward side of the mountains; it was very dry, and burnt well all night, and would have been a good beacon for any one near the island.

As soon as the weather moderates we must go and see if we can get another seal or two, if they are only black ones. I am trying to tan the largest of the last two skins we got. Whether I shall succeed or not I cannot tell; but we have found a bark which I have great hopes of, and, if it answers, the skin of this fellow would make excellent sole leather. We are not yet reduced to wearing seal-skin clothes entirely, but those which we do wear look most deplorable, although they are neither ragged nor dirty; but they are patched to such a degree that in scarcely any piece of garment that any of us wear is there a particle of the original visible. Joseph's coat would scarcely be a circumstance of comparison with some of ours. Old canvas, old gunny bags, anything we can get hold of, goes in for patches, and we use canvas ravellings for thread, and sew everything with a sail-needle. We are certainly a motley group. I have cut up all my bed sheets for patching with, and I expect I shall have to use canvas, gunny bags, &c., also shortly. Raynal and I keep on doing a little at our new place, but the greater part of our time, when we are down there, is occupied in straining our eyes in looking down the harbour. The barometer has been all the week between 29·10 and 29·90, and is now 29·52. Thermometer 38°.

Sunday, October 30, 1864.—Here we are yet, closely clasped in Sarah's Bosom. I don't think I shall have any reason to dread purgatory after this ; I trust that my purgations are now being performed, and are almost completed, for things appear to be drawing rapidly towards a crisis. The proverb says, when things are at their worst they must mend ; but how bad that worst may be is beyond the reach of human knowledge. I must now forego about the last bit of comfort that was left me, which is writing a little on Sundays ; for if I continue to do so, my only remaining book of blank paper will be filled up. I may yet have something of moment to insert, for which purpose I must reserve the few remaining pages. So, my dear old book, I must bid you good bye, for God only knows how long. If nothing comes after us, we shall commence at the New Year to pull the ' Grafton ' to pieces, and try what we can do with her bones. It is an undertaking the success of which I am exceedingly doubtful of. If we had had tools I should have tried what we could have done long before this time ; but who expected that we should be left here unlooked for like so many dogs !

     *   *   *   *   *   *

It is folly for me to get into this vein. Let it pass. Our stock of tools is, as I think I have said before, an American axe, an adze, a hammer, and a gimblet—a mighty assortment to take our ship to pieces, and build another one with, if even there was any carpenter or blacksmith among us, which there is not. The idea is almost farcical ; but, as I have said before, I shall go to sea on a log in preference to dragging out a miserable existence here : besides, I am not sure that we shall be able to do that much longer. We have had very bad weather all the week, with the exception of Wednesday. It was constant heavy rain until Friday evening, and blowing a gale from the westward. On Friday evening it shifted suddenly to S.S.W., and the rain turned into snow, which fell heavily, and now lies thick on the ground ; and the weather is dark, gloomy, cold, and miserable. On Wednesday, although a dirty wet day, and blowing too hard to take the boat, we were obliged to turn out, almost without breakfast, to look for something to eat. Four of us went out together, taking the gun, expecting to get a few widgeons ; and I returned very ill, and I have not been right since. Until the evening we were very unfortunate. We travelled about ten miles without getting anything. Here there were a few mussels ; but it was high water, and we could not get to them, so we set to work fishing, but only got two very small ones, about the size of sprats. About three o'clock in the afternoon, by wading into the water, we were able to get a few mussels, which we at once roasted and ate, but afterwards we got as many as we could eat. I think I ate too many, and this, with walking and fasting so long, very likely made me ill. This is picnicing in reality. God protect us from having much of it to do ! but He is still good to us.

On our way home we fell in with and killed two tiger seals, without which I think we should positively have starved, for the weather has been such as to prevent us from getting any since. On Tuesday morning we launched the boat, although it was blowing a heavy gale, with heavy rain, and with a fair wind went to the place where the seals were. We had taken a small piece of one home with us on the previous evening, to make our supper and breakfast with. We got our seals into the boat very comfortably, but with four oars we were five hours pulling back home (a distance of two miles and a half!) where we arrived drenched to the skin, and I have had a severe cold ever since. The barometer has been from 29 inches to 29·50 ; thermometer, 34°.

November 28.—Strong gale from N.W. ; hail, sleet, and snow falling. Barometer, 29·35.

December 1.—Ice on the mountains. 6th.—Very low tide and easterly wind. 8th.—Frost ; thermometer at 32°. 19.—Thermometer 56° ; 1° above temperate. 21st.—N.E.

gale for 12 hours; barometer 29·90. Throughout the month of December the weather has been exceedingly fine. A ship could come in here at any time during the whole month, and from last Christmas till to-day (New Year's Day) the weather has been as fine as ever I saw it anywhere. Barometer about 30 inches, and thermometer 60° at noon.

CHAPTER VII.

SHIP-BUILDING COMMENCED.—FAILURE OF THE SAME.—THE BOAT PLACED UNDER REPAIR.—SAND-FLIES.—DISCOVERY OF A CAVERN.—WINTER AGAIN.

Sunday, January 1, 1865.—A whole year has now passed since I first anchored in this place, and in all probability another will at least pass before I get away, unless by chance of some sealers coming in the meantime. I have got quite grey-headed. My hair is now all coming out. Whether I shall get it again or remain bald-headed remains to be seen. I have also, since I last wrote, been very much troubled with boils, a number of which have been about my face; but these are going away again. The men continue quite healthy, which is well, for I have not even a dose of salts to give them or take myself, whatever happens. The only medicine we have is plenty of exercise, which is not only conducive to health, but dispels gloom, and makes people really cheerful. I take plenty of this medicine myself, and encourage it in others as much as I possibly can; and I am happy to say the result has proved so far satisfactory. I manage to keep the men almost constantly employed at something which is at the same time useful and amusing. We shall shortly commence to pull the schooner to pieces, and I have no doubt but we shall feel truly interested in the work of trying to get away. I hope we may succeed. It is quite true that by energetic perseverance men may perform wonders, and our success would by no means constitute a miracle. The men are all very sanguine, and I have no doubt but we shall be able to make something that will carry us to New Zealand. We are not quite ready to commence yet. Raynal and I have not finished our new place, where we intend to live, and this house must be thatched, so as to preserve the sails, which, up to the present time, have covered it.

Providence continues good to us, for since I last wrote, when the prospect of getting food looked so gloomy, the bull seals have returned. They came at the beginning of November. They appear to pay annual visits to the cows, but unfortunately there are not more than three or four in the harbour. They have not yet had their calves. The bulls remain, however, and we are able to get one almost at any time; for they are very bold, and will come out of the water and chase us, in which manner we get them on shore and kill them; but they are particularly fierce. We are obliged to be very cautious in attacking them. There are some exceedingly large ones—quite as large, if not larger, than the largest we killed at Campbell's Island. These bulls, wherever they have been—whether about the roads outside or at other islands—have evidently had better food, or it has been much more plentiful than they find it here, for they have fallen away immensely since they came. I should not have been at all surprised at their losing fat after coupling time; but that is not yet come, so I conclude that it is owing to the nature or quantity of food which they get.

In November some of the birds lay their eggs—the blackbird; the robin, which is the first; and the green bird, which is the famous songster; and the seagull. We thought one day to have a treat, and spent the whole day in the boat hunting after and getting gulls' eggs. We got twenty altogether, out of which, when boiled, we got five good ones; the remainder were all addled. These are all the eggs we have been able to get. I am sorry to say the shag, or what we call widgeon, have all deserted the harbour. Very likely they are gone elsewhere to hatch their eggs. On the night of the 23rd November we had a severe gale, accompanied with rain, from north, and it was one of the heaviest we have had. The barometer fell in seven hours 1 inch and 14·00, from 29·92 to 28·78. The heaviest part of the gale was from midnight until 3 A.M., when it hauled to N.W. At 9 A.M. it fell instantaneously calm, and continued so twenty-four hours, with dark, gloomy weather and showers.

Sunday, February 5, 1865.—Since I last wrote we have had some very severe weather. We had a rotatory gale, which continued without cessation from the 10th to the 25th of last month, during which time we were reduced to the point of starvation. It was impossible to launch the boat, and, although we traversed the shores as far as we could every day, we were unable to procure anything to eat. It rained heavily nearly all the time during the gale. I never suffered as I do now; it is no use talking about what I have suffered—God alone knows the extent of that since I have been here. I shall talk, or rather write, about something else; but, by-the-by, my hands are so stiff and swollen with hard work that I can scarcely guide my pen, for this is the first day's rest I have had for five weeks.

We have commenced in earnest the work of building a vessel to get away in. This will not prevent me from observing the Sabbath, but during the time mentioned it has been impossible to do so. Two Sundays we were out after grub; the next we were thatching the house; and last Sunday we were working at the wreck, trying to get her higher on the beach, to do which, with the means at my command, I have exhausted my ingenuity without success. We stripped the lower masts and bowsprit, and cut them away: took every ounce of ballast out, and disburthened her of all possible weight, without taking away any of her upper work, as I did not know what I might have done with her had I succeeded in moving her. But this can only be done by lifting her bodily up. I had seventeen empty casks secured round her bows, but they had not the slightest impression on her. She is built of very heavy hard wood, principally greenheart and coppy. She was built from the wreck of a Spanish man-of-war; but I am sorry to say they took care not to put any copper bolts in her : but perhaps there were none in the original wreck. But they have not been at all sparing with the iron. She has got any quantity of that about her, which will be of more service to me than any other part of her, excepting the plant, which is already full of bolt-holes ; but we must make it answer our purpose. The vessel I am going to build will be a cutter of about ten tons. We have got the blocks laid down, and a quantity of timbers cut. All the frame we shall have to get out of the woods, excepting the keel, which the ' Grafton's' mainmast will supply. Mr. Raynal is Vulcan ; he has had some little experience in blacksmithing, which will now be of the greatest service to us, as we shall have to make nearly all our own tools. He has got a forge up ready for going to work at, as soon as we get some charcoal made. We have now a quantity of it in the ground, undergoing the process of burning. The schooner had a quantity of old iron in her bottom for ballast, amongst which we found a block, which will answer the purpose of an anvil. Mr. Raynal has undertaken to make a saw out of a piece of sheet iron. When we found the old sealers' camp on Figure-of-Eight Island, we found an old saw file, but the teeth were all rusted off it. This has been carefully reserved ever since, and Mr. R. ground it smooth on a grinding stone, which was our principal ballast, and with an old chisel, made out of an old broken flat file, cut fresh teeth in it ; but unfortunately, as he was cutting almost the last tooth, he broke it—the part which goes into the handle—and about two inches of the file went. I think he can manage to cut teeth in the saw with it. I am afraid that augers will be the most difficult tools to make ; but, now that the job is fairly undertaken, I have not the slightest doubt of final success in some shape or other. Every one works cheerfully and well : I sincerely hope nothing will occur to damp either. We work from six in the morning until six in the evening.

We have been able to work the whole of the past week,

but to-day it is blowing a hard northerly gale, with constant heavy rain, and threatens to continue. The barometer is low (28·70), which is the only sign of a change. We may expect the gale to haul to the N.W. whenever it shifts. Weather permitting, and God continues His goodness in supplying us with food, which we can manage to get in moderate weather, we shall get along very well—a critical position to be placed in, not knowing the moment all means of subsistence may be withdrawn from us.

Some time ago I mentioned a bark we had found, which I thought would tan, and I am now glad to say that it does make an excellent tan. We are now all wearing shoes of the leather it has made. It is very good leather, and if allowed to remain long enough in the tan would be excellent. I am inclined to think that the skin of these seals (which are the sea-lion), properly tanned, will make a very superior leather. What we are wearing now was about four months in tan, and it appears as if it will wear very well. This bark is from the hard wood, which I have said is good for ship timbers and knees.

Almost a year ago I mentioned a small fish, something like the anchovy, which were found in shoals. These fish appear to come annually, and are followed by the Australian mutton bird, which bird went away from here about May last. A great many were killed by the cold before they left; they returned again about the 20th January. I dare say these birds are eatable, but they are small. We have not had a chance of getting a shot at them this year, but we intend to try them when we can get one. We find that some of the cow seals have had calves, but not all, so that the latter part of January, and the beginning of February, is evidently the time for calving, and not December, as I have thought before. How long the building of our craft will occupy I am at present unable to judge, having had no previous experience in ship-building. I must see how the work progresses before I can form any idea.

Sunday, March 12, 1865.—It is now more than a month

G

since I last wrote, during which time we have been busily employed in our projected work of ship-building, although I myself have been unable to do anything with my hands, because for about three weeks I have had one or both of them in a sling with boils. I am now beginning to get the use of them again. We have got the keel, stem, and stern-post of the craft, and a number of timbers ready for bolting them together; but also here we are stuck fast, and find ourselves unable to go any farther. Mr. Raynal has made a saw, chisels, gouges, and sundry other tools. His ingenuity and dexterity at the forge have indeed surpassed my expectation, but making augers has proved a hopeless failure. Assiduously he wrought at one for three days, and it was not until there was not a shade of hope left that he gave it up; and if he had had the material to make them out of I feel confident he would have succeeded. The only steel he had was two picks and some shovel blades, which tools we took from Sydney, in hope of having some mining operations to perform at Campbell's Island. Yes! that is the rock I split upon.

But to my subject. It was truly deplorable to view the faces of all as we stood around him, when he decidedly pronounced it impossible for him to make one: they all appeared, and I have no doubt felt, as if all hope was gone. It went like a shot to my heart, although I had begun to anticipate such a result, and had made up my mind for immediate action accordingly; but when I saw positively that I must, as a last card, put my project into practice, I felt I was tempting Providence; for my tacit project and unalterable resolution is to attempt a passage to Stewart's Island in the boat. When I communicated my intention to the men, with the exception of the cook they unhesitatingly desired to go with me, which request I did not object to on this occasion; and the cook, rather than remain behind by himself, is going also. It would have been better for them in the boat if some had remained behind, but humanity prompts me to take them all with me ; for it is very doubtful whether those remaining on the island would find sufficient food or not to subsist upon through the fast approaching winter. The seals are very scarce, and in all probability abandon the place entirely about the latter end of April, at which time they began to disappear last year, although they had previously been so exceedingly numerous. The truth is, starvation is staring us in the face, which, it will be admitted, is enough to drive men to desperation. And this fact has moved me to the resolution which I have taken, and I think I am acting prudently. I have given it my serious and deliberate consideration for the last three months, as I have all along had my doubts about being able to make augers, without which it is utterly impossible to build anything better than the boat ; and I think I can make her so that if she could carry two persons in safety she can carry us all. I shall make some alterations in her before we go, as I do not intend to start before next month, when, after the equinoctial gales, we may reasonably expect fine weather. And as up to the present time the weather in this year corresponds exactly to that of the same months in last year, I am in good hopes of being able to get away and arrive in safety. The boat is a clinker-built dingy, 12 feet on the keel, and, I am sorry to say, very old and shaky. I intend to strengthen her as much as possible ; to raise her about a foot, and lengthen her about three feet ; all of which we must contrive to do between this and the 1st of April, so as to be ready to embrace the first favourable opportunity of starting.

Since December, as I have before noticed, the weather resembles very much that of the corresponding months of last year ; and I must not forget to remark that during the last nine days we have had some of the finest weather that we have experienced since we came here. This we cannot expect to last much longer, on account of the equinox. On the 8th and 9th instant we had a sharp frost in the night, with light north-east airs, and clear weather ;

indeed, a more favourable opportunity of going in the boat could not possibly have presented itself. We could have pulled all the way to New Zealand. May it please God to grant us such another chance when we may expect it, and are ready! On the last occasion of my writing, I forgot to mention having seen a comet to the southward. It was visible from the 23rd up to the 26th January, after which date, for some time, the weather was so cloudy as not to admit of its being seen. Barometer has been nearly stationary for the last nine days, at 29·80.

Sunday, March 26, 1865.—The sea booms, and the wind howls. These are sounds which have been almost constantly ringing in my ears for the last fifteen months; for during the whole of this time I dare venture to say that they have not been hushed more than a fortnight together. There is something horribly dismal in this boom and howl; sometimes it makes my flesh creep to hear them, although I am now so well used to it. Had the romantic admirers of this sort of thing been in my place, I would have been thankful; and they, I have no doubt, would have been quite satisfied. I could not wish my greatest enemy to be similarly situated. Well, I have said I am about to leave. Yes; this, I hope, will be the last Sunday but one that we shall spend in this part of Sarah's Bosom; and perhaps by that time we may have had the good luck to have got out of it altogether. Yes, we go in now for death or freedom! But I have good hope of our success; in fact we are all in high spirits about it. This, however, is natural enough, I have no doubt; for men, after suffering such an imprisonment as we have done, are ready to regain their liberty at any price, especially when grim starvation is urging them on.

Since I last wrote, we have worked steadily and industriously at the boat, and have got along as fast as our skill and tools will permit; and I think we shall be able to launch her in about ten more days from this. We have worked from daylight in the morning until half-past nine at night, Raynal at his forge, and I, after dark, at the sails in the house. We have had sails, masts, and everything to make. But the other day I thought we were ruined, for I broke the gimblet, without which our only means of making holes would have been to have burned them, which would be a most tedious process, for we required a great number of them; but, fortunately for us, Mr. Raynal managed to make it so that we can make a hole with it.

I have not said anything about the blow-flies and sand-flies lately. I may briefly state that they are equally as bad as they were when we first came here; and in consequence of having to work on the beach we are constantly exposed to the virulence of the latter, which surpasses my powers of description. I have seen mosquitoes very bad. I knew an instance, in a place called Nicarie, on the coast of Surinam, of a sailor being driven mad by them, and, seeking relief by plunging overboard, was drowned. I have also been in many other places, where I found them as troublesome as the Nicarie; but never have I seen anything in the shape of mosquitoes to equal those sand-flies in malignity. If the wind is moderate in the least degree —that is to say, if it is not blowing a whole gale, they are flying about in myriads, from daylight to dark (fortunately they modestly retire in the night), and alight on you in clouds, literally covering every part of your skin that happens to be exposed, and not only that, but they get inside our clothes and bite there. I do not think that at the present moment I could place the point of a needle on any part of my hands or face clear of their bites. I remember on one occasion, when working at the boat, a long time ago, having to abandon my job and come into the house. But there is no abandoning it now—we must grin and bear it, and persevere to get the job done. When the boat is launched, which she must be as soon as possible (as we are not able to get much to eat without her), we shall have to leave this place, and go down to

Camp Cove, where she can lie at anchor. We shall there be in a convenient position for popping out on the first opportunity. The seals are getting very scarce; indeed we have not seen one in the water for a long time. The few cows that had calvés here this year took them to the island (Figure-of-Eight), as they did last year, but I think we have got them all.

On the 17th and 18th we had a hurricane, which was actually the heaviest that I have ever experienced, either at sea or on shore. Mr. Raynal, who has resided in Mauritius for a period of seven or eight years, says that these gales are frequently much more severe than the Mauritius hurricanes. They are, indeed, terrific. Notwithstanding all this, there have been two opportunities of going away in the boat during the past or rather the present month; and I hope and trust we shall get another one as soon as the *packet* is ready. Before we leave I shall write my whole story—at least sufficient of it to be well understood, and leave it sealed up in a bottle, so that whoever comes here next—which, undoubtedly, some one will, although that event may not happen for a long time—may be enabled to discover what has happened to us. * * * * * * *

Sunday, April 2, 1865.—The past week leaves us but little farther advanced with our work, as the weather has been very wet and boisterous, which has prevented us from working outside. Indeed, with the best of weather we only get along slowly, and I find we shall not be ready as soon as I expected. There is a great deal to be done, and our tools are such that it is almost impossible to get along at all. I allowed ten days from last Sunday, and I find I may yet allow that time at least. Mr. Raynal is constantly employed at the forge, as there is a great deal of blacksmith's work to be done. We have everything to make— even the nails, of which, and small bolts, we require a great many. Since we have not been able to launch the boat, and particularly during the last week, we have been very much pinched for food, for there is little or nothing to be

picked up in the neighbourhood.   We have had one hand
out all the time grub-hunting.   But he had very poor success, and things were looking very gloomy, when to-day

Heaven, all bounteous ever, its boundless mercy sent.

I will recount the day's proceedings.   First thing after
breakfast we all started off, taking different directions, and
about one o'clock we began to return, one coming in after
another without having met with anything (one brought
two small fish), and we were all looking very blue at each
other, when in came the only remaining man, carrying on
his back a load of meat, weighing about one cwt.   He had
met with, and killed, two large cow seals about five miles
from the house.   We at once got something to eat, and all
started off to bring the meat home.   We had to make all
possible haste, as we had only just sufficient time to go and
come back again before dark ; and we had also the risk of
being caught by the tide, and being unable to get back
again to-night at all, as there are several places on the
way we had to go where there is six feet of water when
the tide is up, and it would be almost impossible to get by
going any other way.

On the way, Mr. Raynal and one of the men parted
company with us, they going through the bush in passing
the point, whilst we went round the point.   They fell in
with a young seal, and in chasing him he fell or leaped
into a deep narrow gully, about thirty feet deep, with perpendicular sides, and at the bottom runs a stream of water
which occupies the whole width of the chasm, and at a distance of about 100 yards from the beach is filled up at the
top, and the stream is lost sight of, as it runs underneath
the ground, and comes out of a small hole on the beach.
One of them ran down to get to the hole before the seal
would get there, but he did not come out, so Mr. Raynal
went down after him, whilst the men kept guard over the
outlet.   He found, to his great surprise, after getting down
to the bottom, that there was plenty of room to walk in

under what we have always termed the bridge. (We have some very strange names for distinguishing places by.) He saw the seal lying at the outlet, and watching the man who was outside waiting for him. When he found Raynal coming towards him he showed fight, but on getting a knock bolted for the hole, and was duly received by the man outside. He was a one-year-old bull; a very nice addition to the two cows already killed. But the place underground, where Raynal was, proved to be a spacious cavern, divided into two apartments by the stream running through the centre, each of which was about forty feet long and twenty wide. The roof was about twenty feet high, and through the centre was a round hole which had escaped our previous notice, and by which a flood of light was admitted to the cavern. Mr. Raynal describes it as a very comfortable place to live in. In the meantime we had gone on. After killing the seal and making these discoveries they followed and missed us, but fortunately fell in with a cow and calf. The calf they killed, after having a severe battle with the cow, and then returned. But they were behind us about an hour, and had to swim with their load across some of the six feet places, as the tide was up. We were wet also, for it rained heavily since noon, and still (9 p.m.) continues to do so. After all, we have been kindly dealt with, for Providence has always at the last push provided us with something.

Sunday, April 16, 1865. —Since I last wrote hoary winter has set in in earnest, and with the utmost severity. It has blown an incessant gale, with constant hail, snow, and pelting rain, since the 3rd inst., and has almost entirely prevented us from working at the boat since that time. We have, however, by dint of great perseverance and many a wet jacket, managed to get all done except putting on the planks, and I have no doubt but we shall finish in two or three days; but we must have better weather to launch her. Small as she is, there has been a great deal of work about her. There are about 180 clinch bolts in her, and there will, when finished, be about 700 nails and spikes in her. Raynal has had to make all these out of short bolts of all sorts and sizes, belaying pins, &c., welded together and drawn out. But I must be brief to-day, as I intend to insert here a copy of the letter which I am going to leave here, and which I have just finished writing, and the blank space is getting very small.* However, I cannot omit taking notice of a small bird which appears to be an annual visitor to this island, as they have been here about the same time both last year and the present one. They come in immense flocks, fly rather high, and in waves. They are evidently a seed bird of the sparrow species, and very much resemble the wild canary, both in colour and size. They only remained here a few days, and I fancy they went away on the 3rd of this month, which was a fine day, with a light southerly breeze—in fact, one of the most pleasant days we have had since we came here, and we have had only one anything like it before. So much for this wretched land; but it has made up for that fine day since, by blowing a continuous and one of the heaviest gales that it is possible to imagine. I have been round both capes (*i. e.*, Cape Horn and Cape of Good Hope), and crossed the Western Ocean many times, but never have I experienced, or read, or heard of anything in the shape of storms to equal those of this place.

---

* The copy does not appear to have been made.—Pub.

CHAPTER VIII.

LAUNCH OF THE BOAT.

Friday, June 23, 1865.—It is now more than two months since I wrote, and anticipated being away in three days, but 'man proposes and God disposes.' Since that time we have had our greatest trials and difficulties to contend with. In the first place, when we got an opportunity of putting the plank on to the boat, we found that it would not stand bending, although well steamed. We were then obliged to almost remodel the boat entirely, and cut planks out of the bush, which, with our saw, which required sharpening every half-hour, was an exceedingly tedious operation. In the next place, everything was buried in snow for three weeks; then followed heavy rains and continued wet stormy weather up to the present time, in which we, and myself in particular, persisted in working; and we were all seized with a violent attack of dysentery about the same time. This we have all recovered from; but I am left with rheumatic pains and cramps, which will in all probability cling to me through life. This is not to be wondered at. I am very much surprised that I have stood it at all, for my clothing is in a most wretched and deplorable state. It is useless for me to describe it—it is a complete bundle of rags; and by adding to these troubles grim starvation, which all along has been gnawing at our bowels, we have a summary of our calamities, the details of which would be sickening. But, thank God! we are now in reality on the point of surmounting or ending our wretchedness and misery.

The boat is finished, rigged, sails bent, and ready for launching; but the weather is at present so dreadfully bad that it is impossible to launch her. In the meantime we are keeping body and soul together by eating roots and drinking water. The meat that we salted and dried eighteen months ago, and which has long been shrivelled up like chips, has now come into requisition, and is used sparingly and with a relish. We also shoot sea-gulls or any other scavengers that come within reach of us. Everything that is really fit to eat keeps out of our reach. We have had one seal since I last wrote, and this one affords another and more striking instance of the savage manner in which these animals fight. It was found by one of the men in a place where I have no doubt it had gone to die. One of its fore flippers was entirely torn away from its body; the other one was cut or broken off by the lower joint; the lower jaw broken, and the flesh torn away from underneath, and with a strip of skin about two inches wide torn off all the way down the belly, and another strip was torn off its back, from the top of the head to its tail, which was left quite bare to the bone. How it had managed to crawl out of the water I cannot imagine, and whether it had been set into by more than one seal I am unable to conjecture. It was a cow, and was with calf.

This great scarcity of meat has not been for want of searching after it. We have constantly had one, and sometimes two, men out on the forage. If the boat was afloat, I have no doubt but we should be able to find as much as we could eat. When we get her afloat, we shall at once lay in a sea stock, and be off with the first slant of wind. I consider, now that we have finished, we have made an excellent job of the boat, and she is not at all unsightly. Indeed, she may be pronounced a neat, substantial-looking, but small yacht, and what we have done is indeed substantially done. I wish the old bottom was half as good as the new work. Here remains the only doubt of our safety. If that stands we are safe; if not, we sink, which will be preferable to the bodily sufferings and hellish mental tortures I suffer here. But a truce to all ideas excepting that of being shortly restored to all that is dear to me on earth. We are all in first-rate spirits, considering the misery with which we are surrounded. It is only this evening that we have got the boat ready for launching, and indeed there are several little preparations uncompleted yet.

Mr. Raynal is still making his hammer ring in the forge, although it is now half-past one o'clock in the morning. He is just finishing his last job, and I have snatched this opportunity for writing a little. Raynal has all along worked until eleven o'clock or midnight. There has been an amazing quantity of blacksmith work required for that small boat, which he has executed in a surprisingly skilful manner, and he has worked very hard. For my part, I have worked harder with my hands for the last nine months than ever I did in my whole previous lifetime; but I must not complain of this, for had I not done so I don't suppose I should now have been above the earth to write about it. I shall not be able to write much more, for my book is full, and I do not know whether I shall be able to muster up another scrap of paper or not.

In some part of my journal I have noticed an animal burrowing in the earth. About six weeks ago we caught a young cat of the common domestic species. We caught her in a trap in the forge, where she, no doubt, went to warm herself, after everything was quiet. We first kept her in a box for a few days, and then tied her up in the house near the fire, where in a few days she appeared to have become quite contented and reconciled to her lot. The strap about her neck by some means got broken, but still she remained about the house for some time, keeping under the floor in the daytime, and coming out in the evening; and she soon cleared the house of mice, with which we were dreadfully infested: but after a short time she was missing, and we saw nothing of her for some time, when she again made her appearance in the forge, where she continues to be a regular nocturnal visitor, and is quite tame, and likes to be petted and played with; but she never makes her appearance until after dark. Cats may be very numerous on the island, and still not be out in the daytime; therefore we do not see them. Whether they are the only animal that makes holes in the ground here or not I am yet unable to say positively; but if such be the case (judging from the number of holes), they are numerous, and are all round the shores of this vast bay.

On the 27th June we launched the boat, and took with us such things as we might require whilst lying at Camp Cove. Fortunately it was perfectly calm, for on getting the boat into the water we found her so tender, the least movement put her almost on her beam ends; indeed some of the men were quite frightened, and would gladly have gone on shore again. I explained to them that she would not turn over entirely so long as the ballast, which was composed chiefly of salted seal skins, did not shift, which was impossible; but at the same time I felt sadly disappointed in her myself, and I felt doubtful as to whether it would be prudent to venture forth in her or not—certainly not in her present condition; but I thought I should be able to make such alterations as would render her more fit to go to sea. We pulled her down to Camp Cove, a distance of about seven miles, and arrived there at dark in the evening, and after some little trouble, on account of the darkness, we succeeded in landing some sails, which we had brought for making a tent with, and other articles.

From this date, until the 11th July, we had very severe weather, and heavy gales from all points of the compass. I have proved this to be an excellent anchorage, perfectly sheltered from all winds, and good holding-ground. We altered the disposition of the ballast in the boat, as also her rig, from that of a cutter to a lug sail and jib, which latter rig I find is the most suitable; but I found that five of us were too many to attempt going to sea in her. I pointed this out to the men, and proposed that two should remain on the island, whilst I and two others tried to reach New Zealand, when, if I arrived safe (of which I had very grave doubts), I would immediately find some means of sending for those who remained. This proposal appeared to be opposed by the whole party, some of them saying, 'Well, if any of us are to be drowned, let us all drown together.' I endeavoured to convince them of the folly of risking all our lives, and told them that, had any one else been capable of navigating the boat, I would have preferred remaining behind, as, should those in the boat be lost, I and whoever was with me would still have a chance of being rescued, sooner or later ; but, seeing my arguments had little effect, I let the matter drop. We had frequently been out in the boat hunting for food, which about this part of the harbour was very scarce ; and the oftener I went out the more I felt convinced that the boat was unfit to carry all of us ; still I felt anxious that we should all get away together, although at the same time I saw the imprudence of such a step.

On the morning of the 11th we got a fair wind, and in anticipation of the event had to set to work in the night and cooked up all the seal and shag—which birds I heretofore dignified with the name of widgeon—that we had, and which I considered sufficient to take us to Stewart's Island. About eight o'clock in the morning a fine breeze was blowing ; the boat was hauled to the rocks by me and Mr. Raynal, and everything was ready for putting the provisions on board and starting. I went up to the tent and told them to bring down what was to go in the boat, and we would be off at once ; when, to my astonishment, they all begged of me not to start, as they were afraid that it was going to blow hard. I now found that I was going to have some trouble with them ; they were afraid to go, yet they objected to being left behind. I saw the necessity of having three hands in the boat, or Raynal and I would have gone by ourselves. I now saw that I must alter my tactics, and at once determined not to take them all ; and on the 13th (two days later) I took two of them back to the old camp at the wreck, and left them there. Their names were George Harris and Henry Folgee. These two had always agreed very well, and the latter had evinced a strong disinclination to going in the boat at all ; therefore I considered these the proper men to leave behind, giving them everything that we could spare. After landing them, we returned to Camp Cove, so as to be ready for starting with the first fair wind.

Several days of very bad weather succeeded, and we got very short of food ; but on the 18th the weather moderated, and we managed to get a young seal and a few shag, which we cooked on that evening, expecting a fair wind on the following day.

CHAPTER IX.

WE LEAVE THE ISLAND AND LAND AT PORT ADVENTURE.—
ARRIVAL AT INVERCARGILL.—DESPATCH OF THE 'FLYING
SCUD' TO AUCKLAND ISLAND.

The morning of the 19th July, 1865, broke ne and
promising ; at 8 A.M. a light air came from the southward,
and at 11 A.M. we set sail from Camp Cove with the first
squall of a sou'wester, which winds never blow with any
degree of moderation for more than 12 hours, and invariably end in a hard gale ; but by taking the very first of it
I expected to have got some distance away before the
strength of the gale would overtake us. We did not, how
ever, get more than 20 miles from the island before we
felt the full fury of a south-west gale, which continued
until our arrival at Port Adventure, Stewart Island, on
the morning of the 24th instant, after a miserable passage
of five days and nights, during the whole of which time I
stood upon my feet, holding on to a rope with one hand
and pumping with the other. The boat was very leaky, and
kept the pump almost constantly going. As my anxiety
would not permit me to leave the deck, I performed this
part of the work while the other two relieved each other at
the helm. The wind, although fair, was so strong that we
were obliged to lay-to nearly half the time, and the sea
was constantly breaking over the little craft ; and how she
lived through it I scarcely know. I had not eaten an
ounce of food from the time of leaving until we arrived,
and only drank about half a pint of water ; yet I felt
no fatigue until the night before we landed, when I suddenly became quite exhausted, and lay down on the deck,
over which there was no water washing for the first

time since we left the island. We were now close to the land. I lay for about half an hour, and then got up again, feeling that I had just sufficient strength remaining to enable me to hold out till the next day ; but had we been out any longer I feel convinced that I should never have put my foot on shore again.

On the following day, however, we landed at Port Adventure, where we were kindly received by Captain Cross, of the 'Flying Scud.' When we landed I could not stand, but was led up to that gentleman's house, where something to eat was immediately prepared for us, of which I partook very sparingly ; for I felt very ill and unable to eat, and my companions were almost as much knocked up as myself. After this meal I had a warm bath and went to bed, where I remained till late in the evening, and on the following morning, after a good night's rest, I felt much better. Captain Cross was this day going to Invercargill. I made him a present of our boat, and we went with him in his vessel to Invercargill. I requested him to name our boat the 'Rescue,' and he informed me that early on that morning they had hoisted English colours on board, and given her that name.

On the morning of the 27th July, 1865, I landed in Invercargill, and, in company with Captain Cross, walked up the jetty and entered, I think, the first store we came to—that of Mr. J. Ross. I had not been there more than five minutes when Mr. John Macpherson, of the firm of Macpherson and Co., came in. He heard my tale, and at once, without the slightest hesitation or consideration, offered to assist us by every means in his power, and said that one of his vessels would most likely be in Invercargill in a month or so, and could we not devise some means of getting the other two men up before that time, she should go down for them. He took me at once to Mr. Ellis, Collector of Customs, who was the first person that I should see, and deliver to him my ship's papers, and who, as agent for the general government, was the first person

H

to whom Mr. Macpherson addressed himself on our behalf. It appeared, however, that he could do nothing for us on the part of the government. Mr. Macpherson then waited upon the Deputy-Superintendent, and he, on behalf of the provincial government, could also do nothing for us. Mr. Macpherson then took me to his own house to lunch, after which he most generously got up a subscription for the purpose of giving immediate relief, and chartering a vessel to go down and bring up the two men whom I had left behind; and before 6 P.M. had succeeded so far as to have raised about £40 in subscriptions of £5 each.

In the meantime Mr. Collyer, of the Princess's Hotel, had invited me, Mr. Raynal, and the other man to come and stay at his house free of charge, which kind offer I accepted. Mr. Macpherson also kindly invited me to his house to spend the evening. In the morning of the 28th, at the earliest business hour, Mr. Macpherson recommenced his work of disinterested goodness and charity, and until after dark in the evening trudged round the wet and muddy streets of Invercargill soliciting subscriptions for our aid; and on this evening had raised over £100, besides clothing and blankets for the men on the island. I consider it unquestionably the work of Divine Providence which has guided me safely thus far, and placed me in the hands of such a humane and sympathetic gentleman as Mr. Macpherson, by means of whose untiring endeavours the public of this little town have acted with so much bounty towards us poor castaways. I did not think it just or proper that I should accept of their charitable offerings so far as to clothe myself afresh, and begged of Mr. Macpherson to advance me a sufficient amount for that purpose, and accept a bill for the amount on Sarpy and Musgrave, of Sydney, which he most generously did.

A vessel was this day chartered to go down to the island, which vessel happens to be the 'Flying Scud,' owned and sailed by Captain Cross, who kindly entertained

us at Stewart Island, and brought us here in the said
'Flying Scud;' and a sufficient quantity of provisions
for the trip was collected, either by way of subscriptions
or purchase; and it was considered by those most interested
in the affair incumbent on me to accompany Captain Cross,
so as, from my knowledge of the place, to be in some
measure a guarantee for the safety of the vessel, as she is
not insured. To this I did not object, much as my heart
yearned to return at once to my deserted family; for my
conscience tells me that this little self-denial is justly
due to all parties, and I humbly pray that we may have a
safe and successful voyage and speedy return, when I may
consider that I have fully discharged my duty.

Saturday, July 29, 1865.—This day also was occupied
by the indefatigable Mr. Macpherson in running about
town, prosecuting his work of despatching the 'Flying
Scud.' I took luncheon at his house again to-day, and at
about four o'clock in the afternoon he walked down to the
vessel with me to see us off; we were also accompanied by
his brother, Mr. William Macpherson. A number of the
townspeople were assembled on the wharf, from which, at
about 5 P.M., we cast loose and sailed, amidst the cheers,
and accompanied by the well-wishes, of the assembled
crowd. The wind was moderate from west; the weather
had been gloomy and showery during the day, but the
evening was fine. As the vessel could not go over the
bar, we brought up for the night in a snug anchorage, at a
place on the west side of the river called Sandy Point,
about six miles from town: another small vessel was also
anchored there.

CHAPTER X.

THE VOYAGE TO AUCKLAND ISLAND IN THE 'FLYING SCUD.'

Sunday, July 30.—At the peep of day we weighed anchor and proceeded down, and although the bar was breaking, Captain Cross perseveringly attempted and succeeded in crossing it without any further accident than the loss of one of the sweeps, along with which, however, Captain Cross had a very narrow escape from going overboard; the wind was so light, though fair (north), that it required the sweeps to keep her in the channel. A very light northerly air carried us across the Straits, and we got under the land of Stewart Island at dark. The wind then came from N.W., and gradually increased, hauling to the westward, giving us a speedy run down along the land, and at 11 P.M. we were off Port Adventure, where Captain Cross had occasion to call; but as the wind was now W.S.W., we should have been obliged to take shelter in any case, as it is useless to go out and buffet against foul winds when it can be avoided. At midnight we anchored in a cove at the neck of the peninsula which forms the southern entrance point of the Port, and where the 'Flying Scud' was anchored on my first arrival, just a week ago.

Monday, July 31.—Brisk gale at W.S.W. and cloudy squally weather, with occasional showers. People on board variously employed. I have been very unwell to-day; indeed, I fear that I am going to be attacked with some serious illness.

Tuesday, August 1, 1865.—Strong gale at S.W., with squalls and frequent showers of hail and rain. It is very cold, although the thermometer is not lower than 37°. The people on board have all been variously employed. Captain Cross sent a man to pull me round the Port, as I wished to look at the different anchorages. In a small but snug cove on the south side of the bay, which is called Oyster Cove, we found a party consisting of an Englishman, a half-caste Maori, and two Maori women, who (with five ragged and somewhat ferocious looking dogs) were dwelling in a cave in the rocks, their business there being that of dredging for oysters, which they dispose of in the Invercargill market. They presented me with four or five dozen, which I must pronounce the finest I have met with in the Southern Hemisphere.

I was very much gratified with our pull round Port Adventure. I carefully inspected the timber, which is abundant and of considerable variety ; but saw only one tree which at all resembles that on Auckland Islands. It is that of the hard-wood, and is here very appropriately called iron wood ; but it grows much straighter and larger than that of the Auckland Islands. Amongst the herbage I saw nothing resembling in any way that of the Auckland Isles, excepting some of the tufty grass ; and amongst the feathered tribes I only saw one little chirruper such as we had down there—this is the robin ; neither have I seen any of the boggy earth such as is down there, and the rocky formations which I saw are quite dissimilar. On returning to the vessel in the evening I found the crew as busily employed as I had left them, in putting everything in order for a sea voyage, which I believe the vessel has not yet been called upon to perform. She is nearly new, and has been wholly employed in the coasting trade.

Wednesday, August 2.—Heavy S.W. gale, with bitter squalls and showers of hail. It is very fortunate that we are in a good harbour during this heavy weather and head winds ; the little vessel would have got a severe thrashing had she been out in it, as it would be right in our teeth. Everything on board is snugly arranged, and she is now properly ready for the prosecution of her undertaking. However, there are at present no indications of a change. I am particularly anxious to be off, but must only endeavour to wait as patiently as I can till the favourable opportunity offers. I am quite well again; so much so that I had quite forgotten my late indisposition.

Thursday, August 3, 1865.—The gale still continues, but the showers have subsided, and the weather is finer. I have been wandering about the woods to-day, and have been to where I could see the sea, which is very rough. I find an herb growing here which grows plentifully at the Auckland Islands, and which the Maoris on a pinch substitute for tea. I have tried it, but it makes such miserable insipid stuff that had I been aware that it could be converted to this purpose I should decidedly have preferred the pure water, which *was* our beverage.

Captain Cross entertains me at his house, which is superior to those at the village, and at some distance from it, standing quite alone on the top of a hill. I find that he holds himself very much in reserve from the rest of the villagers, who appear to look towards him with considerable respect. He has a very interesting family of three children. His wife is a half-caste Maori, and it is curious to hear them conversing together. He speaks English, and she speaks Maori, as it appears that neither can speak the language of the other, although they both understand that of the other perfectly well ; consequently I can hold no conversation with Mrs. Cross. If I pass any slight remark, she will only smile without attempting to make any response, and to a question will simply answer yes or no. The children speak both languages, but always converse in Maori. I was highly amused to-day ; we had a visit from the magistrate of the village, who is an aged Maori. This distinguished personage would not presume to sit at table with us at dinner, but persisted, out of deference to us, in waiting until we had done ; neither does Mrs. Cross sit at table with us, which I consider very strange; but Cross informs me that he cannot prevail on her to sit at table, excepting when he is entirely alone. She is a very young woman, and as light in colour as a European; the Maoris, indeed, are very light coloured down here.

Friday, August 4, 1865.—The wind is still from the southward, but appears to be moderating; it is yet blowing a brisk gale, and is again very showery. I went to look at the sea to-day, which is still running very high. There is not the slightest indication of a change, further than a rising barometer; but I fear it will not come before the full of the moon, which takes place on the 6th.

Saturday, August 5.—There is no change in the direction of the wind, but its force is considerably abated, though it is still very squally, with occasional showers. To-day I visited the last resting-place of the oldest and first inhabitants of this island. The village burying-ground is on a lonely point jutting out into the bay, and thickly covered with trees and thick scrub, and is at a considerable distance from any of the dwellings, which is very wise and proper; but it is done from superstitious notions. They are very much afraid of the ghosts of their departed brethren paying them a visit. They are exceedingly superstitious. I was aware of this fact before, but I had not the slightest idea of its extent. I think to-morrow and the full moon will bring us a favourable change; the barometer is above 30 inches.

Sunday, August 6. — The morning was calm and the weather clear; every appearance of a northerly wind. At 2 P.M. we made a start with the first breath of a northerly wind, which, as we cleared the Port, seemed inclined to increase and haul to the eastward; but at 4 P.M. it again backed to N.W., and at 7 o'clock was at S.W., very light, and the weather continued clear and fine. It is now mid-night; the appearance of the weather has changed; it is dark and gloomy, the clouds are coming up from the southward, and I fear much that we shall have the wind from that quarter. However, the barometer keeps high ; perhaps it may continue light. We are now between Port Adventure and Port Pegasus, beating down along the land ; and should the wind continue from this quarter, we shall take shelter in the latter Port.

Monday, August 7.—At 4 A.M. the breeze freshened ; the weather was dark and gloomy, but the wind seemed inclined to back to the westward, which induced us to proceed on, and not go into Port Pegasus ; and as we approached the South Cape it went to N.W., which is for us a fair wind. At 8 A.M. we were about 14 miles south of the said Cape. It is now noon, the weather is thick and foggy, the breeze is strong, and the sea is running high, and the little vessel is dancing about like a cork. I am obliged to get myself chocked up in a corner to write, as it is impossible to sit, or stand, or even lie, without holding on, or being well chocked off. 9 P.M.—In the afternoon the weather bore a very threatening aspect, and the wind increased and hauled to the southward.

At 4 P.M. it was at S.W. (which is dead ahead), and blowing hard, and a very high and ugly sea running ; and as to beat against it is a task for which the little craft is not calculated, we bore up again for Port Pegasus. She is now running at the height of her speed, which is about 10 knots, and in another hour I expect to make the land. We were within 10 miles of the Snares Islands, but the weather is very thick, and we did not see them. It is the most prudent plan to run back, as we were no great distance away, and by lying-to we should only have lost ground.

Tuesday, August 8.—As we proceeded to the northward again, the wind moderated and the weather cleared a little. It is now 3 A.M. We have just hove the cutter to, and will wait for daylight, as we have not yet made the land, although we have run 20 miles farther than where we should have *found* it. I feel very uneasy about it, as all on board do. We have only one compass on board, which I have every reason to believe is out of order and is leading us astray, and where we are, or which side of the channel we are on, it will be impossible to ascertain until I can get sights in the morning. Unless we see the land at daylight, this is one of the most awkward positions that ever I remember being placed in. It is quite likely that we are in the vicinity of those ugly dangers, the Traps Reefs; and if the sea is running high and breaking all over, it will be impossible to see them before we should be on the top of them. We are now under double-reefed sails: the little vessel appears to lie-to very well. 9 A.M.—When daylight came nothing was in sight, so we continued to lie-to until 8 A.M., as the weather was thick and hazy. At 8 we stood to the N.N.W.; wind west. I have just had sights, but they are very indifferent, for the vessel is tossing about and throwing so much water over, and the sea is so rough, that it is impossible to get good ones. However, I find by using an assumed latitude that she is to the eastward of the island, but how far it is difficult to judge, as a few miles in latitude make a great difference; but she is no doubt between 60 and 70 miles from the South Cape. We are now lying-to again, as I consider it prudent to do so until noon, when I can get the true latitude.

We are all very miserable, everything wet, and we can get nothing cooked; for the man whom Captain Cross engaged, who was to have done the cooking, is a sea-sick, lazy, good-for-nothing fellow, and can't or won't do it; and Cross and the other men have to be almost constantly on deck. She is very wet and uneasy, and all this is bad enough, and we all wish the cruise well ended; but still it is pleasure compared with what I suffered on coming up in the boat, and I think now that these sufferings should have deterred me from undertaking the trip again in so small a vessel, if at all. 1 P.M.—I got the sun at noon, and find that the vessel is about 60 miles S.S.E. from the East Cape of Stewart Island, which is the nearest land. The compass must have led us nearly three points out of our course. This was yesterday, no doubt, when we were steering S.W. by S. At noon, when the vessel was heading to the northward, the compass was right, or nearly so, as no doubt it will be while she is heading so near the north point. A pretty pickle poor Cross would have been in had he had neither navigator nor chronometer on board, which Captain Gray, the harbour-master of Invercargill, proposed, saying that 'he could go down there very well without a chronometer,' and undertook to explain to me how it was to be done ; which was simply in the manner that some stupid Yankees, who don't know big A from a chest of drawers, take their vessels to the West Indies, viz., running down their latitude and steering *west.* He seemed to think he was doing a stroke by explaining this mode of navigation, but, as matters have turned out, it would not have answered in this instance.

It is very fortunate that we turned back yesterday, otherwise we might have got far to leeward of our destination before the error had been detected. It now threatens to blow a very hard gale (we are now under reefs), and whether we shall be able to get in anywhere to the northward of Otago I don't know, but we must get into the first port and get another compass, and find out how this one is disturbed, or get the deviation. It is now midnight ; we are getting into smooth water ; at 4·30 P.M. we made the land, East Cape of Stewart Island bearing W.N.W. about 25 miles distant. We are now beating up for it under double reefs, and intend going into Port Adventure again, where Captain Cross thinks he can procure another compass. The one I had in the boat has been destroyed by salt water. The weather looks very threatening. I fear it is going to blow very hard from S.W. I hope we shall be able to get in.

Wednesday, August 9.—It has been blowing a very heavy gale from S.S.W. since 2 o'clock this morning, which is now accompanied with frequent heavy showers of rain. At 5 A.M. we had the good fortune to get an anchor in Port Adventure, in the same place we left on Sunday. We find that there is not a compass to be got here; the only place where we are likely to get one on the island is at Paterson's Inlet, about 12 miles from here. Captain Cross appears confident of getting one there. If we cannot we shall be obliged to return to Invercargill, and get one there. As soon as ever the wind moderates we shall leave here. This trip is becoming so protracted that I am thoroughly sick of it, and am getting quite down-hearted about it; indeed, the question arises in my mind, am I doing an injustice to my family by prosecuting it?

Thursday, August 10.—It is still blowing a heavy gale from S.S.W., and it would have been madness to have thought of going out to-day. The sea is very heavy out-side, and a very great swell is rolling on the beaches in the harbour; and, what is worse, there is not the slightest indication of a change. The glass keeps high—much higher than ever I saw it during several gales while I was at the Auckland Islands. We had the honour of a visit again to-day from the magistrate whom I have mentioned before, and his daughter. They were followed by a numerous train—viz., three dogs, one cat, an innu-merable lot of poultry, and a pig. This happy family no doubt were the escort of the lady, as they did not accompany his honour on his previous visit. But when Captain Cross saw this motley train coming into his garden he seized a stick and laid about them lustily, and such a discord and confusion I never witnessed. The cackling fowls took the air; the dogs, howling, took the fence; and the pig, screaming, ran in all directions, looking for a place to get through it; whilst the cat vanished like a shadow—which direction she took I can't say. At all this the old magistrate laughed heartily, but the young lady did not appear to be so well pleased, for a frown dis-turbed her beautiful face—and such a frown! Her broad

thick lips, which seemed to have a natural antipathy to
each other, rose and fell—one touching the end of her nose
and the other covering her chin; her eyebrows fell, and
the hair on her low forehead gave chase, and almost over-
took them; whilst her nostrils distended so that her flat
nose almost covered the diameter of her interesting face:
but she did not condescend to say a word.

Friday, August 11.—10 P.M.—It continues to blow a
very heavy gale; it has been from S.W. since noon, and it
is now raining heavily, with thunder and lightning. There
is no possibility of moving in such weather as this, and
when it will end there is no telling—the Maoris here say
that it will continue throughout this moon. I wish there
was any means of getting letters across to Invercargill;
but it appears that the 'Flying Scud,' on our return, will
be the first vessel to go across.

Saturday, August 12.— First thing this morning we
started for Paterson's Inlet, and anchored at the neck of
the Peninsula at 2 P.M. We left Port Adventure with a
S.W. wind blowing hard and squally; on reaching the
East Cape the wind was W.N.W., and before we reached
the Inlet it was at N.W., squally and showery. We were
under double-reefed courses, and found some difficulty in
beating up. A Mr. Lowrie furnished us with a compass,
which was the object of our visit, and while there I had
the honour of being introduced to *Toby*, the Maori chief
of Ruapuke and Stewart Islands. This distinguished in-
dividual was over on a visit, as Ruapuke Island is his
place of residence; he very kindly offered us the use of
the compass belonging to his boat, and, as it appeared to
be a better one than either of the two we had, I accepted
it. Toby is by far the most intelligent-looking Maori I
have yet seen; he is, I should judge, about forty years of
age, and is what may be termed a good-looking man. He
informs me that he had a party sealing on the Snares
Islands, and that there is a snug cove on the eastern side

of the large island, where a boat or small vessel may lie in perfect safety from all winds. I have not heard of any such place before.

When these islands were surveyed by Drury, in H.M.S. 'Pandora,' they did not attempt a landing, but presumed that one might be effected on the north side of the large island under very favourable circumstances. If Toby's information be correct, this might prove a place of refuge for us in case of necessity, and save us from having another run back to Stewart Island; but I hope and trust that when we do get another chance of starting we shall get a run right down, or if we have to run back here again I shall feel inclined to abandon my undertaking, for I am getting out of all patience with it. Mr. Lowrie, who is one of the oldest hands — that is, one of the oldest European residents—on the islands, thinks that we may have a favourable change on Monday or Tuesday next, but strongly advises us not to attempt starting again until the wind gets in to the northward, after passing round by south and east, as in any other case a northerly or N.W. wind cannot be depended on for an hour.

At 3 P.M. we weighed anchor again, and returned to Port Adventure. We arrived at 8·30 P.M., but we were obliged to pull to the anchorage with the sweeps, as it fell calm when we were off the port. It is our intention to go down to Port Pegasus in the morning, if the weather be still favourable, and lie there till we get a wind to start with. Now we have got three compasses on board, and they all differ from each other—two of them differing as much as two points ; so that it is evident that there is some local attraction which acts upon one more than another. Before we go to sea I shall be obliged to swing the vessel and ascertain their deviation, and this can only be done in a calm, and I fear will give us some trouble ; but we cannot go to sea with compasses in this state ; we should be as well without any. The wind has been to the southward of east in Port Adventure all day, while to the northward of the East Cape it has been N.W., which, I believe, is very frequently the case. The barometer is falling rapidly. I have little doubt but we shall have a gale from S.W. to-morrow.

Sunday, August 13, 1865.—At daylight a breeze sprang up from W.S.W., and suddenly increased to a gale; we let go a second anchor. Since noon it has blown as hard as ever I saw it do, the wind about west. The bay has been one continual sheet of foam all the afternoon, and since nightfall it has been thundering and lightning, with frequent showers. The New Zealand coast pilot says that ' thunder and lightning during a gale is indicative of its long continuance.' We have had a good deal of it lately; so what may we expect now?

Monday, August 14.—From the time of writing last night (10 o'clock) until one o'clock this morning the thunder and lightning was incessant, peal rolling upon peal and keeping the earth in a continual tremor, and it rained very heavily the whole time. I don't remember ever seeing a heavier thunderstorm, not even in Australia. After this the wind died away, and during the night came from south, where it continued throughout the day, with almost constant sleet and snow, and the ground is now quite white, and it is freezing. The weather will be much more severe down at the Auckland Islands than it is here. I hope the two poor fellows down there will take no harm until we can reach them.

Tuesday, August 15.—The wind has been S.S.W. during the greater part of the day; moderate on the whole, but squally, with snow, which this morning was about two inches thick on the cutter's deck. Since nightfall the wind has fallen light, and the clouds, which still come from the southward, are not flying so rapidly as they have been doing; but still I fear the breeze from that quarter is not yet ended. The cutter ' Ellen' sailed to-day; the captain thought he *might* go to Invercargill, but he was not sure. I sent a letter by him to Mr. Macpherson, and was very sorry that I could not send others, on account of the uncertainty of his going across.

Wednesday, August 16.—A moderate southerly wind, with occasional showers of hail and drizzling rain. The weather is milder, and the snow has disappeared in a great measure. We might have started for Pegasus to-day, but as it would perhaps take 24 hours to beat down there we are better where we are. I fear that the prediction of the Maoris, that we shall have no change during this moon, will prove true.

Thursday, August 17.—It has been raining all day; the wind has been light and baffling from between south and west, and the barometer is rising. I trust that a change is near at hand.

Friday, August 18, 1865.—Light southerly airs, and gloomy dark weather, with frequent showers of mist. I am getting truly miserable. I can find nothing to occupy my mind with, for my reading is all done; in fact I could not take an interest in it if I had more. My attention is entirely taken up in watching any slight change that takes place in the weather. This afternoon we went to Oyster Cove, and got about 30 dozen oysters. The barometer indicates a favourable change. I trust we shall get away to-morrow.

Saturday, August 19.—Calm and dull cloudy weather until noon, but every appearance of a N.E. wind. At 11 A.M. we picked the anchor up, and pulled the vessel towards the Heads. At noon we got a light air from E.S.E., and had to beat out. The wind continued very light, and at 8 P.M. died away altogether, after which, having the tide in our favour, we pulled and got into Port Pegasus at a quarter to 12 (midnight). It is now close to one o'clock in the morning; calm and cloudy. I am off to bed.

Sunday, August 20.—Calm all this day. First thing in the morning I attended to the compasses, one of which I am very well satisfied with, as it shows little or no deviation, and I feel that we may trust to it; the others are very much out. In the morning we went on shore, and a dog which we have caught a penguin. They also went in the boat, and in a very short time caught three dozen beautiful fish (trumpeters). Port Pegasus is one of the finest harbours I have ever been in, and there is abundance of heavy timber all over its shores. If the land be good, which the abundance and verdure of its vegetation seem to indicate, it must, in the course of a few years, become a port of considerable importance. After dinner we got the anchor up and pulled the cutter outside, in hope of finding a breeze, but we were disappointed; there was not a breath of air, so we pulled in again, and in the evening anchored about six miles to the southward of where we lay last night. The barometer keeps high, 30·20.

Monday, August 21, 1865.—First part calm. At 9 A.M. a light air came from the northward, and we at once got under weigh, and came out by the southernmost entrance, and got a light N.E. breeze, which, by sundown, had run us to about eight miles south of the South Cape, where it died away, and at 7 P.M. came out from S.W. very light, just enough to give the vessel steerage way. This is very disheartening; I almost begin to doubt whether we shall ever accomplish this trip or not. Here is an instance of the uncertainty of the weather in these regions. All day the weather and barometer bore every indication of easterly wind, and a more easterly-looking sunset I never saw; and now, in one hour and a half, we have the wind from the direct opposite point, and all the indications of one hour and a half ago are entirely reversed. All the clouds have settled down to the N.E., and the sky is now clear, with the exception of a low, thick, black, arched bank of clouds, which are slowly, but surely, rising from S.W.; but the barometer is too high—30·15—for a strong breeze from that quarter. It has never deceived me in regard to a S.W. gale, and I yet have a hope that it will back into the northward again; at least, to the northward of west.

Tuesday, August 22.—I am once more tossing about on old Ocean. The little vessel is dashing the laughing spray from about her bows, and galloping away, with a fair wind from N.W., and I think we have a fair prospect of a speedy, and in some measure comfortable, run down to the Auck-lands. It is now 2 P.M. ; the Snares, which we passed at 10 A.M., are now out of sight astern. At 11 o'clock last night the wind came from W.N.W., as I had anticipated, and afterwards backed farther to the northward, gradually increasing to a fine steady breeze. At daylight, Stewart Island and the Snares were both in sight.

Wednesday, August 23, 1865.—After writing yesterday until midnight, the breeze freshened to a strong breeze, and at 2 A.M. we had double reefs in. At 3 A.M., having run far enough to be able to see the land in the morning, if the weather had been clear, we hove to under close-reefed sails, and lay till daybreak; but no land being in sight, we ran on again, and before I could get sights I began to feel very uneasy. At half-past eight, however, the sun peeped through the fog and gave an observation, by which I found that we were about twenty miles to the eastward of the island. We at once hauled up S.W. We had evidently been set to the eastward by a very strong current, and at least a point and a half out of our course. I have no notice of this current, but I had reason to suspect that there was such a thing, and endeavoured to guard against it; which had I not done it would certainly have put us more than fifty miles to the eastward. At 11 A.M. we made the land, and as the weather was so thick we were obliged to stand close in before we could make out which part of the islands it was. It proved to be the islands at the north end of the group. We then saw a line of breakers to lee-ward of us, stretching out from the land farther than we could see. These are the reefs which I have mentioned in my journal while down here. We at once hauled off, and stood at about ten miles from the land before we felt sure that we were clear of them, and then went through a heavy tide race, which broke on board in all directions. These reefs are very ugly dangers, and cannot be too carefully avoided until surveyed.

After clearing these dangerous reefs we hauled in again, and sailed down close along the shore; and on the side of one of the mountains, about eight miles north of the entrance of 'our harbour,' we saw, or thought we saw, smoke. Captain Cross and the others were positive that it was smoke, but I was not so sure of it, although I think it quite probable that my two men may have been up there and set fire to the grass. This we shall ascertain when we reach them. At 4 P.M. we entered the heads of the desired harbour, and the wind, which while we were running along shore was blowing a strong double-reef breeze, drew down the sound with great fury, and we felt doubtful whether we should be able to beat up against it or not. However, we hauled her up to it, standing by the halyards, and lowering away everything in some of the squalls, which would otherwise have capsized her, or blown away the canvas. We thrashed her up, and nobly did the little craft do her work. She was frequently down, hatches in the water, while the spray flew in clouds over the mast-head, smothering and nearly blinding us all. It was quite as much as I could do to keep my eyes clear enough to penetrate the darkness and fog, so as to keep her off the shore and find the way up. And as we advanced up the sound the gale kept increasing, which caused the greatest anxiety; for had we not been able to beat up, in all probability we should have been blown away to the eastward, and perhaps not been able to reach the island again at all. But Providence favoured us, and two hours ago—at 8 P.M.—we brought the brave little vessel to an anchor in the smooth unruffled waters of 'Camp Cove,' from which place

I sailed on this very day five weeks ago. How very different are my feelings to then! It is now blowing a living gale from N.W. Had we been one hour later we could not possibly have beat up. Now the greatest part of my anxiety is over, but I fear it will be two or three days before we can get up to where the men are. Barometer 29·50.

CHAPTER XI.

ARRIVAL AT AUCKLAND ISLAND.—JOYOUS MEETING WITH OUR
FELLOW-CASTAWAYS.—DOG VERSUS SEAL.

Thursday, August 24.—We were up and on shore as
soon as it was daylight this morning, and to my great
surprise the tent, which we had left standing, and many
things which we had left about, had all disappeared. It
was evident that the men had been down here, but what
means they had employed in taking the things away I
could not conjecture, unless they had constructed a raft
for the purpose. We walked across the neck to the back
of Masked Island, where we found further evidence of
their having come down on a raft—half a tent hanging to
a tree, and a rudely constructed oar and mast. Fortunately these latter were placed above high-water mark, or
I should at once have concluded that they had been
washed off the raft, and that the poor fellows had been
drowned. We then went back to the cutter, had breakfast, and went round to Masked Island in the boat, so as to
have a look up the harbour, which was white with foam,
and showed the impossibility of getting up at present.
We found two seals on shore and killed them—a cow and
calf—put them in the boat, and went on board to dinner.

It was very showery in the forenoon, but at noon the
showers took off, and at 3 P.M. the wind moderated a
little, and we at once got under weigh, and under double-
reefed canvas beat up to our old house ; and as we did not
come in sight of it until within about a mile from it, the
boys did not see us until we were close upon them. Then

the one who saw us ran into the house to tell the other, and before they reached the beach Captain Cross and myself had landed, leaving the cutter under weigh, as there was too much wind and sea to anchor her. One of them, the cook, on seeing me, turned as pale as a ghost, and staggered up to a post, against which he leaned for support, for he was evidently on the point of fainting; while the other, George, seized my hand in both of his and gave my arm a severe shaking, crying, ' Captain Musgrave, how are ye, how are ye ? ' apparently unable to say anything else.

The excitement of the moment over, I hurried them off to get anything they might want to take on board with them for the present; for it was now getting dark, and we wanted to get back to the cove as soon as possible : the distance is seven miles. In a very few minutes we were all on board the ' Flying Scud,' and off before the wind down the harbour again, and reached the anchorage in Camp Cove at half-past 6. Immediately after anchoring we had supper, which consisted of fish and potatoes, tea, and bread and butter, and which the two poor fellows set about with such a zest as I have seldom seen exhibited over a meal. My first meal in Port Adventure bore no comparison to this of theirs (although I had been five days without food); and *I* did ample justice to it. They tell me that they have been very much pinched for food since I left them, and on one occasion they were obliged to catch mice and eat them. Moreover, it appears that they could not agree, and, strange as it may seem, although there were only the two of them on the island, they were on the point of separating and living apart ! Snow has been two feet thick. They tell me that they have not been on the mountains since I left them ; therefore if it was smoke which we saw the other day, there must have been some other unfortunates on the island, and it is our intention to run along the shore as we go back, and endeavour to find out whether there is anyone else on the

island or not. 10 P.M.—barometer 29·50; weather dark
and misty; wind N.W., inclined to moderate.

Friday, August 25, 1865.—At midnight last night it fell
calm, and about an hour before the break of day we took up
anchor and pulled the cutter up to Epigwaitt. This is the
name we gave to the place where our house stands, and
where the ' Grafton ' was wrecked. It is an Indian word,
and means ' a home by the wave,' or ' a dwelling by the
water.' In naming it we all chose a name, wrote it on a
slip of paper, folded them all up alike, placed them in a
bag, and shook them up ; then one man put in his hand
and drew out a slip, which was to have on it the name that
we were to give to the place. Epigwaitt—which was mine
—came out. We were about four hours in getting up
there. My boys picked up what things they wanted, and
Captain Cross also took anything that he could pick up
that might be of any service to him, and we started off
again from the cove, where we anchored about 5 P.M. We
had a light air from the westward to come down with. I
furnished my boys with pipes and tobacco, and gave them the
clothing which was sent down for them, with which they
were highly delighted, and, like myself, I think they can
appreciate the kindness of those who sent them ; but I
find on opening the parcels that there were no shirts, and
as I know that I ordered *two* Crimeans, I am sorry they
have omitted sending them, for they are very much in
need of them.

I have now got one great burthen off my mind, but a
gigantic source of uneasiness yet remains—my wife and
family. God grant that it may be speedily removed, and
that I may soon enjoy their society again, and once more
breathe the air of civilization, from which I have now so
long been exiled ! The men had constructed a raft with
four empty casks, and come down and taken away everything that we had left, amongst which was an oar, which
they substituted for the one that I found yesterday. The
mast they had left, as it was calm, and they had no use for

it, and the half seal they could not very well carry, and
they happened to have a good stock at home at the time.
Barometer, 29·50.

Saturday, August 26.—Light northerly and N.E. airs
all this day. Captain Cross is very desirous of having
a knock down amongst the seals; he and my men have
been pulling round in the boat to-day, and the dog killed
two young ones, but they did not fall in with any more.
The other day, when we got the two on Masked Island, I
had shot the young one, as I wanted to make sure of him,
so as to give them a taste of young meat. After I fired,
Cross saw the old cow running towards him, and at once
bolted down a cliff and made for the boat. The cow,
however, turned in another direction, and the other man
and I followed, and killed her. Cross, not seeing the seal
follow him, took courage, and went up the hill again; and,
seeing the young seal lying there, thought he was asleep,
and set on him with his club, and cried out in a joyous
tone of excitement—'Where are you, boys? I've killed a
seal.' 'Are you sure you've killed him?' said I. 'Killed
him? yes,' he said, 'his brains are coming out of his
mouth.' On looking at him I saw that the calf had been
vomiting milk; and on showing him the hole where the
ball had gone through its head, he was quite crest-fallen.
'Well,' he said, 'I thought I'd killed a seal.'

Sunday, August 27.—Light N.E. airs, and moderate
pleasant weather. This is an extraordinary spell of fine
weather; it is very seldom that we have three fine days
together down here. This morning we went for a pull in
the boat up the western arm. We killed three young seals.
Cross and one of his men fell in with an old cow, but she
escaped from them, and got into the water. They had the
dog with them, too, who fastened boldly to the seal, but
only came off second best, with part of one of his ears
torn entirely off. He is a large, noble dog; such a one
would have been of the greatest service to us while
down here. He held fast to the seal until she dragged

him into the water, and would not have let go then
had not one of the men hit him on the head with his
club, instead of the seal. I was at some distance from
the scene of action, but it appears they were afraid to
go near the seal, or they might easily have killed it.
We went to the very head of the western arm. I had
never been so far up before, and I find that there is a
good ship entrance on the *west* side of Monumental · Isle,
not less than 300 yards wide, and the sea does not
roll so heavily through it as through the east one, which
I have before recommended. Strong tides rush through
them, and neither should be attempted by a stranger
without first sending in a boat, although I have no
hesitation in saying that they are both safe ; and good
anchorage may be had immediately after entering, by
hauling into the north-east basin and shutting in the
entrance, or running half a mile up.

Monday, August 28.—Light N.E., wind and fine
weather until sundown, when the wind hauled to the
N.W., with rain, and it is now (10 P.M.) blowing hard
from that quarter, and raining heavily. I have been
employed the whole of the day in skinning a young
lion, and it is not yet finished. I am taking the skin
off complete. It is the first seal I have skinned in this
way, and I find it a very tedious job. I don't know
any other animal that would be so difficult to skin. I
have promised one to a gentleman in Invercargill for
stuffing. The other people have been skinning other
seals, and trying out the blubber. They have got about
20 gallons of oil. There is no appearance of a favourable change in the wind, and I fear much that we shall
not get one before full moon, and next month will, in
all probability, be stormy. Barometer falling, 29·30 ;
thermometer 48°.

Tuesday, August 29.—Strong northerly wind and dark
cloudy weather until evening, when, as yesterday, it
hauled to N.W., and now blows hard, with rain. It

has taken me nearly all day to finish my skinning. They have been away in the boat to-day, and got another seal.

Wednesday, August 30.—Heavy N.W. gale, and gloomy dark weather. They have been out with the boat to-day, and got two seals. The poor dog got dreadfully torn with one of them, but I believe it did not damp his courage in the least. He fastened to the next one more savagely than he has ever done before. He is a noble brute, weighs about 90 lbs., and is as courageous as a lion ; still he is no match for those large seals, one of which would soon kill him were not some person on the spot imme-diately to knock it down. He is, however, of the greatest service in finding and holding them. It is one month to-day since we left Invercargill, and a long dreary month it has been to me ; and how much longer we shall be humbugging till we get a chance of starting I don't know. Barometer 29·15.

Thursday, August 31.—Strong northerly gale, and con-stant heavy rain till 6 P.M., when the rain ceased and died away, and the sky broke, showing every indication of a S.W. wind, as also a low barometer, 29·80, which I have never known to fail here. Notwithstanding the heavy rain, Captain Cross and two men went in the boat to look for seal, and had the good luck to kill six. I have undertaken to skin another young one for stuffing. This I intend to present to Mr. Macpherson, if he will accept of it.

CHAPTER XII.

DEPARTURE HOMEWARD.—EXPLORATIONS AT THE NORTH OF THE
ISLAND.—PORT ROSS.—LAURIE COVE.—A BARREN SETTLE-
MENT.—DISCOVERY OF A DEAD BODY.

Friday, September 1.—At about ten o'clock last night
the wind came from S.W., and blew with very great
violence till midnight, and it rained heavily : as the sailors
say, it came 'butt-end foremost.'   After midnight the gale
moderated considerably, and at daylight had moderated to
a strong breeze, with clear weather, broken detached
clouds (wind S.W.) ; but Captain Cross was afraid there
would be too much sea outside, and hung on till 10 A.M., at
which time we shipped the anchor, and are now (11 P.M.)
bundling out of the Bosom (Sarah's Bosom) in whose
folds I have experienced the greatest misery of my life ;
but I fear much that the wind will haul to the N.W. again.
At noon we cleared the heads.   I brought the seal on
board that I am skinning, but the vessel is too unsteady
to admit of my finishing it till we get into port again ; I
hope it will not spoil.   From the S.E. point of the island
—where the entrance of our late ' prison house ' is—to its
N.E. extreme, the direct line is about N. by W. and S. by
E., and the distance about 25 miles ; while the land, from
about five miles north of the former up to the latter point
(the coast line), falls back to the westward, forming a
bight about seven miles deep, along which are the numerous indentations and gullies, described in my former
journal, with here and there a small sand or shingle
beach.   Shelter from westerly winds might, probably, be

found in some of these places ; but they are all open to the eastward. There appear to be no off-lying dangers along this line of coast until reaching the N.E. point, off which, in an easterly direction, lie the numerous dangerous reefs which I have so often had occasion to mention. There are two small low islands amongst them, and they extend, perhaps, ten miles from the point. There appear to be clear passages through amongst them, but they are evidently connected with the shore by a ridge of foul ground, which causes an ugly swell and strong tide-rips, and until they are properly examined are well deserving a *wide* berth.

As we proceeded to the northward the wind hauled to the northward also, so we kept the land on board as close as possible, intending to go into Port Ross if we could find it, as we now had a head wind (W.N.W.) ; and Laurie Harbour—which, I suppose, is in Port Ross—has been represented to be such a snug port, and as it lay somewhere at the extreme north end of the island we should at least have shortened our journey some thirty or thirty-five miles. Besides, I had a strong desire to see this Port Ross, Sarah's Bosom,* Caroline, Rendezvous, or Laurie Harbour—for I believe they are all one and the same place ; having received a different name from different persons who have visited it, in their ignorance of its proper one, which I should imagine is *Laurie Harbour* in Port Ross. Most likely the former was given to it by Captain Bristow, who discovered the islands in the year 1806 ; and in the year following left on shore in Laurie Harbour a number of pigs, which my informant remarks had, up to the year 1851, thrived remarkably well. And it no doubt received the latter from the explorer Ross, who at a subsequent period visited nearly all the islands in the Southern Ocean ; and, in my humble opinion, names given by such

---

* I am now of opinion that the name of the place where I lost the 'Grafton' is Carnley's Harbour.

men are the proper ones to apply, and should be retained. It is the site of a settlement and whaling station which was formed about the year 1848, but shortly afterwards abandoned, from what cause I am unable to say; but most likely the scarcity of whales. I believe the company sank some £20,000 over it, and some of the people in Invercargill were quite surprised that I had not found out this place while we were on the island, as we should have been quite provided for had we got there; as we should have found good houses, plenty of pigs, and abundance of vegetables growing in wild profusion. Alas! for us that the distance was so great, and the nature of the country such as rendered travelling over it next to impossible. I now felt very curious to see this wonderful place, and Captain Cross was particularly anxious to get his vessel to an anchor before a N.W. gale came on, which does not appear to be far off. At half-past four in the afternoon we passed the N.E. point of the island, giving it a good berth (say a long ¼ mile), as it is low, and shallow water appears to run off it; and a ridge of foul ground evidently connects it with a small island which lies about 2¼ miles east from it, and over which there was a nasty confused sea and heavy tide-ripples. One breaker came on board, but did no damage, and immediately we were in smooth water.

We now commenced to look anxiously for this said port. Here we were, amongst a whole host of small islands and rocks—the names of which we were quite ignorant of—night and probably a gale coming on, no place in sight in which there was any probability of obtaining shelter, and our only directions for finding the desired port were the following, which I copied from a letter which has found its way into print, in a little book, entitled 'A History of Gold,' by James Ward, and, slender as it may appear, served us in some measure as a guide to the place. He says—'Port Ross is at the extreme north of the island, and contains secure anchorage for vessels. From the entrance to the head of the port, the distance is about four miles. Entering the harbour from the north, you pass Enderby Island on the right, the Ocean Island and Ocean Point, until you reach Laurie Harbour, which is not visible to the line of sight, as it runs behind the back of a small wooded peninsula, which projects into the sea. After passing Ocean Island, a ship may anchor in perfect safety in any part, but the upper end of the inlet (Laurie Cove) is the most suitable for ships wanting to heave down or undergo extensive repairs. It is perfectly land-locked, and the steep beach on the southern shore affords the greatest facility for clearing and reloading vessels.' And also— ' The buildings are at the head of Laurie Cove, perhaps one of the most beautiful inlets on the wide range of ocean.'

From these brief remarks I at once concluded that the desired haven was a small snug basin, whose waters the fierce winds of the Southern Ocean found it impossible to ruffle. Such a place would indeed be suitable for clearing or discharging, heaving down, repairing, and reloading vessels ; and such, in fact, is absolutely necessary, unless in a case of great emergency. But of this anon. I have not yet seen the place with daylight ; when I have I shall be better able to describe it. Now (10 P.M.) we are at anchor in two fathoms of water, at the head of what may be termed a lagoon, with a clear drift for an easterly wind of at least 4½ miles. It is about a quarter of a mile wide where we are, and widens to about three-quarters of a mile at the entrance. On three sides of us are hills rising abruptly from the water to the height of about 900 feet. Now I will endeavour to describe the manner in which we reached this place ; its name I must omit, for the simple reason that I don't know whether it has one or not ; it cannot possibly be Laurie Cove.

The evening was fine and beautifully clear, and with a nice whole-sail breeze and smooth water we beat in amongst the islands, finding clear passages between them, until we had the largest and most northernmost of the small group (its centre or thereabout), which I take to be

Enderby Island, bearing N.N.E.; the highest hill on the north end of Auckland Island, which is somewhat remarkable, having on its summit a bare peak, something in the shape of one's thumb when pointed upwards, bearing S.S.W. On the right, when heading for the latter bearing, is an island, lying close off a bluff-looking point, and between them is a small, low islet.

This is no doubt Ocean Island and Ocean Point. On the left, with a clear passage between it, and a low, thickly-wooded point, is another island, while straight ahead Port Ross lies open before you, the head of its waters washing the base of the high hills. Between Ocean Island and a small, low peninsula, with some naked, dry trees upon it —a great deal of timber having been cut down—which lies on the west side, there is a beating width of from three to two miles smooth water, with westerly or southerly winds, but subject to a swell with northerly ones, as there is a long fetch for any wind between N.W. and N.E.

Having got the vessel into the position mentioned, with the said bearings on, we stood up for this small and once thickly-wooded peninsula; but before reaching it the wind died away, and left us becalmed. We at once put out the boat, and Mr. Wheeler (Cross's mate) and myself went ahead to look for Laurie Cove, leaving them to row the cutter up after us. The night was then fine and moonlight, which is but an uncertain light to strangers in a strange place; however, away we went, frequently taking a cast of the lead, and on getting round the peninsula we found an arm running in farther than we could see, in a S.W. direction. Up this we pulled, expecting to find the strongly-desired Laurie Cove, when 'lo! and behold,' we found ourselves in one fathom of water, and close up to a point which juts out from the southern side. We now pulled over for the northern side, and finding deeper water, went back to the cutter, which was not very far behind. She had then a light air following her up. We directed them which way to go, and then went ahead again, thinking we should find the place above the point. But no; above the point there was not more than two fathoms water, and that only between the point and the northern shore: there is about a cable's length between them. Here we anchored, and here the cutter now lies. A very unsatisfactory place; perhaps we shall find the right one in the morning. Just before anchoring it commenced to rain heavily and continuously. Barometer 28·63.

Saturday, September 2, 1865.—It was calm during all last night. The sky, at daybreak, had a very wild and threatening appearance, and the sun rose red and watery-looking, and a light air sprang up from the northwards. We at once got under weigh, and proceeded in search of Laurie Cove. We beat down the arm, or lagoon, again; but the wind suddenly increased, with every appearance of a heavy gale. We brought up in a small bight in 4 fathoms on the S.W. side of the 'low-wooded peninsula,' with its extreme point bearing N.E. by N., and a bluff point at the other extreme of the bight bearing S.W. by S.-half-S. The distance between them is about half a mile, and the other surrounding land (to the eastward) is from half a mile to two miles from where we are anchored, and a S.E or easterly gale would come with considerable force on a vessel lying at anchor here. We are, however, land-locked, and well sheltered from any westerly wind; but a swell comes round the peninsula which causes the vessel to roll about a good deal.

After breakfast Captain Cross, Wheeler, and myself went on shore to have a look round. We found that a great quantity of timber had been cut down on the peninsula, and the north side of it is evidently the site of the old settlement, and that the 'Flying Scud' is now riding at anchor in Laurie Cove, and rolling about almost as much as if she was at sea. What a disappointment! In place of getting into a perfect dock, as we expected, we find it almost an open road. And the buildings, and

vegetable gardens, where are they ? All gone ; scarcely a
vestige of a house remains ; bare levelled places point out
where many of them have stood, as remaining traces of
rude fences also point out where innumerable small gardens have been ; but the ground everywhere, except where
some of the houses have apparently stood, is choked up
with a vigorous growth of thick long grass, and there is
not the slightest sign of any edible vegetable, or even a
single shrub that is not a native of the island, if we except
a few flax bushes, which appear to thrive well, and two
small trees. As for the pigs, we have found no traces of
them.

While we were on shore it came on to rain heavily, and
blew a hard gale from N.W. After strolling about for an
hour or so, and getting thoroughly wet, we went on board
and ran out the second anchor. It has continued to blow
and rain heavily up to the time of writing (9 P.M.). I
consider it extremely fortunate that I knew nothing of
there ever being a settlement here, or most likely we
should have been tempted to try and make our way to it,
in which case it is highly probable we might have starved
to death, for there appear to be no seals here. We have
only seen one, which was in the water, and there are very
few of the roots here which we used to eat. The formation of the soil is the same here as at the other end of the
island. I have seen some rock which is different, but
much that is similar, while the timber and other vegetation is precisely the same. Barometer, 8 A.M., 29·60 ;
noon, 29 ; 8 P.M., 28·95 : thermometer, 42°.

Sunday, September 3, 1865.—About midnight last night
the wind came from W. or W.N.W., and blew very hard,
drawing down the arm where we were at anchor the other
night, and sending a heavy roll round the point, so that
it was necessary to pick up the anchors, and haul farther
into the bight. She is sheltered from the wind, but lies
very uncomfortably. After breakfast Captain Cross, my
boy George, and myself went on shore. It came on to

rain, and I took shelter under a flax bush, while they proceeded in another direction, and I lost sight of them. I now commenced another survey of this deserted spot, but saw nothing that I had not seen yesterday, except that I find they have made stone pathways here and there—no doubt the earth was so soft that they required them ; we made similar ones at Epigwaitt—and over these walks the grass has shot up with more vigour than in other places : it is so thick and long that it is almost impossible to trace them. After wandering about for a couple of hours, I returned on board, bringing with me some specimens of rock and earth. I have just arrived on board. Cross and George have not yet returned.

8 P.M.—I had scarcely finished writing when Captain Cross came on board, and they informed us that they had found a man lying dead on shore, who had apparently died of starvation, and had evidently not been long dead, as flesh remained on his hands. They brought with them a slate—a common roof slate — on which were scratched some hieroglyphical zig-zags, which had no doubt been written by the deceased man, probably when dying, but which we found impossible to decipher any further than the Christian name, James. I reserve the slate, as some one will be able at least to make out the whole name. They had not disturbed anything about him further than removing an oil-coat which was lying over the upper part of the body. After dinner, Captain Cross, George Wheeler, George Harris, and myself went ashore to see and examine the body, taking with us a spade to bury it with.

On arriving at the place indicated—the second bight to the northwards of the peninsula—we saw the remains of a dead man. When he died he was, no doubt, under the shelter of an old frame-house, *then* partly in ruins ; and since his death, and very recently, it has fallen down entirely, but without touching the body, and leaving it exposed to the weather. The body lay on a bed of grass, with some boards underneath raising it a few inches from

K

the ground, and was close up against the west end of the
house, which end and the sides had fallen outwards, while
the roof, being pressed by the wind towards the other end,
had just fallen clear of the body, which, with the exception
of ordinary dress, had no other covering than the before-
mentioned oil-coat, which Captain Cross had removed.
Within his reach were two bottles containing water, one
nearly empty, the other was full. Close by lay a small
heap of limpet and mussel shells, which fish appear to
have been his sole sustenance. He has no doubt died from
starvation. The unfortunate man lay in a very natural
and composed position. His feet, which were off the side
of his bed, lay across each other; the body was on its
back, and the hands were laid on the lower part of the
body, with the fingers quite straight. The finger nails
were quite perfect on the right hand, and on both hands
some flesh still remained. The skin and flesh had disappeared from the other parts of the body, excepting the head
and face, on which the skin remained, and was parched
and dry and of a blackish colour. The deceased has been
a man of slender frame, height about 5 feet 7 inches or
5 feet 8 inches; hair light brown, or approaching auburn;
forehead low; high, prominent cheek bones; upper jaw
protruding, and had one front tooth out; the remainder
were perfectly round and beautifully regular, and the chin
was pointed. He had on a sou'wester hat, three woollen
mufflers, a dark brown cloth coat, with an almost invisible
stripe in it, and trowsers to match; a blue serge vest, a
brownish-coloured Guernsey shirt, a red and black check
Crimean ditto, and a blue Guernsey ditto next the skin.
Cotton drawers next the skin, trowsers and woollen drawers
over all, and three or four pairs of woollen socks and stock-
ings. One old shoe was partly on the right foot, and the
left one was tied up with woollen rags, as if it had been
sore. Round his neck hung some Roman Catholic relic
in the shape of a heart, made out of two small pieces
of leather sewn together, with something sacred placed

between them. This and a lock of the unfortunate man's hair I have brought with me, as it is not impossible but we may yet, by some means, discover who the poor man was ; and these may be claimed and valued by some relative or friend as the last memento of *one gone.*

After a gloomy and somewhat lengthened examination of the lamentable object of our present visit, we dug a grave, in which we placed the mortal remains of the unfortunate unknown, and, after offering up a brief prayer, his bones were mingled with their mother earth. There was not a vestige of clothing to be found about the place other than that described, which he had on. How he has come here I cannot conjecture. Has he been the only one saved from some ill-fated ship ? or, have there been others who saved their lives also, and have *they* undertaken to travel over the inhospitable island in search of something where-upon they might subsist, while he, poor man—perhaps sick, or lame, or both — preferred remaining here to take his chance ? or, worse than all, has he been turned ashore by some inhuman brute of a captain ? Such things have been done, or the idea would not suggest itself to me. The only fact which presents itself is, that he has died of starvation, and been alone in this solitary spot. We raised the fallen roof from the ground to see that no one was underneath it. As we sailed along the shore the other day, we kept our eyes and glasses fixed on it, but did not see any smoke, or the slightest sign of there being a human being on the island. After performing the last melancholy ritual to the remains of our unfortunate brother tar, we returned pensively and gloomily towards the vessel.

This lamentable spectacle would undoubtedly give rise to serious thoughts in anyone, but how infinitely more in me, whose bones might at the present moment have been lying above the ground under similar circumstances, had not the hand of Providence showered such great mercies upon me, perhaps the least deserving. What a field for serious reflec-tion! And it is not impossible that at the present moment there are other poor men lying dead, or perhaps dying, on other parts of these desolate islands. Throughout the day the wind has been at W.N.W.; hard gale and showery; barometer 29·15. I should have noticed that the deceased had not a single article in his pockets, or about his person —not even a knife or matches, although not far from the remains, and under the fallen roof, were evident signs of fire having recently been burning there.

Monday, September 4.—This morning we took a pull in the boat round the weather shores of the bay, and I found marks of habitations for a distance of about two miles along the shore, to the northward of the peninsula. We also went up into the bush at several places, but saw no further signs of anyone having been about here recently. In the afternoon we all remained on board, and I proceeded with skinning my seal; but the weather was so bitterly cold that before I got the skin off I was obliged to lay it aside again. It has continued to blow a very heavy gale from W.N.W., with frequent showers of hail; thermometer 34°, barometer 29·20. This evening the weather appears to be clearing up a little. I have every hope that the wind will be more to the southward in the morning, and we shall be able to get away.

CHAPTER XIII.

LAST VIEW OF THE ISLAND.—AN UNCOMFORTABLE VOYAGE.—
ARRIVAL AT STEWART ISLAND.—CONCLUSION OF JOURNAL.

Tuesday, September 5.—First and middle part of this day heavy gales from W.S.W., with frequent bitter squalls, with snow. In the afternoon Condors and I took a walk up the hills at the back of the harbour, but found it very difficult to penetrate the scrub, which is very dense from the water's edge to the summit of the hills, and is of the same description as that on the southern part of the island. We saw no clear land, neither do I think that there is any near this end of the island. On our return we passed the grave of the departed stranger, and arrived on board again at 5.30 P.M. The wind had moderated, and we made up our minds to make a start; so at 7 P.M. we unmoored and sailed down the bay with a strong breeze, weather clear, with good moonlight, and we are now, 8.30 P.M., again tossing about on the boisterous ocean, with Enderby Island nearly astern. As we came round it, we suddenly were into one of the most ugly seas that ever I got into. The craft is kicking and jerking so dreadfully that it is almost impossible for me to scribble— writing is out of the question altogether. I begin to fear that we have done wrong in coming out, for the wind is no better than west. She does not lie her course, and we are already under double-reefed canvas, and very likely to be under smaller sail very shortly; but she must face it now—there is no turn back this time. I guess the little craft will be able to buffet it out, and, no doubt, we shall get a fair wind some day.

Wednesday, September 6.—Since midnight last night we have had a very hard gale, and till eight o'clock this evening we managed to carry close reefs ; but since that time we are lying-to under the balance-reefed mainsail and a small jib.   There is a very dangerous sea running, but the vessel seems to ride very comfortably—much better than I would have expected her to do ; still a sea falls on board now and then, and the water is finding its way to almost every part of her ; but she is not making any water in her bottom. The wind is at W.N.W., and inclined to back to the northward.   I fear that the heaviest of the gale is yet to come. Since noon it has rained heavily, with gloomy dark weather, and it is very cold—thermometer 42·37.

Thursday, September 7.—Hard gale and high dangerous sea.   The little vessel is being knocked about unmercifully. Heavy rain.   No place to lie down.   Blankets and every stitch of clothing wringing wet.   Can't get anything cooked, not even a cup of tea.   Second edition of our trip in the boat. *Misery.* 4 P.M.—Blowing a hurricane ; sea frightful ; vessel labouring, and straining immensely ; if not very strong she cannot stand this long ; consider her in a highly dangerous situation.   Just taken in mainsail and jib, and set a small boat's sail, under which she feels somewhat easier ; but if one of the high seas that are coming round her in every direction falls on board, she is gone ; it would knock her into ten thousand pieces. *Frightful.*   Midnight : at 6 P.M. the gale began to moderate, and, fortunately, the sea quickly followed suit.   We set the mainsail, but carried away the traveller, and tore the sail.   8 P.M.—The wind came from the S.W., and continues very light, but sufficient to keep her steady, while the sea is rapidly running down ; hope soon to be able to make her stretch her legs again. She has weathered this storm bravely, and without sustaining any visible damage about the hull.   Surprising what these little vessels will stand : but she is an amazingly good sea-boat, rides like a sea-gull, and holds her ground well.   Bravo, ' Flying Scud ! '

Friday, September 8.—Noon; strong and increasing breeze; double reefs in. We have just made the Snares Islands, bearing W.N.W., distant about 15 miles. The ' Flying Scud' is again bounding merrily off before the wind; she is now going through the water at the rate of 11 knots, which I think is the height of her speed. If the wind will only stand just as it is at present, we shall be up to Pakiwia, Stewart Island, before dark. 5 P.M.—Sorry to say that at 3 o'clock the wind, which previously was inclined to back to the westward, went in to S.E., and now blows very hard. At 3.30 we made Stewart Island, South Cape bearing north. We are carrying all the canvas that the poor little craft will bear, and the sea is now and then making a clean breach over her. We want to make Port Pegasus, and get in there, if possible ; but I fear we shall not be able to do it, for the ebb tide is setting her to the westward, and the wind is hauling to the eastward, with every appearance of a hard N.E. or easterly gale. 8 P.M.—Stiff gale (E.N.E.), and an ugly, confused sea. South Cape bearing N.W. about 6 miles. I fear much that she will not do it; we shall have to run to leeward of the Cape.

Saturday, September 9.—We thrashed her at it all night last night, endeavouring to get up to Port Pegasus ; sometimes two, and sometimes three reefs in. The little craft got a severe drubbing, and would with another hour or two's perseverance have got in ; but at 8 A.M., when within a mile and a half of the entrance, the gale freshened, and hauled to N.E. This was thoroughly disheartening, and, considering the severe weather and misery we have had to contend with, and going without sleep (I have had the smallest share of hardship, and I can safely say I have not slept half-an-hour since we left the Aucklands ; and at the present moment, 4 P.M., I am sitting by a fire on shore, comfortably smoking my tobacco, and might have been asleep for the last four hours, but I have not the slightest inclination to do so), it is no wonder that we gave it up, and ran round the Cape, and made for Port Easy, where we anchored at a quarter past eleven this morning. Port Easy is ten miles to the northward of the South Cape, and by passing between the islands and the shore, and keeping the shore close on board, within three-quarters of a mile, you are bound to sail right into the port, which I must pronounce the snuggest and easiest of access that ever I have entered in the southern hemisphere. There is room for fifty ships of any size to swing to their anchors, well sheltered from all winds, and a convenient depth of water, three to four fathoms. Immediately after anchoring, Captain Cross and I took the boat, and bundled all our clothes and bed-clothes into her, and went on shore, where we lit a fire that would roast half-a-dozen bullocks, and hung our clothes round it to dry. We then went on board, got dinner, and came on shore again, bringing with us a saucepan for heating water in, and a tub for washing in, and since performing our ablutions from top to toe we feel like new men, and we are now, as I have said, comfortably smoking our tobacco, quite regardless of the N.E. gale which is now howling outside. Our clothes are getting dry nicely, and I have no doubt but we shall sleep without rocking to-night, since we could not sleep with it.

Sunday, September 10.—Strong N.E. gale, and fine clear weather all this day. As I anticipated, I had a fine night's rest last night, and at the peep of day Cross and I got up and went on shore to try and get some game, as our meat is done. Wild fowl are abundant here ; we got duck, teal, wood-hen, and red-bill. After breakfast the boat went, and they soon got a lot of fine fish, which are also abundant here. After dinner they went on shore and cut firewood, and filled up the water on board. Although it is Sunday, these things were absolutely necessary, in order to be in readiness to proceed on our voyage as soon as the weather will permit, which we have every reason to hope will be in the morning. It is now eight o'clock in the evening, and I am just going in for a repetition of last night's dose.

Monday, September 11, 1865. — First part, calm clear weather throughout. In the morning the people were busy scraping the spars and cleaning the vessel up. There were two very large whales playing about in the port; here would have been a windfall for anyone who had gear to kill them with. I went close up to one of them in the dingy, and when he went down we pulled the boat right over him. I have seen many whales in my travels, but I never was so near one before, neither did I think that they were such large monsters as they proved to be when close to them. At 11 A.M. a light air sprang up from the N.W. We at once got under weigh, and at 11.30 left the port, with a fine breeze, which, in fifty minutes, ran us down to the South Cape, and we anticipated a speedy and comfortable run along the east side of the island; but, on arriving off the South Cape, what was our disappointment when met there, slap in the teeth, by a brisk north-east gale, which, with the flood tide running against it, created a most dangerous, confused, and breaking sea. We were at once obliged to reduce sail to double reefs; and, by giving the invincible 'Flying Scud' one more severe thrashing, we got her into Wilson's Bay, where we found a snug anchorage on the west side of the bay. At 4 P.M. brought up in it, in four fathoms water, well sheltered from all winds, and from the swell which I have no doubt rolls into the bay almost constantly. This is another excellent harbour of refuge, and anyone who had been here once could bring a large ship in with safety. Barometer 29·60.

Tuesday, September 12.—Strong N.E. breeze, and fine clear weather until noon. From noon till 8 P.M., clear weather and calm. Latter part, heavy rain and calm. Before breakfast Captain Cross and I went in the boat to try fishing. We were not more than an hour and a half away, and returned with six dozen fine codfish. I never had such sport in fishing: we were hauling them up two and three at a time, just as fast as we could haul in the

lines.   After breakfast three of us went to try our luck,
and before noon returned with eight dozen more, chiefly
trumpeters.   There are very few ducks or wild-fowl here.
The barometer is very low—28·10.   I expect we shall have
more wind than we want to-morrow.

Wednesday, September 13.—It rained heavily until day
broke this morning, when the rain ceased; but it continued calm, with dark, gloomy, threatening weather.
Soon after daybreak Cross and I took the boat and pulled
round to a small bay to the northward of the one the cutter
lay in.   We knew that many years ago there were some
Maoris living somewhere in Wilson's Bay, but we did not
know in which part of it.   This small bay, however, proves
to be the spot, and a lovely spot it is.   It is certainly the
most beautiful site for a settlement that I have seen in New
Zealand, and seldom elsewhere.   The basin in which this
charming site is situated is perhaps two miles in circumference, with a small, round, wooded island in its centre,
and its waters are as calm and smooth as a millpond.   It
is impossible for any wind to ruffle or disturb them, and the
swell, which seems to reach almost every other nook and
corner of this extensive bay, is effectually shut out from it
by two reefs, which stretch out from each entrance-point,
overlapping each other, but leaving a deep and safe channel
between, through which the largest ship could be warped,
and find a sufficient depth when inside for mooring in.   Its
shores, on all sides, excepting the north, are rocky, and
clad from the water's edge to the top of the hills with an
abundant growth of large timber of various kinds.   The
northern side is where the people have lived.   It has a sand
beach about half a mile long, and the land next the beach
is slightly elevated, and level for a short distance back to the
foot of the hills, which rise without undulation to the
height of about 300 feet.   From the quantity of land which
has been cleared, I judge that a good many people have
lived here.   At 9 o'clock in the morning we up anchor

and pulled the cutter out of the bay with the last of the
ebb tide, expecting to find some wind when we got outside,
from some quarter or other, for we are all heartily sick of
the protractions of this voyage. When we got outside we
got into a most tremendous heavy sea rolling down from
the eastward, and it came on to rain heavily, with light
baffling airs from between north and west, which, with the
flood tide, put us along our own course ; but as we advanced
so the head sea increased. We had every reason to appre-
hend an easterly gale, and we were glad to get into Port
Pegasus, in the north arm of which we anchored at 3 P.M.
Rain continued till 7 P.M., weather threatening, and barometer very low, 29·80.

Thursday, September 14, 1865.—Calm till 8 A.M., when a
light air came from W.S.W., with which we started out of
the Port by the northern passage. We found a very heavy
sea still running from the eastward, which is indicative of
recent heavy easterly gales on the coast. The wind continued
light, and came from the same quarter until evening, and at
6 P.M. we once more anchored in Port Adventure ; and I feel
truly thankful that this much of our hazardous and miserable
voyage has been safely accomplished. I have no doubt
but the remainder will be easily performed, and from the
appearance of the weather I am in hope of our reaching
Invercargill to-morrow ; and if the weather be favourable
Captain Cross intends to tow the 'Rescue' (the boat I
came up in) over, and let the good people of Invercargill
look at her. Since anchoring the weather has been calm
and clear. The barometer keeps very low (29·5), which I
cannot understand.

Friday, September 15, 1865.—We sailed from Port Adventure in the 'Flying Scud,' having the 'Rescue' in tow,
with a moderate S.W. breeze, until in crossing Foveaux
Straits the wind increased, and the sea ran high, and on
arriving at the New River bar the sea was breaking right
across. The 'Rescue' had got full of water, parted the
tow rope, and was left to her fate.

And thus, with a grateful heart, I end my journal; with what deep thankfulness to a gracious Providence for saving myself and my companions from a miserable fate, I trust I need not set down here.

THOMAS MUSGRAVE.

APPENDICES.

I.

AN ACCOUNT OF THE SEA-LION

AND ITS HABITS.*

BY CAPTAIN THOMAS MUSGRAVE.

It is universally understood that the seal is an amphibious animal, sleeping and frequently basking in the sun on shore, and finding and eating their food entirely in the water. Four flippers, on the underneath side (on which there is no fur, but a hard black skin), only sufficiently long to raise them so that their belly is clear of the ground, serve the purpose of legs and feet when on shore, and as propellers when in the water. They are clad with fur, which varies very much in texture and value. They are considerably sought after, both for their fur, and the skins of some species, which make a very superior leather; and they also yield a considerable quantity of valuable oil.

There are many species of seal (*phoca*), some of which are found in nearly all parts of the world beyond the limits of the tropics; but as man appears so they disappear, hence they are seldom seen but by navigators.

But the sea-lion, which I am about to describe, and to endeavour to convey some idea as to his habits, &c., is only found in high north or southern latitudes, and is perhaps never seen nearer the Equator than 48°.

---

* This account was originally written in *seal's blood*, as were most of Captain Musgrave's journals.

The females are of a grey, golden buff, or beautiful silver colour, sometimes spotted like the leopard, and are called tiger seals. Their fur is about an inch long, not very soft, but very thick, and particularly sleek and smooth. Their nose resembles that of the dog, but is somewhat broader; their scent appears to be very acute. The eyes are large, of a green colour, watery, and lustreless; when on shore they appear to be constantly weeping. I have heard sealers say that they have a very sharp eye, and can see a great distance; but I beg leave to correct those who are of that opinion, for I have every reason to believe, and am fully convinced, that such is not the case. On the contrary, their eye is not sharp, neither can they see far when on shore; but, as I have already noticed, their sense of smell is very keen. In the water—for which element chiefly their eye is evidently formed—I have no doubt but they see well. The ears are particularly small, tapering, and are curled in such a manner as to exclude the water; and their sense of hearing is not very acute. The mouth, which is prodigiously large, is furnished with teeth, four of which (the canine teeth) are an immense size. I have seen one of these measuring $3\frac{7}{8}$ inches long by $3\frac{1}{2}$ in circumference at the base. On the upper lip, on each side, are thirty bristles (they seldom deviate from this number) of a hard horny nature, and resembling tortoiseshell in appearance, from 6 to 8 inches long, gradually decreasing as they approach the nose to $1\frac{1}{2}$ or 2 inches in length, and the regularity with which these bristles are arranged is strikingly admirable.

The females and young seals generally remain in the bays, and they appear to select bays which have wooded shores, most probably for the sake of the shelter which they and the long coarse dried grass afford, and which most likely they and their young require in those tempestuous regions, where only they are to be found; whilst during the greater part of the year the males, which are naturally much more hardy, remain outside, and fish amongst the rocks along the sea coasts, where, judging from their condition when they come in, they fare by far the best.

The males, or—as we sailors call them—the bulls (although I believe they are more commonly designated dogs and bitches), are uniformly of a blackish grey colour. One of a medium size will measure about six feet from nose to tail (which latter is about three inches long), and about six or seven feet in circumference, and weigh about 5 cwt. They by far exceed these dimensions ; I have seen one seal produce forty gallons of oil. The fur and skin are superior to those of the female, being much thicker ; and the former finer from the shoulders backwards, though not so pretty. On the neck and shoulders he has a thicker, longer, and much coarser coat of fur, which may almost be termed bristles. It is from three to four inches long, and can be ruffled up and made to stand erect at will, which is always done when they attack each other on shore, or are surprised,—sitting, as a dog would do, with their head erect, and looking towards the object of their surprise ; and in this attitude they have all the appearance of a lion ; and adding the enormous teeth already described, which they invariably display on these occasions, gives them (in appearance) all the ferocity and formidableness which their name seems to imply.

They begin to come into the bays in the month of October (in the southern hemisphere), and remain until the latter end of February, each one selecting and taking up his own particular beat in a great measure ; but sometimes there are several about the same place, in which case they fight most furiously, never coming in contact with each other (either in or out of the water) without engaging in the most desperate combat, tearing large pieces of skin and flesh from each other. Their skins are always full of wounds and scars, which, however, appear to heal very quickly.

From November until the beginning of February they lie in the sun a great deal, generally selecting a sand or shingle beach to land and lie upon, and are easily killed during this season ; for they frequently, when in the water, on seeing a man on shore, will land and charge him, or rather chase him if he will run away ; but on facing the seal he will generally stand, when the man must go very quietly up to him and kill him ; but sometimes, on the man facing him, he will retreat quickly into the water.

Another mode of getting them on shore, which during this season never fails, is to retire into the bush out of their sight, and imitate the lowing of a cow, which is the natural cry of a female seal. To kill them it is usual to strike them on the nose with a wooden club, and if hit in the proper place a very slight blow stuns them, when they must at once be stuck. This method of killing them is quite proper when they can be taken whilst asleep ; but when they are not plentiful, and it is necessary to get them up out of the water in the manner described, the surest plan is to put a ball into their head, before moving to-wards them ; then go up, give them a blow with a club, and stick them ; for if they escape after getting a blow they will not be got out of the water in the same manner a second time, and it makes the others shy also. Although they are so ferocious amongst themselves, and so for-midable in appearance, when attacked by man they will, as a general rule, escape into the water if possible ; yet in striking them it is necessary to make sure of the blow, otherwise they are very likely to get hold of the party at-tacking them, in which case he will not escape without, at least, broken bones. It requires some nerve to face these monsters, which is only acquired by practice.

Having treated pretty fully on the character and habits of the males, or bulls, we must now turn our attention to the females, or cows, which are proportionately smaller and much more timid than the bulls. They will scarcely in any case confront a man ; but, like the bulls, if not knocked down by the first blow, will *snap* and break anything that happens to get between their powerful and capacious jaws. Their appearance I have already described.

In the latter part of December, and during the whole of January, they are on shore a great deal, and go wandering separately through the bush (or woods), and into the long grass on the sides of the mountains above the bush, constantly bellowing out in a most dismal manner. They are undoubtedly looking for a place suitable for calving in ; I have known them to go to a distance of more than a mile from the water for this purpose. Their voice is exceedingly powerful, and in calm weather may be heard to the almost incredible distance of four and a half or five miles. Why they bellow so much before calving I am scarcely able to judge ; but after that event, which does not take place until after the first of February,* it is undoubtedly to call their young, which they generally get into the water a few days after they are born, and assemble them in great numbers at some particular place, selecting such places as a small island or a neck of land with a narrow junction. This, no doubt, prevents them from getting straggled about and lost, as they do sometimes in the bush ; while in these places they cannot very well get away without going into the water, to which, when very young, they have a great antipathy.

The means employed by the cow of getting her young into the water for the first time, and taking it to a place of safety, is, when witnessed, highly amusing.

It might be supposed that these animals, even when young, would readily go into the water—that being one of their natural instincts—but strange to say such is not the case ; it is only with the greatest difficulty, and a wonderful display of patience, that the mother succeeds in getting her young in for the first time. I have known a cow to be three days getting her calf down half a mile, and into the water ; and what is most surprising of all, it cannot

---

* They have only one calf at a birth.

L

swim when it is in the water. This is the most amusing fact; the mother gets it on to her back, and swims along very gently on the top of the water; but the poor little thing is bleating all the time, and continually falling from its slippery position, when it will splutter about in the water precisely like a little boy who gets beyond his depth and cannot swim. Then the mother gets underneath it, and it again gets on to her back. Thus they go on, the mother frequently giving an angry bellow, the young one constantly bleating and crying, frequently falling off, spluttering, and getting on again; very often getting a slap from the flipper of the mother, and sometimes she gives it a very cruel bite. The poor little animals are very often seen with their skins pierced and lacerated in the most frightful manner. In this manner they go on until they have made their passage to whatever place she wishes to take the young one to; sometimes they are very numerous at these places, their numbers being daily augmented until the latter end of March. Here the young remain without going into the water again, for perhaps a month, when they will begin to go in of their own accord; but at first they will only play about the edge, venturing farther by degrees; and until they are three months old, if surprised in the water, they will immediately run on shore and hide themselves; but they always keep their heads out, and their eyes fixed on the party who has surprised them, imploring mercy in the most eloquent language that can be communicated by these organs.

During the months of February, March, and April, the cows are on shore the greater part of the time, and lie in the bush in mobs of from twelve to twenty together, at the places where their calves are assembled. They do not appear to have any particular time for going into the water to feed; and they allow their young to suck whenever they please; and when they are satisfied they immediately leave the cows and play in small groups, at some distance from the old ones. The mothers appear to take scarcely any notice whatever of their young, which, added to the fact of their being so cruelly bitten sometimes, as already noticed, led me at one time to think that they had no natural affection for them. This, however, I found was quite a mistaken idea. One instance came especially under my notice of a cow whose calf had been killed and taken away from her, roaming about the place where she lost it, incessantly bellowing, and without going into the water—consequently going without food—for eight days. After the first few days her voice gradually became weaker, and at last could scarcely be heard. I made sure that she was dying. She survived it, however, and on the eighth day went into the water ; but for more than a month afterwards she paid a daily visit to the spot, bellowing in the most doleful manner. I have cited this case, which is not an isolated one. It may be considered as the rule, not an exception.

Before they have their calves, or from the beginning of January, the cows lie sometimes in small mobs in the sun, as well as while giving suck, and there are generally one or two bulls in each mob ; the latter leave the bays after the beginning of April. The cows are evidently by far the most numerous ; they begin to breed when two years old, and have a calf when three years old ; they carry their calves eleven months. Their teats are four in number, and are placed on the belly about equi-distant from each other and the flippers ; the nipple (excepting when in the mouth of the young seal) recedes inwards, leaving nothing visible save a small black spot ; thus there is nothing to obstruct or impede them when in the water. The teat is about as big as a person's little finger from the middle joint to the end.

The tongue of the seal is split, or rather has a notch in the end, about an inch deep, leaving a point on each, the only utility of which appears to be that of pressing out the teat when they are sucking.

When the young seals are about three months old they

leave off sucking, and, with the cows, leave the places where they were suckled; and now all the seals keep in the water nearly altogether in the daytime, and in the night they are on shore. They do not appear to choose any particular place for sleeping in, further than taking shelter in the bush, or in the long grass close to the water. They do not go far from the water, and sleep in small mobs of six or eight together; never going on shore until after dark, and going into the water again at the very peep of day. Sometimes the same mob will sleep in the same place for several nights in succession, if they are not disturbed; it may be thus ascertained where they are to be found.

About this time (*i. e.*, May), or shortly after beginning to breed, the cows are very much troubled with vomiting, when small pebbles are often disgorged, which are very likely snapped up when catching fish on the bottom, and would at any other time have been digested. I have picked up a number of very remarkable little stones (if they are stones, for I have not as yet been able to ascertain) which have been brought up from the deep in this manner. On one occasion I found a deposit of these curiosities six and a half feet below the surface of the earth—or, more strictly speaking, the decayed vegetable matter of which the place was composed; and some of them are particularly curious and pretty. And supposing that the accumulation of this decomposed vegetable matter is half the sixteenth of an inch (which is scarcely possible) every year, it is more than 2,500 years since they were brought up from the sea, and vomited there by a sea lioness. I would describe some of them, but as the matter is foreign to my subject I will at once return to it. I am inclined to think that these seals prey more upon small fish than large ones, and they·very frequently eat crabs and mussels, and they will sometimes seize upon birds, such as the widgeon and duck; but they do not prey upon each other, neither will they eat anything that they find dead. Their greatest speed in the water does not exceed twenty miles an hour; and when going through the water at the height of their speed they have the extraordinary power of stopping themselves instantaneously. Sometimes, when anything surprises them, as a boat for instance, they will come towards it at the top of their speed, and when within perhaps a yard of it, they will, without the slightest diminution of velocity, raise their head and half their body out of the water, and at once become motionless as a statue. I have known bulls to attack a boat, but this is not a frequent occurrence.

When they are on shore they can run surprisingly fast; on a hard, smooth beach, they can run nearly as fast as a man; and in the bush, or long grass, they can get along much faster. They can also climb up rocky cliffs and steep slippery banks which would be inaccessible to man, and very often they fall backwards down these places and bruise themselves severely. In conclusion, I must observe that the above notes have been deduced from experience gained entirely in the southern hemisphere, in latitude about 51° S. But I have not the least doubt but my remarks may be applied to the same species of seal in the northern hemisphere in the corresponding seasons. Perhaps few persons have had so good an opportunity of observing the habits of this animal as myself; as I had during the prosecution of a voyage to the Southern Ocean (partly for sealing purposes) the misfortune to be shipwrecked, and left upon one of those desolated islands for a period of twenty months, and our food during that time consisted almost entirely of seals' flesh; and I may add that that of the suckling, which is the best, is far from being unpalatable; and if it could be had with the necessary accompaniment of meat, it might be made a most delicious dish.

It will be obvious from a perusal of these observations that the months of February, March, and April, are the best suited for sealing purposes. May and June are also good months; but the whole business of the day's killing must be done at the very dawn of day, so that it is necessary to know where different mobs are encamped, and a party of men must be at the place where each mob is to be attacked at the peep of day, as they nearly all go into the water within a few minutes of the same time.

THOMAS MUSGRAVE.

A SHORT ACCOUNT

OF

THE AUCKLAND ISLANDS.*

OUR first knowledge of this group of islands is due to the commercial enterprise of British merchants. They were discovered by Captain Abraham Bristow, in the ship 'Ocean'—a vessel belonging to the late Samuel Enderby, Esq.—during a whaling voyage, August 16th, 1806. This was in his third voyage round the world, and the following extract from his log-book, quoted by Sir James Ross, announces the discovery :—'Moderate and clear; at daylight saw land, bearing west by compass, extending round to the north as far as N.E. by N., distant from the nearest part about 9 leagues. This island or islands, as being the first discoverer, I shall call *Lord Auckland's* (my friend through my father), and is situated, according to my observation at noon, in lat. 50° 48′ S. and long. 166° 42′ E., by a distance I had of the sun and moon at half-past ten A.M. The land is of a moderate height, and from its appearance I have no doubt but it will afford a good harbour in the north end, and I should suppose lies in about the latitude of 50° 21′ S., and its greatest extent is in

---

* See further Findlay's 'Pacific Directory,' a book no navigator in these seas should be without, though it is not to be got in the ports of Melbourne or Sydney. The books from which this account has been compiled are all to be found in the Melbourne Public Library.

a N.W. and S.E. direction. This place, I should suppose,
abounds with seals, and sorry I am that the time and the
lumbered state of my ship do not allow me to examine it.'

Captain Bristow visited them in the following year
(1807) in the 'Sarah,' also belonging to the Messrs.
Enderby, when he took formal possession of them for the
British Crown, and left some pigs there, which afterwards
increased to a surprising extent, but seem, by Captain
Musgrave's account, to have since become quite extinct.*
The islands remained untenanted during the subsequent
years, being visited occasionally by vessels in search of
whales and seals—the former coming into the bays to calve
during the months of April and May, and the latter consisting chiefly of sea lions. Among those who came hither
in 1829 was Captain Morrell, an American navigator, to
whom, among other things, we owe the discovery of
the deposits of guano at Ichaboe, and whose description
of the port of Carnley's Harbour is given presently.

In the year 1840 the island was visited by the vessels of
three nations— the English ships 'Erebus' and 'Terror,'
under Sir James Clark Ross and Captain Crozier ; † the
French corvettes 'L'Astrolabe' and 'La Zelée,' under
Dumont D'Urville; and the United States Exploring
Expedition, under Captain Charles Wilkes. From the
narratives of these voyages we have chiefly derived the
subsequent particulars.

The islands were without permanent inhabitants during
all the periods of the above visits ; but, subsequently, a
body of New Zealanders, about seventy in number, came
over from Chatham Island in a whale ship, and were
landed on the N.E. or Enderby Island. Bringing with
them their warlike spirit, their quarrels soon led to an

---

* A few pigs of a very small breed appear to have been seen by the
shipwrecked crew of the 'Invercauld' in the north part of the island.

† Afterwards lost whilst commanding the same old ship in the Franklin
expedition to the Arctic regions.

outbreak, and some fighting and loss of life ensued. They then divided into two separate bodies, under different chiefs, about thirty remaining in their original locality, twenty-five more going to the southward, the remainder maintaining separate independence. Neither Maori nor European has, however, trodden these desolate shores for many years prior to Captain Musgrave's visit.

From the eminent services rendered to geographical science, and to further those commercial enterprises in which the Messrs. Enderby for several generations had so largely engaged, the group was granted by the British Government to Messrs. Charles, George, and H. Enderby, and on the formation of the Southern Whale Fishery Company they undertook the establishment of their principal centre of operations here. Accordingly, Mr. Charles Enderby, with an efficient staff of assistants, took possession of his domain in the early part of 1850, finding the New Zealanders before mentioned in possession of a portion of the land. Their claims were soon adjusted, and they became great auxiliaries to the infant colony. This, then, is the brief history of this remote island. It promised to become a most conspicuous point in the wide world of waters. With every advantage of insulation, the possession of numerous and excellent harbours, with every means at command for the relaxation of whale and other fisheries in these seas, it was not unreasonably thought that it must some day become the centre of much trade, and that, too, of a very different character to almost every other part of the South Pacific. But in less than two years the whole scheme of the ' Great Southern Whale Fishery ' fell through. It does not fall within our province to go into particulars, although the story is both curious and instructive. It is sufficient to say that the whole settlement was abandoned in 1852, and the business details became the source of infinite legal difficulties.

Though the group has been visited by the four principal navigators above mentioned, Morrell describing a southern harbour which he calls Carnley's Harbour, and the three others all having confined their remarks to the northern or Laurie Harbour, we had but an imperfect notion of the entire group, even as regards its dimensions, until the recent visit of Captain Musgrave.

From the cursory examinations made by Mr. Enderby, it would appear that the island must be considerably broader than is represented on D'Urville's chart. Of course the very imperfect sketch given by Bristow cannot be taken as giving a correct idea of the island.

The following imperfect notices of the group are collected from the Narrative of the 'Voyage of Discovery, &c., of H.M.S. "Erebus" and "Terror,"' vol. I.; the 'Narrative of the United States Exploring Expedition,' vol. II.; 'Le Voyage de "L'Astrolabe" et "La Zelée,"' par M. Dumont d'Urville; and the 'Narrative of Four Voyages,' by B. Morrell. These sources have been also combined in a *brochure*, by C. Enderby, Esq., F.R.S., 'A Short Account of the Auckland Islands,' &c., London, 1849; and see also the 'Quarterly Review' for June, 1847.

Mr. M'Cormick, the naturalist to Sir James Ross's Antarctic Expedition, remarks that the formation of the Auckland Islands, as well as Campbell Islands, is volcanic, and constituted chiefly of basalt and greenstone. He also calls attention to *Deas Head*, in Laurie Harbour, north of Shoe Island, as being of great geological interest, exhibiting fine columns 300 feet high, which are highly magnetic. The loftiest hill, *Mount Eden*, at the head of Laurie Harbour, attains an elevation of 1,325 feet, is rounded at the top, and clothed with grass to its summit. Another hill in the west rises to nearly 1,000 feet.

PRODUCTIONS.—Dr. Hooker, whose observations have been published in connection with the voyage of the 'Erebus' and 'Terror,' under the title of '*Flora Antarctica*,' remarks that, 'Perhaps no place in the course of our projected voyage in the Southern Ocean promised more novelty to the botanist than the Auckland Islands. Situated in the midst of a boisterous ocean, in a very high latitude for that hemisphere, and far removed from any tract of land but the islands of New Zealand, they proved, as was expected, to contain amongst many new species some of peculiar interest. Possessing no mountains rising to the limits of perpetual snow, and few rocks or precipices, the whole land seemed covered with vegetation; a low forest skirts all the shores, succeeded by a broad belt of brushwood, above which, to the summit of the hills, extend grassy slopes. On a closer inspection of the forest it is found to be composed of a dense thicket of stag-headed trees, so gnarled and stunted by the violence of the gales as to afford an excellent shelter for a luxuriant undergrowth of bright green feathery ferns, and several gay flowered herbs. With much to delight the eye, and an extraordinary amount of new species to occupy the mind, there is here a want of any of those trees or shrubs to which the voyager has been accustomed in the north; and one cannot help feeling how much greater the pleasure would be to find new kinds of the pine, the birch, willow, or the oak, than those remarkable trees which have no allies in the northern hemisphere, and the mention of which, suggesting no familiar form to compare them with at home, can interest few but the professed botanist. Eighty flowering plants were found—a small number, but consisting of species more remarkable for their beauty and novelty than the *flora* of any other country can show, no less than fifty-six being hitherto undescribed, and one-half of the whole peculiar to this group, as far as is at present known.'

THE TREES on the island have been stated by some as rising to 70 feet in height, by others only to 30 feet. Captain Musgrave gives the latter. Both may be right, for they are most generally found to have been overturned by the strong gales, which is readily done, from the nature of the soil they grow in—a very deep, light, peaty earth, which affords but little support for the roots. The trunks attain a diameter of four and five feet at times, but, from the above-mentioned cause, the stems are seldom straight enough to afford timber of any magnitude. For knees, or such purposes, it may be very valuable. Abundance of fuel from this source, then, may be relied on. The peat, too, which covers the greater portion of the land, might be made available for this purpose, but not perfectly so, by the usual mode adopted in Ireland.*

WATER, as an article of consumption, is very abundant. The stream which falls into the head of Laurie Harbour had sufficient water to form a noble cataract after a month's dry weather, and, indeed, abundance of streams are to be met with in all parts. The nature of the soil is such that, whatever quantity of rain falls, it very quickly sinks below the surface, and then, probably, percolates away on the volcanic and impervious rock beneath. From the moisture of the climate, and the igneous character of the rock, this peaty formation arises. This vegetable formation is found to be several feet in thickness, and consists of a mass of decomposed black vegetable fibre, which, if properly compressed, makes good fuel. Great difficulty was experienced in forming a foundation for the observatory, at the time of the 'Erebus' and 'Terror's' visit; they had to dig twelve feet through the peat to gain the solid rock on which to erect the instruments. The magnetic observations made here were found to be singularly affected by the nature of the island. Some of the magnets were found entirely to depend for their direction of the north and south poles on the fragments of rocks around them. The compasses in the 'Terror' were so much affected by Shoe Island as to mask the local attraction of the iron in the ship. These phenomena led to the opinion that the island may be taken as one great magnet itself.

---

* As an evidence that the wood will burn—a quality not always found in these latitudes—it is mentioned by Sir J. C. Ross that some of his officers set fire to the dense brushwood to clear a path for their explorations of the interior.

Respecting the ZOOLOGY of these islands, Mr. McCormick observes 'there is no species of land animal, with the exception of the domestic pig introduced several years ago in the island by Captain Bristow.' Their food consists of the *arabia polaris*, described by Dr. Hooker as ' one of the most beautiful and singular of the vegetable productions of the island it inhabits ; growing in large orbicular masses on rocks and banks near the sea, or amongst the dense and gloomy vegetation of the woods. Its copious bright green foliage and large umbels of waxy flowers have a most striking appearance.'* ' The whole plant,' he adds, ' has a heavy and rather disagreeable smell, common to many of its natural order, but it is nevertheless greedily eaten by goats, pigs, and rabbits. It is so abundant in marshy spots that these animals frequently live entirely amongst it, particularly when it grows near the margin of the woods, where they form broad tracks through the patches, grubbing up the roots to a great extent, and, by trampling down the soft stems and leaves, make soft and warm places for themselves to litter in. One of these animals was shot by Mr. Hallett, and, although in poor condition, its flesh was considered well flavoured, though by no means equal to that of our own well-fed pigs.'

LAURIE HARBOUR and the north part of the island are thus described in the narrative of the United States Exploring Expedition in the ship ' Porpoise,' dated 7th March, 1840 :—

' On the 7th we anchored in the harbour of Sarah's Bosom, in twelve fathoms water. During our brief stay here, all were actively employed wooding and watering, for which this harbour affords a fine opportunity. Assistant-Surgeon Holmes made several excursions on the largest island, of which he gives the following account :—"I found it very thickly covered with trees in its less elevated parts. As few of them were of any size, I found no small

---

* Flora Antarctica, p. 20.

difficulty in penetrating and making my way through them; in many places it was absolutely impassable. It was only after a long and fatiguing walk that I succeeded in reaching the summit of that part of the island near which the brig was anchored, when I found the trees less numerous. A thick growth of underwood and dwarf bushes, intermingled with ferns, concealed the surface, rendering it difficult to walk. Even in the places apparently most level, the ground was very unequal, and a single step would sometimes send me nearly up to the neck into a hollow filled with large fern fronds.

' "On the highest parts, the small level spots were covered only with moss and a description of tall grass, and in places also a kind of grain grew abundantly. The ground was dry everywhere, all the water being found in the streams, which were numerous and pure.

' "Near the summit the ground was perforated in all directions, probably by birds who rear their young in these holes. Many of the birds, principally *procellaria*, were sitting on the ground; they made an effort to escape, but suffered themselves to be taken without any attempt at resistance.

' "The forest was full of small birds, of three or four different species, which were perfectly fearless. One little fellow alighted on my cap as I was sitting under a tree, and sang long and melodiously. Another, and still smaller species, of a black colour, spotted with yellow, was numerous, and sang very sweetly; its notes were varied, but approximated more nearly to the song of our blackbird; occasionally a note or two resembled the lark's. Hawks, too, are numerous, and might be seen in almost all the dead trees in pairs. Along the sea coast were to be seen the marks of their ravages upon the smaller birds. The sea birds were very numerous on the opposite side of the island, sitting upon the cliffs or hovering over the isles. On the western side of the Auckland Island the underbush and young trees are exceedingly thick."

' Dr. Holmes remarks that he was occupied fully an hour in making his way for 100 yards, where to all appearance a human step had never before trodden. There was not a vestige of a track; old trees were strewn about irregularly, sometimes kept erect by the pressure from all sides. Some trees were seen upwards of 70 feet in height, although they were generally from 15 to 20. Every part of the island was densely covered with vegetation. The soil, from the decomposition of vegetable matter, had acquired considerable richness. Specimens of all plants were collected; some resembling the tropical plants were found here.

' These islands have in many places the appearance of having been raised directly from the sea.

' The whaling season occurs here in the months of April and May. Near the watering-place a commodious hut has been erected by a French whaler. Near by there was another in ruins, and close to it the grave of a French sailor, whose name was inscribed on a wooden cross erected over it. Some attempts at forming a garden were observed at one of the points of Sarah's Bosom; and turnips, cabbages, and potatoes were growing finely, which, if left undisturbed, will soon cover this portion of the island: to these a few onions were added.

' Many of the small islands in this group were visited. They closely resemble the larger ones. The cliffs consist of basalt, and are generally from 50 to 60 feet perpendicular.

' These islands have a picturesque, wild, steep, and basaltic appearance. The highest peak was estimated to be 800 feet; the smallest has a less elevation. The general aspect of the land resembles the region round Cape Horn.'

CLIMATE.—No very accurate knowledge of the general climate of the group is as yet acquired, though the full and exact observations made by Captain Musgrave during his twenty months' stay are valuable on this head. It has been supposed to be similar to Chiloe, but in one particular the climate differs from that of Chiloe, viz., in the strong winds which it would appear the islands are subject to. The trees are evidence of this, as they bend from the general westerly direction of the violent squalls. Mr. Enderby experienced one very remarkable phenomenon in the early part of 1850, at the station in Port Ross. A most violent gust of wind struck, with the force of a solid body, the spot near where he was, and this not for any continued period, or over an extended space, but only for about five seconds of time, and a few yards in diameter. After passing onward, the percussion of the repeated shocks could be heard at short intervals as it went. There was no apparent cause for it, and the intervening spaces were comparatively calm. This would form an important consideration with vessels unprepared for such a visitation when at anchor.

THE AUCKLAND GROUP, according to Sir James Ross, consists of one large and several smaller islands, separated by narrow channels. The largest island he states to be about 30 miles long and 15 miles in extreme breadth; but this cannot be considered as exact. It contains, he continues, two principal harbours, whose entrances are both from the eastward, and whose heads or termination reach within two or three miles of the western coast.

ENDERBY ISLAND is the north-eastern island of the group; it forms the northern side of the entrance to Laurie Harbour, or Port Ross. It was upon this island that the principal portion of the stock landed by the Whale Fishery Company was kept. They immediately began to improve in their new position—an evidence of the good quality of the land. The island, two or three miles in length, is capable of sustaining a large quantity of cattle. It is covered with peaty mould, which is capable of being rendered very productive. The New Zealanders, who were established here, raised vegetables, turnips, potatoes, cabbages, &c.—the first of excellent quality, excelling most others; the latter equal to any European productions. This augurs well that other fruits and plants may flourish. The island is not high, and is well supplied with water.

There is a narrow entrance to Laurie Harbour, between the west end of Enderby Island and Rose Island, which is only a channel fit for boats. The sea was breaking right across the opening when the 'Erebus' passed; but in calm weather it might be mistaken by strangers for a safe passage.

As is frequently the case, the tidal currents meet off Enderby Island, and on this Sir James Ross says:—' On rounding the north-east cape of Enderby Island, we passed through some strong whirlpools occasioned by the meeting of the tides off the Point, and although we did not at first find soundings with our ordinary hand lines, it is by no means improbable that some shoals or rocky patches may have some influence in producing these strong and dangerous eddies.'

LAURIE HARBOUR, or PORT ROSS.—Captain Bristow, the discoverer of these islands, who also drew the first sketch of the group, named this, the principal harbour, Laurie Harbour, after the gentleman who first issued this knowledge to the world, in 1810. On a chart of the Western Pacific, by Captain Butler, and published by Mr. Laurie, this sketch will be found. A copy of this chart, by the late Mr. Purdy, presented to Captain Hurd, R.N., was published by the Admiralty in 1823, and these composed our entire knowledge of them until the visits of Captain Sir James Ross and Admiral Dumont D'Urville.

D'Urville has given a rough survey of them, and Captain Sir James Ross has given a survey of the harbour in question, under the name of Rendezvous Harbour; but, following the recognized principle, we have retained the name applied by its discoverer in 1806. Mr. Enderby has given a third appellation, that of Port Ross, which, as it may be in some use, we have also retained. The other names are chiefly as given by Captain Bristow.

M

There are two surveys of this excellent harbour, the one by Sir James Ross, the other by Admiral D'Urville. That of the latter is the most complete, and exhibits more in detail the character of the locality.

The entrance to the harbour is between Enderby Island on the north side, on which was once a pilot station, and *Green Island*, or Ewing Island of Sir James Ross, their distance apart being little above a mile. *Ocean Island* is three-quarters of a mile west of *Green Island*, and is connected by shoal water to the S.E. point of the harbour. *Rose Island*, which forms a continuation of the north side of the entrance, lies to the N.W. of Ocean Island, and from between these the harbour runs 2½ miles to the S.W., having a depth of ten to twenty fathoms over it, and the shores bold-to.

Deas Head, to the S.W. of Rose Island, is an interesting feature, formed of basaltic columns 300 feet high.

Shoe Island, in the middle of the harbour, and three-quarters of a mile south, *true*, of Deas Head, is a bold and picturesque island; it is highly magnetic, and is bold-to.

Terror Cove is to the west of this, and is separated from *Erebus Cove*, to the south of it, by a projecting point of land.* Sir James Ross's observatory was in Terror Cove. In the former charts this is called the *Harbour of Sarah's Bosom*,† being thus named by Captain Bristow when he came here on his second visit in 1807. He anchored here in the 'Sarah;' hence its appellation. In his brief account he states that ' ships may be safely land-locked all round. Here may be had plenty of fine water, wood in the greatest abundance, winged game, &c. The

---

* By the side of a small stream of water, and on the only cleared spot we could find, the ruins of a small hut were discovered, which I have since learnt formed for several years the wretched habitation of a deserter from an English whale ship and a New Zealand woman.—*Sir James Ross.*

† Captain Musgrave, not having any accurate particulars of localities, in compiling his charts and journal, fell into the error of calling the Carnley's Harbour ' of Morrell by the name of ' Sarah's Bosom.'

islands are annoyed by the most powerful gales in winter.'

The result of the observations made by Sir James C. Ross at *Sarah Harbour*, or Terror Cove, gave for the observatory, lat. 50° 32′ 30″ S., long. 166° 12′ 34″ E. ; variation 17° 40′ E. ; dip, 73° 12′. High water, full and change, at 12h. ; the highest spring tides scarcely exceed 3 feet.

A remarkable oscillation of the tide, when near the time of high water, was observed ; after rising to nearly its highest, the tide would fall 2 or 3 inches, and then rise again between 3 and 4 inches, so as to exceed its former height rather more than an inch. This irregular movement generally occupied more than an hour, of which the fall continued about 20 minutes, and the rise 50 minutes of the interval.*

The establishment of the Southern Whale Fishery Company was fixed at the south side of Erebus Cove. This cove is bounded on the south side by a small peninsula projecting in an E.N.E. direction,† and connected by a narrow isthmus. This beach allows of easy landing, and the land, being level, is suitable for the purposes of wharfage, whaling stores, &c.

From this part the head of the harbour extends nearly two miles farther in a W.S.W. direction to its head, into which a fine and copious stream of fresh water falls. In its upper part Mr. Enderby found a large and valuable bed of cockles, little inferior to oysters. The southern side of the harbour does not require any particular notice.

The following is Sir James Ross's account of the harbour :—

'Rendezvous Harbour, which is at the north extreme of the island, contains several secure anchorages. The outermost of these, though convenient for stopping at a short time only, is a small sandy bay on the south side of

---

* Voyage of Discovery, vol. I., p. 153.

† *Pig Point* of Bristow.

Enderby Island, and about one and a half miles from its
N.E. cape.

‘It is well protected from all winds except those from
the S.E., and the holding ground is a good tenacious clay.
It is probable that there may be found good anchorage
also to the west of Enderby Island. After passing Ocean
and Rose Islands, a ship may anchor in perfect safety in
any part, but the most convenient will be found to be
between those islands and Erebus Cove, where abundance
of wood and water may be obtained, as also at Terror
Cove.

‘The upper end of the inlet, called Laurie Harbour, is
the most suitable for ships wanting to heave down or to
undergo any extensive repairs. It is perfectly land-locked,
and the steep beach on the southern shore affords the
greatest facility for clearing and re-loading the vessel.

‘I was so struck with the many advantages this place
possesses for a penal settlement over every other I had
heard named, to which to remove convicts from the now
free colonies of New South Wales, New Zealand, and Van
Dieman’s Land, that I addressed a letter on the subject to
Sir John Franklin on my return to Hobart Town, recom-
mending its adoption.

‘This letter was forwarded to the Secretary of State for
the Colonies ; but I believe Chatham Island, as being
seated in a milder climate, has been preferred, although I
am not aware of any other advantage it possesses, whilst
the want of good harbours will be found a great drawback ;
and the two tribes of New Zealanders, from Port Nichol-
son, who took possession of it in 1835, after eating one
half of the aborigines they found there, and making slaves
of the other half, will prove a difficult people to dispossess
of the land they have gained by conquest.

‘Laurie Harbour is well calculated for the location of an
establishment for the prosecution of the whale fishery.
Many black, and several sperm whales, came into the

harbour whilst we were there, and from such a situation the fishery might be pursued with very great advantage.

'We arrived there in the spring of the year, November being equivalent to the latitude of Hobart Town. We found a very great difference in the temperature, amounting to about 10° of the thermometer, but still greater to our feelings, owing to the increased humidity of the atmosphere, the temperature of the dew-point being nearly the same in both places. It cannot, however, be considered severe, when we remember that in England, which is very nearly in the same latitude, the mean temperature for April, the corresponding month, is 46°.* Our stay was too short to justify any further remarks on the climate of these islands; but a series of well-conducted observations, continued for two or three years, could not fail to prove highly interesting and important to the advancement of meteorological science.'.

Sir James Ross made the islands during a fog, and had some difficulty in rounding to the northward. 'As we opened the harbour the squalls came down the western hills with much violence, threatening to blow us out to sea again, and it required the utmost vigilance and activity of the officers and crew in beating up at times to maintain the ground we had gained. There is, however, ample space, and no concealed dangers. The belts of sea-weed which line the shore and rocks point out the shallow or dangerous parts. After five hours of hard contending with the fierce westerly squalls, we anchored at 1 P.M., November 20th, 1840, in a small cove on the west shore, in 10 fathoms.'

Captain Wilkes says—'The harbour of Sarah's Bosom is not the most secure. That of Laurie's is protected from all winds, and has a large and fine streamlet of water at its head. The rocks are covered with limpets, and small

---

* At the Auckland Islands, during Ross's stay, the average temperature was 45° 27'.

fish of many varieties are caught in quantities among the kelp. The crew enjoyed themselves on chowders and fries. No geese were seen, and the only game observed were a few grey ducks, snipe, cormorants, and the common shag. The land birds are excellent eating, especially the hawks. On the whole, it is a very desirable place in which to refit.'

Some officers of the French expedition, under Admiral D'Urville, made a boat excursion to Laurie Harbour. They thus speak of that part of the east coast lying between the two harbours :—

'These banks are very full of fish. The bottom is regular, varying from fifteen to twenty fathoms. The coast is indented with numerous creeks, surrounded by basaltic rocks, where boats can easily approach.'

'If ever,' says M. Dubouzet, one of the French officers, in his journal, 'the fine harbours of these islands should attract colonists thither, Laurie Harbour would be the most suitable point for the site of a town.'

Another, M. Jacquinot, says—' The vast bay is encircled everywhere by elevated land, clothed with trees from the sea-board to the summit. The soil, of volcanic formation, is covered with a thick layer of vegetable *débris*, producing a vigorous growth of large ferns.'

The eastern side of the island is but little known as yet. From the chart by Admiral D'Urville, it has several most excellent harbours, a fact confirmed during some of the visits made by Mr. Enderby. That one will be found superior to Laurie Harbour is not likely, but they may prove of great service. One of them was named Chapel Bay, from a rock, the form of which gave its appellation, near its entrance.

ADAM ISLAND appears on Bristow's Chart, and to the northward of it must be Carnley's Harbour, of Captain Morrell (the Sarah's Bosom of Captain Musgrave).

CARNLEY'S HARBOUR makes in about four miles to the eastward of the South Cape, and the entrance is formed by two bluff points, from which, to the head of the lagoon, the distance is fifteen miles. The passage is above two miles wide, and entirely free from danger, within twenty-five fathoms of each shore.

' It runs in first N.N.W., then N.N.E., forming at the head of the lagoon a beautiful basin, with sufficient room for half a dozen ships to moor ; the least water from the entrance, until we came near the anchorage, was twenty-five fathoms mid-channel. We anchored in four fathoms, clay ground.

' The western side of this island is a perpendicular, bluff, iron-bound coast, with deep water within 100 fathoms of the shore, while the eastern coast is principally lined with a pebbly or sandy beach,* behind which are extensive level plains, covered with beautiful grass and refreshing verdure, extending back about five miles, and then rising into elevated hills.

' All the hills, except a few of the highest, are thickly covered with lofty trees, flourishing with such extraordinary vigour as to afford a magnificent prospect for the spectator.

' The large trees are principally of two sorts ; one of them is of the size of our large firs, and grows nearly in the same manner : its foliage is an excellent substitute for spruce in making that pleasant and wholesome beverage, spruce-beer. The other resembles our maple, and often grows to a great size, but is only fit for ship-building or fuel, being too heavy for masts or spars of any dimensions.

' The quality of the soil in this island is sufficiently indicated by the uniform luxuriance of all its productions. Were the forest cleared away, very few spots would be found that could not be converted to excellent pasturage or tillage land.

' The valleys, plains, hill sides, and every spot where

---

* This description entirely agrees with the accounts of D'Urville and his officers.

the rays of the sun can penetrate, are now clothed with a strong, heavy, luxuriant grass, interspersed with many natural specimens of the countless beauties of Nature's vegetable kingdom. This extraordinary strength of vegetation is, no doubt, greatly assisted by the agreeable temperature of the climate, which is very fine.

'The climate is mild, temperate, and salubrious. I have been told by men of the first respectability and talent, who have visited the island in the month of July—the dead of winter in this island, corresponding to our January—that the weather was mild as respects cold, as the mercury was never lower than 38° in the valleys, and the trees at the same time retained their verdure as if it was midsummer. I have no doubt but that the foliage of many of the trees remains until pushed off in the following spring by the new crop of buds and leaves.

'At the time we were there the mercury seldom rose higher than 78°, although it answered to our July. The weather is generally good at all seasons of the year, notwithstanding there are occasional high winds, attended with heavy rains.' *

The WESTERN side of the Island, according to Captain Bristow, is very high and precipitous, and may be seen, in clear weather, 16 or 17 leagues off. Towards the northern part are two remarkable natural pyramids or columns, called the Column Rocks.†

The N.W. Cape is a very remarkable headland, with a rocky islet, and a curious conical rock just off it. Just to the east of it is a dark-looking promontory, called *Black Head*, with a deep cavernous indentation at its base. This was afterwards found to be only a short distance from the westernmost part of Laurie Harbour. It was reached by Mr. McCormick, and some other officers from the 'Erebus' and 'Terror,' by following the stream which

---

* Narrative of Four Voyages, by Capt. B. Morrell, 28th Dec., 1829.

† Purdy's Tables, p. 89.

empties itself into the head of the harbour, and whose source is in the hills above *Black Head*. These hills are from 800 to 900 feet high.*

DISAPPOINTMENT ISLAND lies off the western side of the Island, and is shown on Bristow's Chart.

BRISTOW ROCK, which must be very dangerous, is also given from the same author as lying 8 miles north of Enderby Island, and is just even with the water's edge. It was not seen by Sir James Ross, and therefore requires great caution.

CAMPBELL ISLAND.—This island was discovered by Captain Fred. Hazelburgh, of the brig 'Perseverance,' belonging to Mr. Robert Campbell, of Sydney, in 1810. According to his account the island is 30 miles in circumference, the country is mountainous, and there are several good harbours, of which two on the east side are to be preferred. The southernmost of these two he named Perseverance Harbour, and in it Sir James Ross anchored in the 'Erebus' and 'Terror,' December, 1840.

The highest hill seen from the harbour is on its north side, and has an elevation of 1,500 feet.

The shores on either side are steep, and rise abruptly to between 800 and 900 feet. The hills, from being less wooded, have a more desolate appearance than those of the Auckland Islands; and though there is abundance of wood in the sheltered places, the trees are nowhere so great as in those islands. These trees especially indicate, by their prostrate position, the prevailing power of the westerly storms. This occurrence of sudden and violent rushes of wind is a remarkable characteristic phenomenon of all the islands about this latitude. This is observed at Kerguelen Land, at the Aucklands, and especially here.

Sir James Ross had been advised, when at Hobart Town, to take his ships into the harbour near the northeast point, but, from the entrance, it appeared so exposed

---

* Sir James Ross.

to winds from that quarter that he bore away for the southern harbour.

Perseverance Harbour is about four miles in depth, running for more than two miles in a W.N.W. direction, and thence, after passing a shoal point, with a warning bed of sea-weed off it, on which the 'Terror' grounded, about W.S.W. to its head. In the outer part of the harbour the water is too deep for convenient anchorage, but in the upper part, which is completely land-locked, there is abundant room for a hundred ships to lie in the most perfect security, and excellent water can be had in any quantity. The remains of some huts were found on each side of a cove, to the north of the 'Erebus' anchorage, as also the graves of several seamen, and one of a French woman, accidentally drowned. There had been also an establishment at the side of a stream in the north-west corner of the harbour, but the position was not so good as that of the cove. The observation spot on the beach, near the shoal point, was found to be in lat. 52° 33′ 26″ S., and long. 169° 8′ 41″ E. ; variation, 17° 54′, E. ; mag. dip. 73° 53′. High water, full and change, at 12 h., but presenting the same irregularities as at Laurie Harbour, Auckland Isles. The rise and fall at neaps was 43 inches.*

---

* Sir James C. Ross : *Voyage of Discovery, &c.*, vol. I., pp. 154 *et seq.*
A detailed account of its productions will there be found.

THE LOSS OF THE 'INVERCAULD.'

Letter from Captain Dalgarno.

CAPTAIN DALGARNO, writing from Southampton to the owners, says :—' I am at last offered another opportunity of addressing you again in this life, to let you know the sad tidings of the ship "Invercauld," which became a total wreck during the night of May 10, 1864, on the island of Auckland, off New Zealand, during a heavy gale of wind from the northward and thick weather. In about twenty minutes after striking she was in atoms—so heavy was the sea running, and all rocks where the disaster happened. The boys Middleton and Wilson and four seamen were drowned ; the remainder, nineteen of us, getting washed on shore, through the wreck, all more or less hurt, the night being intensely dark and cold. We saved nothing but what we had on our persons ; and before being washed from the wreck I hove off my sea-boots, so as to enable me, if possible, to reach the shore. After getting ashore amongst the rocks, we called upon each other, and all crept as close together as we could, to keep ourselves warm. The spray from the sea reaching us made it one of the most dismal nights ever anyone suffered, and we were all glad when day broke on the following morning, when all who were able went towards the wreck to see what could be saved. All we found was about 2 lbs. of biscuit, and 3 lbs. of pork—the only food we had to divide amongst nineteen ; and after all taking about a mouthful each, we went and collected a few of the most suitable pieces from the wreck to make a sort of hut to cover us from the weather, where we made a fire, the steward having saved a box of matches.

'I have seen and suffered more since the disaster happened than I can pen to you at this time; but if God spares me to reach you, I will then give you all particulars. We remained four days at the wreck; and, having no more food, nor appearance of getting any more at the wreck, we proceeded to go on the top of the island, to see if we could find food or any inhabitants. It was no easy matter to reach the top, it being about 2,000 feet high, and almost perpendicular. When we got there we found no inhabitants; and the only food we found was wild roots that grew on the island, of which we ate, and fresh water. At night we made a covering of boughs, and, lighting a fire, crept as close together as possible. On the following morning we made towards a bay that was on the east side, which occupied some days, the scrub being so heavy to walk amongst. The cook and three seamen died during this time, and all of us were getting very weak for want of food and from cold. At length we reached the bay, where we found some limpets on the rocks, of which we ate heartily. We also caught two seals, and found them good food; and had we got plenty of them no doubt all would have lived. After living three months upon limpets, they got done, and all we had again was the roots and water, seeing no more seals.

' By the end of August the only survivors were myself, the mate, and Robert Holding, seaman; the carpenter, and the boys Liddle and Lancefield, being among the last that died—all very much reduced. After we three had lingered for twelve months and ten days, we were at last relieved by the Portuguese ship " Julian," from Macao for Callao, with Chinese passengers. She sprang a leak off here, and sent a boat on shore to see if they could get their ship repaired, when they found us the only inhabitants on the

island.   They proceeded on their passage to Callao, taking
us three along with them.   We were all treated kindly,
and on the 28th June reached Callao, where we were all
treated kindly by the people there.   On the same evening
I sailed by the mail steamer for England, leaving the mate
and the seaman in Callao.   On the 6th July I sailed from
Panama; on the 13th arrived at St. Thomas, and sailed
same day for Southampton by the steamship " Shannon,"
meeting with the greatest kindness from all on board the
several ships I sailed in.'

Note by the Publishers.

The following additional particulars of the loss of the
Invercauld, and the adventures of the survivors, taken
from the *Melbourne Illustrated Post* of the 25th October,
will no doubt be acceptable here, though involving to some
extent a repetition of the above :—

" Information has been received by way of England, of
the wreck, on the Auckland Islands, of the ship *Invercauld*,
a vessel of 888 tons, Captain George Dalgarno, which
sailed from Melbourne for Callao, in ballast, on the 28th
of April, 1864.   The circumstances attending the wreck of
the *Invercauld* are of a peculiarly painful nature, and such
as are likely to excite in the minds of this community
more than ordinary interest, while the details of the
narrative furnished by Captain Musgrave, of the schooner
Grafton, containing so harrowing an account of the
miseries and privations endured by himself and his shipwrecked crew on that barren and desolate isle, are so
fresh in the memories of the inhabitants of this colony.
The *Invercauld* carried no passengers, and her crew consisted (with the captain) of 25 persons.   *Mitchell's Mari-
time Register* of the 5th of August has the following with
reference to the disaster :—

" ' The *Invercauld*, Captain Dalgarno, from Melbourne to

Callao, struck, 10th May, 1864, on the north-west end of the island of Auckland, lat. 53° S., long. 106° E., and went to pieces. Six of the crew were drowned and 19 were washed ashore, of whom the captain, Mr. Andrew Smith, the chief officer, and a seaman named Robert Holding were rescued 12 months and 10 days after.' The saved portion of the crew subsisted together on the island for some time, but through the dreadful scarcity of food the members were speedily reduced by death caused by starvation, until at length only the three survivors remained. They were ultimately rescued from their fearful position by a Portuguese vessel sailing past the island, and in it conveyed to Callao, whence they proceeded to England. Captain Dalgarno has furnished to his owners a complete narrative of the wreck, with a most interesting history of the residence of himself and his companions on the Auckland Islands. They must have been on the island at the same time as Captain Musgrave, and no doubt the smoke seen at a distance by this gentleman must have proceeded from the camp of the castaways belonging to the *Invercauld.* The dead body, and the slate containing some obliterated writing, also discovered by Captain Musgrave, may have belonged to this party, but such was the inaccessible nature of the country that a complete search could not be made on that occasion. Captain Dalgarno, with his mate and Holding, the seaman, met with a most cordial reception at Callao, where the greatest kindness was extended towards them."

THE END.

LONDON
PRINTED BY SPOTTISWOODE AND CO.
NEW-STREET SQUARE

Now ready, at all Libraries, &c, Crown 8vo., with an Engraving of the new Eleanor Cross, price 8s. 6d., cloth gilt,

WALKS AND TALKS ABOUT LONDON.

By JOHN TIMBS, F.S.A.

Author of " Curiosities of London," " Things not Generally Known," etc.

CONTENTS.

1. About Old Lyon's Inn, Strand. 2. Last Days of Downing Street. 3. Walks and Talks in Vauxhall Gardens. 4. Last of the Old Bridewell. 5. The Fair of Mayfair. 6. From Hicks's Hall to Campden House. 7. Talk about the Temple, Past and Present. 8. Recollections of Sir Richard Phillips. 9. Curiosities of Fishmongers' Hall. 10. A Morning in Sir John Soane's Museum. 11. A Site of Speculation. 12. Changes in Covent Garden. 13. The Last of the Fleet Prison. 14. Forty Years in Fleet Street. 15. Changes at Charing Cross. 16. Railway London. 17. Black-friars Bridge. 18. Raising of Holborn Valley. 19. An Old Tavern in St. James's.

☞ This work takes special cognizance of the great changes and improvements now in progress in the Metropolis.

OPINIONS OF THE PRESS.

"The London of the last generation is, day by day, being rent away from the sight of the present, and it is well that Mr. Timbs is inclined to walk and talk about it ere it vanishes altogether, and leaves the next generation at a loss to understand the past history of the metropolis so far as it has a local colouring, as so very much of it has. . . . . Much of this has now gone for ever, but our author has watched the destructive course of the 'improver,' and, thanks to his industry, many a memory that we would not willingly let die is consigned to the keeping of the printed page, which in this instance, as in so many others, will doubtless prove a more lasting record than brass or marble."—*Gentleman's Magazine.*

"Pleasantly communicative as to every relic of the past, and every notability of the present. The present volume is an encyclopædia of local lore, and will be popular far beyond the boundaries of the kingdom of Cockayne."—*Morning Post.*

"This amusing volume contains, as might be expected from its author-ship, much curious information on the changing manners and altered sites of London. The natural extension of the limits of the metropolis, as well as the demolition of buildings which clears the ground for improve-ments, is sweeping away many memorials of the past, over which we may linger in these *Walks and Talks.* . . . . This, and other entertain-ment and instruction of a similar kind, is provided in the present little book of chatty perambulations."—*Reader.*

"In this new and exceedingly pleasant book of Mr. Timbs's, reference is made to the varied aspects under which London appears, and to its being a subject which is always new ; while it seeks to show what has been lost or gained by modern change, the volume is crammed with pleasant gossip about persons, places, and events connected with London."—*City Press.*

London : LOCKWOOD & CO., 7 Stationers' Hall Court, Ludgate Hill.

A LIST

OF

POPULAR WORKS

PUBLISHED BY

LOCKWOOD & CO.

7 STATIONERS'-HALL COURT, LONDON, E.C.

The Boy's Own Book : A Complete Encyclopædia of all the Diversions, Athletic, Scientific, and Recreative, of Boyhood and Youth. With many hundred Woodcuts, and Ten Vignette Titles, beautifully printed in Gold. New Edition, greatly enlarged and improved, price 8s. 6d. handsomely bound in cloth.

N.B.—This is the original and genuine 'Boy's Own Book,' formerly published by Mr. Bogue, and more recently by Messrs. Kent and Co. Care should be taken, in ordering the above, to give the name of either the former or present publishers, otherwise some inferior book, with a nearly similar title, may be supplied.

The Little Boy's Own Book of Sports and Pastimes. With numerous engravings. Abridged from the above. 16mo. price 3s. 6d. cloth.

Merry Tales for Little Folk. Illustrated with more than 200 Pictures. Edited by MADAME DE CHATELAIN. 16mo. 3s. 6d. cloth elegant. Contents:—The House that Jack Built—Little Bo-Peep—The Old Woman and Her Eggs—Old Mother Goose—The Death and Burial of Cock Robin—Old Mother Hubbard—Henny Penny—The Three Bears—The Ugly Little Duck—The White Cat—The Charmed Fawn—The Eleven Wild Swans—The Blue Bird—Little Maia—Jack the Giant Killer—Jack and the Bean Stalk—Sir Guy of Warwick—Tom Hickathrift, the Conqueror—Bold Robin Hood—Tom Thumb—Puss in Boots—Little Red Riding-Hood—Little Dame Crump—Little Goody Two Shoes—The Sleeping Beauty in the Wood—The Fair One with Golden Locks—Beauty and the Beast—Cinderella; or, the Little Glass Slipper—Princess Rosetta—The Elves of the Fairy Forest—The Elfin Plough—The Nine Mountains—Johnny and Lisbeth—The Little Fisher-Boy—Hans in Luck—The Giant and the Brave Little Tailor—Peter the Goatherd—Red Jacket; or, the Nose Tree—The Three Golden Hairs—The Jew in the Bramble Bush.

Victorian Enigmas ; being a Series of Enigmatical Acrostics on Historical, Biographical, Geographical, and Miscellaneous Subjects; combining Amusement with Exercise in the Attainment of Knowledge. Promoted and encouraged by Royal Example. By CHARLOTTE ELIZA CAPEL. Royal 16mo. cloth, elegantly printed, price 2s. 6d.

The idea for this entirely original style of Enigmas is taken from one said to have been written by Her Majesty for the Royal children, which, with its Solution, is given.

'A capital game, and one of the very best of those commendable mental exercises which test knowledge and stimulate study. To the Queen's loyal subjects it comes, moreover, additionally recommended by the hint in the title-page and the statement in the preface, that it is a game practised by Her Majesty and the Royal children, if indeed it were not invented by the Queen herself.'—CRITIC.

' A good book for family circles in the long and dreary winter evenings, inasmuch as it will enable the young to pass them away both pleasantly and profitably.'
CITY PRESS,

JOHN TIMBS'S POPULAR WORKS.

' Any one who reads and remembers Mr. Timbs's encyclopædic varieties should ever after be a good table talker, an excellent companion for children, a " well-read person," and a proficient lecturer.'—ATHENÆUM.

Things Not Generally Known. By JOHN TIMBS,
F.S.A. Editor of 'The Year Book of Facts,' &c. In Six Volumes, fcp. cloth, 15s.; or, the Six Volumes bound in Three, cloth gilt, or half-bound, 15s.; cloth, gilt edges, 16s. 6d. Contents:—General Information, 2 Vols.—Curiosities of Science, 2 Vols.—Curiosities of History, 1 Vol.—Popular Errors Explained, 1 Vol.

*** The Volumes sold separately, as follows:—

Things Not Generally Known Familiarly Explained.
(General Information). 2 Vols. 2s. 6d. each, or in 1 Vol. 5s. cloth.

' A remarkably pleasant and instructive little book; a book as full of information as a pomegranate is full of seed.'—PUNCH.
' A very amusing miscellany.'—GENTLEMAN'S MAGAZINE.
' And as instructive as it is amusing.'—NOTES AND QUERIES.

Curiosities of Science, Past and Present. 2 Vols.
2s. 6d. each, or in 1 Vol. 5s. cloth.

' " Curiosities of Science " contains as much information as could otherwise be gleaned from reading elaborate treatises on physical phenomena, acoustics, optics, astronomy, geology, and palæontology, meteorology, nautical geography, magnetism, the electric telegraph, &c.'—MINING JOURNAL.

Curiosities of History. Fcp. 2s. 6d. cloth; or, with
' Popular Errors,' In 1 Vol. 5s. cloth.

' We can conceive no more amusing book for the drawing-room, or one more useful for the school-room.'—ART JOURNAL.

Popular Errors Explained and Illustrated. Fcp.
2s. 6d. cloth; or, with ' Curiosities of History,' in 1 Vol. 5s. cloth.

' We know of few better books for young persons; it is instructive, entertaining, and reliable.'—BUILDER.
' A work which ninety-nine persons out of every hundred would take up whenever it came in their way, and would always learn something from.'
ENGLISH CHURCHMAN.

Knowledge for the Time: a Manual of Reading,
Reference, and Conversation on Subjects of Living Interest. Contents:—Historico-Political Information—Progress of Civilization—Dignities and Distinctions—Changes in Laws—Measure and Value—Progress of Science—Life and Health—Religious Thought. Illustrated from the best and latest Authorities. By JOHN TIMBS, F.S.A. Small 8vo. with Frontispiece, 5s. cloth.

' It is impossible to open the volume without coming upon some matter of interest upon which light is thrown.'—MORNING POST.
' We welcome this attempt to preserve the bright bits and the hidden treasures of contemporary history. It is with keen pleasure we bear in mind that this learned collector's eye watches our journalism and the daily utterance of scholars, determined that no truth shall be lost.'—LLOYD'S NEWS.

Stories of Inventors and Discoverers in Science and
Useful Arts. By JOHN TIMBS, F.S.A. Second Edition. With numerous Illustrations. Fcap. 5s. cloth.

' Another interesting and well-collected book, ranging from Archimedes and Roger Bacon to the Stephensons.'—ATHENÆUM.
' These stories by Mr. Timbs are as marvellous as the *Arabian Nights' Entertainments*, and are wrought into a volume of great interest and worth.'—ATLAS.

Walks and Talks About London. By JOHN TIMBS,

F.S.A., Author of 'Curiosities of London,' 'Things not Generally Known,' &c. Contents:—About Old Lyons Inn—Last Days of Downing Street—Walks and Talks in Vauxhall Gardens—Last of the Old Bridewell—The Fair of May Fair—From Hicks's Hall to Campden House—Talk about the Temple—Recollections of Sir Richard Phillips—Curiosities of Fishmongers' Hall—A Morning in Sir John Soane's 'Museum—A Site of Speculation—Changes in Covent Garden—Last of the Fleet Prison—Forty Years in Fleet Street—Changes at Charing Cross—Railway London—Blackfriars Bridge—Raising of Holborn Valley—An Old Tavern in St. James's. With Frontispiece, post 8vo. cloth gilt, 8s 6d.

'The London of the last generation is, day by day, being rent away from the sight of the present, and it is well that Mr. Timbs is inclined to walk and talk about it ere it vanishes altogether, and leaves the next generation at a loss to understand the past history of the metropolis so far as it has a local colouring, as so very much of it has. Much of this has now gone for ever, but our author has watched the destructive course of the "improver," and thanks to his industry, many a memory that we would not willingly let die, is consigned to the keeping of the printed page, which in this instance, as in so many others, will doubtless prove a more lasting record than brass or marble.'—GENTLEMAN'S MAGAZINE.

Things to be Remembered in Daily Life. With

Personal Experiences and Recollections. By JOHN TIMBS. F.S.A., Author of 'Things not Generally Known,' &c. &c. With Frontispiece. Fcp. 3s. 6d. cloth.

'While Mr. Timbs claims for this volume the merit of being more reflective than its predecessors, those who read it will add to that merit—that it is equally instructive.'—NOTES AND QUERIES.

'No portion of this book is without value, and several biographical sketches which it contains are of great interest. . . . . "Things to be Remembered in Daily Life" is a valuable and memorable book, and represents great research, and considerable and arduous labour.'—MORNING POST.

'Mr. Timbs's personal experiences and recollections are peculiarly valuable, as embodying the observations of an acute, intelligent, and cultivated mind. "Things to be Remembered" carries with it an air of vitality which augurs well for perpetuation.'—OBSERVER.

School-days of Eminent Men. Containing Sketches

of the Progress of Education in England, from the Reign of King Alfred to that of Queen Victoria; and School and College Lives of the most celebrated British Authors, Poets, and Philosophers; Inventors and Discoverers; Divines, Heroes, Statesmen, and Legislators. By JOHN TIMBS, F.S.A. Second Edition, entirely revised and partly re-written. With a Frontispiece by John Gilbert, 13 Views of Public Schools, and 20 Portraits by Harvey. Fcap. 5s. handsomely bound in cloth.

☞ Extensively used, and specially adapted for a Prize-Book at Schools.

'The idea is a happy one, and its execution equally so. It is a book to interest all boys, but more especially those of Westminster, Eton, Harrow, Rugby, and Winchester ; for of these, as of many other schools of high repute, the accounts are full and interesting.'—NOTES AND QUERIES.

Something for Everybody; and a Garland for the

Year. By JOHN TIMBS, F.S.A., Author of 'Things Not Generally Known,' &c. With a Coloured Title, post 8vo. 5s. cloth.

'This volume abounds with diverting and suggestive extracts. It seems to us particularly well adapted for parochial lending libraries.'—SATURDAY REVIEW.

'Full of odd, quaint, out-of-the-way bits of information upon all imaginable subjects is this amusing volume, wherein Mr. Timbs discourses upon domestic, rural, metropolitan, and social life; interesting nooks of English localities: time-honoured customs and old-world observances; and, we need hardly add, Mr. Timbs discourses well and pleasantly upon all.'—NOTES AND QUERIES, July 20, 1861.

A SERIES OF ELEGANT GIFT-BOOKS.

Truths Illustrated by Great Authors ;   A Dictionary of nearly Four Thousand Aids to Reflection, Quotations of Maxims, Metaphors, Counsels, Cautions, Proverbs, Aphorisms, &c. &c. In Prose and Verse. Compiled from the Great Writers of all Ages and Countries. Eleventh Edition, fcap. 8vo. cloth, gilt edges, 568 pp. 6s.

'The quotations are perfect gems; their selection evinces sound judgment and an excellent taste.'—DISPATCH.

'We accept the treasure with profound gratitude—it should find its way to every home.'—ERA.

'We know of no better book of its kind.'—EXAMINER.

The Philosophy of William Shakespeare; delineating, in Seven Hundred and Fifty Passages selected from his Plays, the Multiform Phases of the Human Mind. With Index and References. Collated, Elucidated, and Alphabetically arranged, by the Editors of 'Truths Illustrated by Great Authors.' Second Edition, fcap. 8vo. cloth, gilt edges, nearly 700 pages, with beautiful Vignette Title, price 6s.

☞ A glance at this volume will at once show its superiority to Dodd's 'Beauties,' or any other volume of Shakespearian selections.

Songs of the Soul during its Pilgrimage Heaven-ward: being a New Collection of Poetry, illustrative of the Power of the Christian Faith; selected from the Works of the most eminent British, Foreign, and American Writers, Ancient and Modern, Original and Translated. By the Editors of 'Truths Illustrated by Great Authors,' &c. Second Edition, fcap. 8vo. cloth, gilt edges, 638 pages, with beautiful Frontispiece and Title, price 6s.

☞ This elegant volume will be appreciated by the admirers of 'The Christian Year.'

The Beauty of Holiness ; or, The Practical Christian's Daily Companion: being a Collection of upwards of Two Thousand Reflective and Spiritual Passages, remarkable for their Sublimity, Beauty, and Practicability; selected from the Sacred Writings, and arranged in Eighty-two Sections, each comprising a different theme for meditation. By the Editors of 'Truths Illustrated by Great Authors.' Third Edition, fcap. 8vo. cloth, gilt edges, 536 pp., 6s.

'"Every part of the Sacred Writings deserves our deepest attention and research, but all, perhaps, may not be equally adapted to the purposes of meditation and reflection. Those, therefore, who are in the constant habit of consulting the Bible will not object to a selection of some of its most sublime and impressive passages, arranged and classed ready at once to meet the eye.'—EXTRACT FROM PREFACE.

Events to be Remembered in the History of England.

Forming a Series of interesting Narratives, extracted from the Pages of Contemporary Chronicles or Modern Historians, of the most Remarkable Occurrences in each Reign ; with Reviews of the Manners, Domestic Habits, Amusements, Costumes, &c. &c., of the People, Chronological Table, &c. By CHARLES SELBY. Twenty-fifth Edition, 12mo. fine paper, with Nine Beautiful Illustrations by Anelay, price 3s. 6d. cloth, elegant, gilt edges.

N.B.—A SCHOOL EDITION, without the Illustrations, 2s. 6d. cloth.

☞ Great care has been taken to render this book unobjectionable to the most fastidious, by excluding everything that could not be read aloud in schools and families, and by abstinence from all party spirit, alike in politics as in religion.

BOOKS FOR NURSERY OR MATERNAL TUITION.

The First or Mother's Dictionary. By Mrs. JAMESON (formerly Mrs. MURPHY). Tenth Edition. 18mo. 2s. 6d. cloth.

. Common expletives, the names of familiar objects, technical terms and words, the knowledge of which would be useless to children, or which could not well be explained in a manner adapted to the infant capacity, have been entirely omitted. Most of the definitions are short enough to be committed to memory ; or they may be read over, a page or two at a time, till the whole are sufficiently impressed on the mind. It will be found of advantage if the little pupils be taught to look out for themselves any word they may meet with, the meaning of which they do not distinctly comprehend.

School-Room Lyrics. Compiled and Edited by ANNE KNIGHT. New Edition. 18mo. 1s. cloth.

La Bagatelle ; intended to introduce Children of five or six years old to some knowledge of the French Language. Revised by Madame N. L. New Edition, with entirely New Cuts. 18mo. 2s. 6d. bound.

This little work has undergone a most careful revision. The orthography has been modernized, and entirely new woodcuts substituted for the old ones. It is now offered to parents and others engaged in the education of young children, as well adapted for familiarizing their pupils with the construction and sounds of the French language, conveying at the same time excellent moral lessons.

' A very nice book to be placed in the hands of children ; likely to command their attention by its beautiful embellishments.'—PAPERS FOR THE SCHOOLMASTER.

' A well-known little book, revised, improved, and adorned with some very pretty new pictures. It is, indeed, French made very easy for very little children.'
THE SCHOOL AND THE TEACHER.

Chickseed without Chickweed: being very Easy and Entertaining Lessons for Little Children. In Three Parts. Part I. in words of three letters. Part II. in words of four letters. Part III. in words of five or more letters. New Edition, with beautiful Frontispiece by Anelay, 12mo. 1s. cloth.

A book for every mother.

Peter Parley's Book of Poetry. With numerous Engravings New Edition, revised, with Additions, 16mo. 1s. 6d. cloth.

This little volume consists, in part, of extracts from various publications, and in part of original articles written for it. It is designed to embrace a variety of pieces, some grave, and some gay ; some calculated to amuse, and some to instruct ; some designed to store the youthful imagination with gentle and pleasing images ; some to enrich the mind with useful knowledge ; some to impress the heart with sentiments of love, meekness, truth, gentleness, and kindness.

Cobwebs to Catch Flies ; or Dialogues in short sentences. Adapted for Children from the age of three to eight years. In Two Parts. Part I. Easy Lessons in words of three, four, five, and six letters, suited to children from three to five years of age. Part II. Short Stories for Children from five to eight years of age. 12mo. 2s. cloth gilt.

. The Parts are sold separately, price 1s. each.

DELAMOTTE'S WORKS
ON· ILLUMINATION, ALPHABETS, &c.

A Primer of the Art of Illumination, for the use of Beginners, with a Rudimentary Treatise on the Art, Practical Directions for its Exercise, and numerous Examples taken from Illuminated MSS., and beautifully printed in gold and colours. By F. DELAMOTTE. Small 4to. price 9s. cloth antique.

'A handy book, beautifully illustrated : the text of which is well written. and calculated to be useful......The examples of ancient MSS. recommended to the student, which, with much good sense. the author chooses from collections accessible to all, are selected with judgment and knowledge, as well as taste.'—ATHENÆUM.

'Modestly called a Primer, this little book has a good title to be esteemed a manual and guide-book in the study and practice of the different styles of lettering used by the artistic transcribers of past centuries....An amateur may with this silent preceptor learn the whole art and mystery of illumination.'—SPECTATOR.

'The volume is very beautifully got up, and we can heartily recommend it to the notice of those who wish to become proficient in the art.'—ENGLISH CHURCHMAN.

'We are able to recommend Mr. Delamotte's treatise. The letterpress is modestly but judiciously written : and the illustrations, which are numerous and well chosen, are beautifully printed in gold and colours.'—ECCLESIOLOGIST.

The Book of Ornamental Alphabets, Ancient and Mediæval, from the Eighth Century, with Numerals. Including Gothic, Church-Text, large and small ; German, Italian, Arabesque. Initials for Illumination, Monograms, Crosses, &c., &c., for the use of Architectural and Engineering Draughtsmen, Missal Painters, Masons, Decorative Painters, Lithographers, Engravers, Carvers, &c. &c. Collected and Engraved by F. DELAMOTTE, and printed in Colours. Fourth Edition, royal 8vo. oblong, price 4s. cloth.

'A well-known engraver and draughtsman has enrolled in this useful book the result of many years' study and research. For those who insert enamelled sentences round gilded chalices, who blazon shop legends over shop-doors, who letter church walls with pithy sentences from the Decalogue, this book will be useful. Mr. Delamotte's book was wanted.'—ATHENÆUM.

Examples of Modern Alphabets, Plain and Ornamental. Including German, Old English, Saxon, Italic, Perspective. Greek, Hebrew, Court Hand, Engrossing, Tuscan, Riband, Gothic, Rustic, and Arabesque, with several original Designs, and Numerals. Collected and Engraved by F. DELAMOTTE, and printed in Colours. Royal 8vo. oblong, price 4s. cloth.

'To artists of all classes, but more especially to architects and engravers, this very handsome book will be invaluable. There is comprised in it every possible shape into which the letters of the alphabet and numerals can be formed, and the talent which has been expended in the conception of the various plain and ornamental letters is wonderful.'—STANDARD.

Mediæval Alphabet and Initials for Illuminators. By F. G. DELAMOTTE. Containing 21 Plates, and Illuminated Title, printed in Gold and Colours. With an Introduction by J. WILLIS BROOKS. Small 4to. 6s. cloth gilt.

'A volume in which the letters of the alphabet come forth glorified in gilding and all the colours of the prism interwoven and intertwined and intermingled, sometimes with a sort of rainbow arabesque. A poem emblazoned in these characters would be only comparable to one of those delicious love letters symbolised in a bunch of flowers well selected and cleverly arranged.'—SUN.

The Embroiderer's Book of Design, containing Initials, Emblems, Cyphers, Monograms, Ornamental Borders, Ecclesiastical Devices, Mediæval and Modern Alphabets and National Emblems. By F. DELAMOTTE. Printed in Colours. Oblong royal 8vo. 2s. 6d. in ornamental boards.

The Fables of Babrius. Translated into English Verse from the Text of Sir G. Cornewall Lewis. By the Rev. JAMES DAVIES, of Lincoln Coll. Oxford. Fcap. 6s. cloth antique.

' " Who was Babrius ?" The reply may not improbably startle the reader. Babrius was the real, original Æsop. Nothing is so fabulous about the fables of our childhood as their reputed authorship.'—DAILY NEWS.

' A fable-book which is admirably adapted to take the place of the imperfect collections of Æsopian wisdom which have hitherto held the first place in our juvenile libraries.'—HEREFORD TIMES.

NEW ANECDOTE LIBRARY.

Good Things for Railway Readers. 1000 Anecdotes, Original and Selected. By the Editor of ' The Railway Anecdote-book.' Large type, crown 8vo. with Frontispiece, 2s. 6d.

' A capital collection, and will certainly become a favourite with all railway readers.'—READER.

' Just the thing for railway readers.'—LONDON REVIEW.

' Fresh, racy, and original.'—JOHN BULL.

' An almost interminable source of amusement, and a ready means of rendering tedious journeys short.'—MINING JOURNAL.

' Invaluable to the diner-out.'—ILLUSTRATED TIMES.

Sidney Grey : a Tale of School Life. By the Author of ' Mia and Charlie.' Second Edition, with six beautiful Illustrations. Fcp. 4s. 6d. cloth.

The Innkeeper's Legal Guide : What he Must do, What he May Do, and What he May Not Do. A Handy-Book to the Liabilities, limited and unlimited, of Inn-Keepers, Alehouse-Keepers, Refreshment-House Keepers, &c. With verbatim copies of the Innkeeper's Limited Liability Act, the General Licensing Act, and Forms. By RICHARD T. TIDSWELL, Esq., of the Inner Temple, Barrister-at-Law. Fcap. 1s. 6d. cloth.

' Every licensed victualler in the land should have this exceedingly clear and well arranged manual.'—SUNDAY TIMES.

The Instant Reckoner. Showing the Value of any Quantity of Goods, including Fractional Parts of a Pound Weight, at any price from One Farthing to Twenty Shillings ; with an Introduction, embracing Copious Notes of Coins, Weights, Measures, and other Commercial and Useful Information : and an Appendix, containing Tables of Interest, Salaries, Commissions, &c. 24mo. 1s. 6d. cloth, or 2s. strongly bound in leather.

☞ Indispensable to every housekeeper.

Science Elucidative of Scripture, and not antago- nistic to it. Being a Series of Essays on—1. Alleged Discrepancies ; 2. The Theories of the Geologists and Figure of the Earth ; 3. The Mosaic Cosmogony ; 4. Miracles in general—Views of Hume and Powell ; 5. The Miracle of Joshua—Views of Dr. Colenso : The Supernaturally Impossible ; 6. The Age of the Fixed Stars—their Distances and Masses. By Professor J. R. YOUNG, Author of ' A Course of Elementary Mathematics,' &c. &c. Fcap. 8vo. price 5s. cloth lettered.

' Professor Young's examination of the early verses of Genesis, in connection with modern scientific hypotheses, is excellent.'—ENGLISH CHURCHMAN.

' Distinguished by the true spirit of scientific inquiry, by great knowledge, by keen logical ability, and by a style peculiarly clear, easy, and energetic.' NONCONFORMIST.

' No one can rise from its perusal without being impressed with a sense of the singular weakness of modern scepticism.'—BAPTIST MAGAZINE.

Mysteries of Life, Death, and Futurity. Illustrated

from the best and latest Authorities. Contents :—Life and Time ; Nature of the Soul ; Spiritual Life ; Mental Operations ; Belief and Scepticism ; Premature Interment ; Phenomena of Death ; Sin and Punishment ; The Crucifixion of Our Lord ; The End of the World ; Man after Death ; The Intermediate State ; The Great Resurrection ; Recognition of the Blessed : The Day of Judgment ; The Future States, &c. By HORACE WELBY. With an Emblematic Frontispiece, fcp. 5s. cloth.

'This book is the result of extensive reading, and careful noting ; it is such a common-place book as some thoughtful divine or physician might have compiled, gathering together a vast variety of opinions and speculations, bearing on physiology, the phenomena of life, and the nature and future existence of the soul. We know of no work that so strongly compels reflection, and so well assists it.' LONDON REVIEW.

'A pleasant, dreamy, charming, startling little volume, every page of which sparkles like a gem in an antique setting.'—WEEKLY DISPATCH.

'The scoffer might read these pages to his profit, and the pious believer will be charmed with them. Burton's "Anatomy of Melancholy" is a fine suggestive book, and full of learning : and of the volume before us we are inclined to speak in the same terms.'—ERA.

Predictions Realized in Modern Times. Now first

Collected. Contents : — Days and Numbers ; Prophesying Almanacs ; Omens ; Historical Predictions ; Predictions of the French Revolution ; The Bonaparte Family ; Discoveries and Inventions anticipated ; Scriptural Prophecies, &c. By HORACE WELBY. With a Frontispiece, fcp. 5s. cloth.

'This is an odd but attractive volume, compiled from various and often little-known sources, and is full of amusing reading.'—CRITIC.

'A volume containing a variety of curious and startling narratives on many points of supernaturalism, well calculated to gratify that love of the marvellous which is more or less inherent in us all.'—NOTES AND QUERIES.

Tales from Shakespeare. By CHARLES and MISS

LAMB. Fourteenth Edition. With 20 Engravings, printed on toned paper, from designs by Harvey, and Portrait, fcp. 3s. 6d. cloth elegant.

The Tongue of Time ; or, The Language of a Church

Clock. By WILLIAM HARRISON, A.M., Domestic Chaplain to H.R.H. the Duke of Cambridge : Rector of Birch, Essex. Sixth Edition. with beautiful Frontispiece fcp. 3s. cloth, gilt edges.

Hours of Sadness ; or, Instruction and Comfort for

the Mourner : Consisting of a Selection of Devotional Meditations, Instructive and Consolatory Reflections, Letters, Prayers, Poetry, &c.. from various Authors, suitable for the bereaved Christian. Second Edition, fcp. 4s. 6d. cloth.

The Pocket English Classics. 32mo. neatly printed,

bound in cloth, lettered, price Sixpence each :—

THE VICAR OF WAKEFIELD.	SCOTT'S LADY OF THE LAKE.
GOLDSMITH'S POETICAL WORKS.	SCOTT'S LAY.
FALCONER'S SHIPWRECK.	WALTON'S ANGLER, 2 PARTS, 1s.
RASSELAS.	ELIZABETH ; OR, THE EXILES.
STERNE'S SENTIMENTAL JOURNEY.	COWPER'S TASK.
LOCKE ON THE UNDERSTANDING.	POPE'S ESSAY AND BLAIR'S GRAVE.
THOMSON'S SEASONS.	GRAY AND COLLINS.
INCHBALD'S NATURE AND ART.	GAY'S FABLES.
BLOOMFIELD'S FARMER'S BOY.	PAUL AND VIRGINIA.

WORKS BY THE AUTHOR OF 'A TRAP TO CATCH A SUNBEAM.'

'In telling a simple story, and in the management of dialogue, the Author is excelled by few writers of the present day.'—LITERARY GAZETTE.

A Trap to Catch a Sunbeam. Thirty-fifth Edition, price 1s.

'*Aide toi, et le ciel t'aidera,* is the moral of this pleasant and interesting story, to which we assign in this Gazette a place immediately after Charles Dickens, as its due, for many passages not unworthy of him, and for a general scheme quite in unison with his best feelings towards the lowly and depressed.'—LITERARY GAZETTE.

☞ *A Cheap Edition of the above popular story has been prepared for distribution. Sold only in packets price 1s. 6d. containing 12 copies.*

Also, by the same Author,

'COMING HOME;' a New Tale for all Readers, price 1s.
OLD JOLLIFFE; not a Goblin Story. 1s.
The SEQUEL to OLD JOLLIFFE. 1s.
The HOUSE on the ROCK. 1s.
'ONLY;' a Tale for Young and Old. 1s.
The CLOUD with the SILVER LINING. 1s.
The STAR in the DESERT. 1s.
AMY'S KITCHEN, a VILLAGE ROMANCE: a New Story. 1s.
'A MERRY CHRISTMAS.' 1s.
SIBERT'S WOLD. Third Edition, 2s. cloth, limp.
The DREAM CHINTZ. With Illustrations by James Godwin. 2s. 6d. with a beautiful fancy cover.

Sunbeam Stories. A Selection of the Tales by the Author of 'A Trap to Catch a Sunbeam,' &c. Illustrated by Absolon and Anelay. FIRST SERIES. Contents :—A Trap to Catch a Sunbeam—Old Jolliffe—The Sequel to Old Jolliffe—The Star in the Desert—'Only'—'A Merry Christmas.' Fcap. 3s. 6d. cloth, elegant, or 4s. gilt edges.

Sunbeam Stories. SECOND SERIES. Illustrated by Absolon and Anelay. Contents :—The Cloud with the Silver Lining—Coming Home—Amy's Kitchen—The House on the Rock. Fcap. 3s. 6d. cloth elegant ; 4s. gilt edges.

Minnie's Love: a Novel. By the Author of 'A Trap to Catch a Sunbeam.' In 1 vol. post 8vo. 6s. cloth.

'An extremely pleasant, sunshiny volume.'—CRITIC.
'We were first surprised, then pleased, next delighted, and finally enthralled by the story.'—MORNING HERALD.

Little Sunshine: a Tale to be Read to very Young Children. By the Author of 'A Trap to Catch a Sunbeam.' In square 16mo. coloured borders, engraved Frontispiece and Vignette, fancy boards, price 2s.

'Just the thing to rivet the attention of children.'—STAMFORD MERCURY.
'Printed in the sumptuous manner that children like best.'—BRADFORD OBSERVER.
'As pleasing a child's book as we recollect seeing.'—PLYMOUTH HERALD.

THE FRENCH LANGUAGE.

M. de Fivas' Works for the Use of Colleges, Schools, and Private Students.

The attention of Schoolmasters and Heads of Colleges is respectfully requested to the following eminently useful series of French class-books, which have enjoyed an unprecedented popularity. A detailed prospectus will be sent on application.

De Fivas' New Grammar of French Grammars;

comprising the substance of all the most approved French Grammars extant, but more especially of the standard work ' La Grammaire des Grammaires,' sanctioned by the French Academy and the University of Paris. With numerous Exercises and Examples illustrative of every Rule. By Dr. V. DE FIVAS, M.A., F.E.I.S., Member of the Grammatical Society of Paris, &c. &c. Twenty-fourth Edition, price 3s. 6d. handsomely bound.

' At once the simplest and most complete Grammar of the French language. To the pupil the effect is almost as if he looked into a map, so well-defined is the course of study as explained by M. de Fivas.'—LITERARY GAZETTE.

*** A KEY to the above, price 3s. 6d.

De Fivas' New Guide to Modern French Conver-

sation; or, the Student and Tourist's French Vade-Mecum; containing a Comprehensive Vocabulary, and Phrases and Dialogues on every useful or interesting topic; together with Models of Letters, Notes, and Cards; and Comparative Tables of the British and French Coins, Weights, and Measures: the whole exhibiting, in a distinct manner, the true Pronunciation of the French Language. Fourteenth Edition, 18mo. price 2s. 6d. strongly half-bound.

' Voulez vous un guide aussi sur qu' infaillible pour apprendre la langue Française, prenez le Guide de M. de Fivas : c'est l'indispensable manuel de tout étranger.'
L'IMPARTIAL.

De Fivas, Beautés des Écrivains Français, Anciens

et Modernes. Ouvrage Classique à l'usage des Collèges et des Institutions. Dixième Édition, augmentée de Notes Historiques, Géographiques, Philosophiques, Littéraires, Grammaticales, et Biographiques. Eleventh Edition, 12mo. 3s. 6d. bound.

' An elegant volume, containing a selection of pieces in both prose and verse, which, while it furnishes a convenient reading book for the student of the French language, at the same time affords a pleasing and interesting view of French literature.'—OBSERVER.

De Fivas, Introduction à la Langue Française;

ou, Fables et Contes Choisis; Anecdotes Instructives, Faits Mémorables, &c. Avec un Dictionnaire de tous les Mots traduits en Anglais. À l'usage de la jeunesse, et de ceux qui commencent à apprendre la langue Française. Seventeenth Edition, 12mo. 2s. 6d. bound.

' By far the best first French reading book, whether for schools or adult pupils.'
TAIT'S MAGAZINE.

De Fivas, Le Trésor National; or, Guide to the

Translation of English into French at Sight. Second Edition, 12mo. 2s. 6d. bound.

☞ Le ' Trésor National' consists of idiomatical and conversational phrases, anecdotes told and untold, and scraps from various English writers, and is especially intended to produce by practice, in those who learn French, a facility in expressing themselves in that language.

*** A KEY to the above. 12mo. 2s. cloth.

THE FRENCH LANGUAGE—*continued.*

Le Brethon's French Grammar: A Guide to the French Language. By J. J. P. LE BRETHON. Revised and Corrected by L. SANDIER, Professor of Languages. Twelfth Edition, 8vo. 432 pages, 7s. 6d. cloth.—Key to ditto, 7s.

VOCABULAIRE SYMBOLIQUE ANGLO-FRANCAIS. Pour les Elèves de tout Age et de tout Degré ; dans lequel les Mots les plus utiles sont enseignés par des Illustrations. Par L. C. RAGONOT, Professeur de la Langue Française.

A Symbolic French and English Vocabulary. For Students of every Age, in all Classes ; in which the most Useful and Common Words are taught by Illustrations. By L. C. RAGONOT, Professor of the French Language. The Illustrations comprise, embodied in the text, accurate representations of upwards of 850 different objects, besides nine whole-page copper-plates, beautifully executed, each conveying, through the eye, a large amount of instruction in the French Language. Eighth Edition, considerably improved, with new plates substituted, 4to. 5s. cloth.

☞ This work in the Anglo-French form having been extensively adopted, not only in Great Britain and on the Continent, but also in America, the publishers have determined to adopt it to other languages in a more portable form. The following is now ready ;—

Symbolisches Englisch-Deutsches Wörterbuch : the Symbolic Anglo-German Vocabulary ; adapted from RAGONOT'S ' Vocabulaire Symbolique Anglo-Français.' Edited and Revised by FALCK LEBAHN, Ph. Dr., Author of ' German in One Volume,' ' The German Self-Instructor,' &c. With 850 woodcuts, and eight full-page lithographic plates. 8vo. 6s. red cloth, lettered.

New Book by one of the Contributors to ' The Reason Why' Series, and Assistant Editor of ' The Dictionary of Daily Wants.'

Now ready, Second and Cheaper Edition, 1 vol. crown 8vo. pp. 384, 2s. 6d. cloth.

The Historical Finger-Post: A Handy Book of Terms, Phrases, Epithets, Cognomens, Allusions, &c., in connexion with Universal History. By EDWARD SHELTON, Assistant Editor of ' The Dictionary of Daily Wants,' &c. &c.

' A handy little volume, which will supply the place of " Haydn's Dictionary of Dates" to many persons who cannot afford that work. Moreover, it contains some things that Haydn's book does not.'—BOOKSELLER.

' It is to the historical student and antiquarian what " Enquire Within" is to the practical housewife—not dispensing with stores of hard-acquired and well-digested knowledge, but giving that little aid which, in moments of hurry and business, is the true economiser of time.'—VOLUNTEER SERVICE GAZETTE.

' The idlest reader would find it convenient to have it within reach.'
PUBLISHERS' CIRCULAR.

' Really a very useful work ; and, at the present day, when everybody is expected to be up in everything, as good a handy-book for cramming on the current subjects of conversation as any that we know. About 3000 subjects have all their place in this extraordinary collection, and although tersely given, the account of each is sufficient for ordinary purposes.'—ERA.

' A very desirable companion, as containing a variety of information, much of which could only be got by diligent inquiry and research. . . . Deserves a place as a book of reference on the shelves of the study or library.'
NAVAL AND MILITARY GAZETTE.

' This most useful and admirably arranged handy-book will in most cases greatly lighten the labour of investigation, and obviate a long and tedious search through voluminous publications.'—WEEKLY TIMES.

THE GERMAN LANGUAGE.

Dr. Falck Lebahn's Popular Series of German School-books.

'*As an educational writer in the German tongue, Dr. Lebahn stands alone; none other has made even a distant approach to him.*'—BRITISH STANDARD.

Lebahn's First German Course. Second Edition.

Crown 8vo. 2s. 6d. cloth.

'It is hardly possible to have a simpler or better book for beginners in German.'
ATHENÆUM.

'It is really what it professes to be—a simple, clear, and concise introduction to the German Language.'—CRITIC.

Lebahn's German Language in One Volume. Seventh

Edition, containing—I. A Practical Grammar, with Exercises to every Rule. II. Undine; a Tale: by DE LA MOTTE FOUQUÉ. with Explanatory Notes of all difficult words and phrases. III. A Vocabulary of 4,500 Words, synonymous in English and German. Crown 8vo. 8s. cloth. With Key, 10s. 6d. Key separate, 2s. 6d.

'The best German Grammar that has yet been published.'—MORNING POST.

'Had we to recommence the study of German, of all the German grammars which we have examined—and they are not a few—we should unhesitatingly say, Falck Lebahn's is the book for us.'—EDUCATIONAL TIMES.

Lebahn's Edition of Schmid's Henry Von Eichen-

fels. With Vocabulary and Familiar Dialogues. Seventh Edition. Crown 8vo. 3s. 6d. cloth.

'Equally with Mr. Lebahn's previous publications, excellently adapted to assist self-exercise in the German language.'—SPECTATOR.

Lebahn's First German Reader. Fourth Edition.

Crown 8vo. 3s. 6d. cloth.

'Like all Lebahn's works, most thoroughly practical.'—BRITANNIA.

'An admirable book for beginners, which indeed may be used without a master.'
LEADER.

Lebahn's German Classics; with Notes and Complete

Vocabularies. Crown 8vo. price 3s. 6d. each, cloth.

PETER SCHLEMIHL, the Shadowless Man. By CHAMISSO.
EGMONT. A Tragedy, in Five Acts, by GOETHE.
WILHELM TELL. A Drama, in Five Acts, by SCHILLER.
GOETZ VON BERLICHINGEN. A Drama. By GOETHE.
PAGENSTREICHE, a Page's Frolics. A Comedy, by KOTZEBUE.
EMILIA GALOTTI. A Tragedy, in Five Acts, by LESSING.
UNDINE. A Tale, by FOUQUÉ.
SELECTIONS from the GERMAN POETS.

'With such aids, a student will find no difficulty in these masterpieces.'
ATHENÆUM.

Lebahn's German Copy-Book: being a Series of Exer-

cises in German Penmanship, beautifully engraved on Steel. 4to. 2s. 6d. sewed.

Lebahn's Exercises in German. Cr. 8vo. 3s. 6d. cloth.

'A volume of "Exercises in German," including in itself all the vocabularies they require. The book is well planned; the selections for translation from German into English, or from English into German, being sometimes *curiously* well suited to the purpose for which they are taken.'—EXAMINER.

Lebahn's Self-Instructor in German. Crown 8vo.

6s. 6d. cloth.

'One of the most amusing elementary reading-books that ever passed under our hands.'—JOHN BULL.

'The student could have no guide superior to Mr. Lebahn.'
LITERARY GAZETTE.

Just published, in a closely-printed Volume, in a clear and legible type,
post 8vo. 6s. cloth.

The Domestic Service Guide to Housekeeping;

Practical Cookery; Pickling and Preserving; Household Work;
Dairy Management; the Table and Dessert; Cellarage of Wines;
Home-Brewing and Wine-Making; the Boudoir and Dressing-
room; Invalid Diet; Travelling; Stable Economy; Gardening, &c.
A Manual of all that pertains to Household Management : from the
best and latest authorities, and the communications of Heads of
Families; with several hundred new recipes.

' A really useful Guide on the important subjects of which it treats.'—SPECTATOR.
' The best cookery-book published for many years.'—BELL'S MESSENGER.
' This " Domestic Service Guide" will become, what it deserves to be, very
popular.'—READER.
' This book is characterised by a kindly feeling towards the classes it designs to
benefit, and by a respectful regard to religion.'—RECORD.
' We find here directions to be discovered in no other book, tending to save ex-
pense to the pocket, as well as labour to the head. It is truly an astonishing
book.'—JOHN BULL.
' This book is quite an encyclopædia of domestic matters. We have been greatly
pleased with the good sense and good feeling of what may be called the moral directions, and the neatness and lucidity of the explanatory details.'—COURT CIRCULAR.

NO MORE LAWYERS' BILLS!

Just published, 4th Edition, much enlarged, and brought down to end of
1865 Session. 12mo. cloth, price 6s. 8d. (saved at every consultation.)

Every Man's Own Lawyer: a Handy Book of the

Principles of Law and Equity. By a BARRISTER. Comprising the
Rights and Wrongs of Individuals, Mercantile and Commercial
Law, Criminal Law, Parish Law, County Court Law, Game and
Fishery Laws, Poor Men's Law; the Laws of

Bankruptcy	Merchant Shipping
Bets and Wagers	Mortgages
Bills of Exchange	Settlements
Contracts	Stock Exchange Practice
Copyright, Patents, and Trade Marks	Trespass, Nuisances, &c.
Elections and Registration	Transfer of Land, &c.
Insurance (Marine, Fire, and Life)	Warranties and Guaranties
Libel and Slander	Forms of Wills, Agreements, Bonds,
Marriage and Divorce	Notices, &c.

Also Law for

Landlord and Tenant	Farmers
Master and Servant	Contractors
Husband and Wife	Stock and Share Brokers
Executors and Trustees	Sportsmen, Gamekeepers
Heirs, Devisees, and Legatees	Farriers and Horse-dealers
Guardian and Ward	Auctioneers, House Agents
Married Women and Infants	Innkeepers, &c.
Partners and Agents	Bakers, Millers, &c.
Lender and Borrower	Pawnbrokers
Debtor and Creditor	Surveyors
Purchaser and Vendor	Railways, Carriers, &c.
Companies and Associations	Constables
Friendly Societies	Labourers
Clergymen, Churchwardens, &c.	Seamen
Medical Practitioners, &c.	Soldiers
Bankers	&c. &c.

' What it professes to be, a complete epitome of the laws of this country,
thoroughly intelligible to non-professional readers. The book is a handy one to
have in readiness when some knotty point requires ready solution, and will be
found of service to men of business, magistrates, and all who have a horror of
spending money on a legal adviser.'—BELL'S LIFE.
' A clearly-worded and explicit manual, containing information that must be
useful at some time or other to everybody.—MECHANIC'S MAGAZINE.
' A work which has long been wanted, which is thoroughly well done, and which
we most cordially recommend.—SUNDAY TIMES.]

THE BOOK FOR EVERY FARMER.

New Edition of Youatt's Grazier, enlarged by R. Scott Burn.

The Complete Grazier, and Farmer's and Cattle Breeder's Assistant. A Compendium of Husbandry, especially in the departments connected with the Breeding, Rearing, Feeding and General Management of Stock, the Management of the Dairy, &c.; with Directions for the Culture and Management of Grass Land, of Grain and Root Crops, the Arrangement of Farm Offices, the Use of Implements and Machines; and on Draining, Irrigation, Warping, &c., and the Application and Relative Value of Manures. By WILLIAM YOUATT, Esq., V.S., Member of the Royal Agricultural Society of England, Author of 'The Horse,' 'Cattle,' &c., Eleventh Edition, enlarged, and brought down to the present requirements of Agricultural Practice by ROBERT SCOTT BURN, one of the Authors of 'The Book of Farm Implements and Machines,' and of 'The Book of Farm Buildings,' Author of 'The Lessons of My Farm,' and Editor of 'The Year-Book of Agricultural Facts.' In one large 8vo. volume, pp. 784, with 215 Illustrations, price £1 1s. strongly half-bound.

'The standard, and text-book, with the farmer and grazier.'
　　　　　　　　　　　　　　　　　　　　　　　　FARMER'S MAGAZINE.

'A valuable repertory of intelligence for all who make agriculture a pursuit, and especially for those who aim at keeping pace with the improvements of the age. . . . The new matter is of so valuable a nature that the volume is now almost entitled to be considered as a distinct work.'—BELL'S MESSENGER.

'The public are indebted to Mr. Scott Burn for undertaking the task, which he has accomplished with his usual ability, making such alterations, additions, and improvements as the changes effected in husbandry have rendered necessary.'
　　　　　　　　　　　　　　　　　　　　　　　　SPORTING MAGAZINE.

'A treatise which will remain a standard work on the subject as long as British agriculture endures.'—MARK LANE EXPRESS.

'The additions are so numerous and extensive as almost to give it the character of a new work on general husbandry, embracing all that modern science and experiment have effected in the management of land and the homestead.'
　　　　　　　　　　　　　　　　　　　　　　　　SPORTING REVIEW.

'It is, in fact, a compendium of modern husbandry, embracing a concise account of all the leading improvements of the day.'—NEW SPORTING MAGAZINE.

The Lessons of My Farm: A Book for Amateur Agriculturists; being an Introduction to Farm Practice in the Culture of Crops, the Feeding of Cattle, Management of the Dairy, Poultry, Pigs, and in the Keeping of Farm-work Records. By ROBERT SCOTT BURN, Editor of 'The Year-Book of Agricultural Facts,' and one of the Authors of 'Book of Farm Implements and Machines,' and 'Book of Farm Buildings.' With numerous Illustrations, fcp. 6s. cloth.

'A very useful little book, written in the lively style which will attract the amateur class to whom it is dedicated, and contains much sound advice and accurate description.'　　　　　　　　　　　　　　　　　ATHENÆUM.

'We are sure the book will meet with a ready sale, and the more that there are many hints in it which even old farmers need not be ashamed to accept.'
　　　　　　　　　　　　　　　　　　　　　　　　MORNING HERALD.

'A most complete introduction to the whole round of farming practice. We believe there are many among us whose love of farming will make them welcome such a companion as this little book in which the author gives us his own experiences, which are worth a great deal.'—JOHN BULL.

'Never did book exercise a more salutary effect than "My Farm of Four Acres." Mr. Burn has followed suit in a very practical and pleasant little work.'
　　　　　　　　　　　　　　　　　　　　　　ILLUSTRATED LONDON NEWS.

Printed by BoD™in Norderstedt, Germany